A Simple Scale

A Simple Scale

David Llewellyn

Seren is the book imprint of
Poetry Wales Press Ltd
57 Nolton Street, Bridgend, Wales, CF31 3AE
www.serenbooks.com
Facebook: facebook.com/SerenBooks
Twitter: @SerenBooks

ISBNs
Paperback – 978-1-78172-470-5
Ebook – 978-1-78172-471-2
Kindle – 978-1-78172-472-9

A CIP record for this title is available from the British Library.

The publisher acknowledges the financial assistance of the Welsh Books Council.

Cover photograph: 'The Best Pianist in the World' is by Noah E. Morrison, an American photographer from New York City, currently based in Los Angeles. He can be found online at noahemorrison.com

Printed in Bembo by TJ International, Cornwall.

A Simple Scale

People say there is no justice on Earth,
But there is no more justice on High. To me
This is as clear as a simple scale.

Alexander Pushkin – *Mozart & Salieri*

Chapter 1:
MANHATTAN, OCTOBER 2001

To begin with, this wasn't her bed, nor anyone else's; it was a sofa. The last thing she remembered: Everyone standing around a piano. Carol playing *Pour, Oh Pour, the Pirate Sherry* and everyone else singing. Typical for one of Carol and Louise's parties. Food, wine, a quasi-highbrow singalong. Except for the chorus, Natalie hadn't known the words, but she sang along regardless.

She opened one eye. Sure enough, this was Carol and Louise's lounge. The bottles and glasses of the night before had been cleared away; the only evidence of a party the dull after-scent of weed smoke. Two black-and-white Boston terriers were staring at her from the centre of the room. From the kitchen: Louise singing along with the radio, the rattle of dry dogfood landing in separate bowls. The terriers bolted for the kitchen, and a moment later Louise appeared in the doorway.

"You're awake," she said.

Natalie sat up. A wave of dizziness, like the sensation of movement hours after swimming.

"What time is it?"

"Eight. Carol had to go in early. Breakfast meeting with students. Coffee?"

Natalie nodded and rubbed the sleep from her eyes. She pulled her t-shirt away from her chest and sniffed. Boozy sweat and smoke. Nice.

"Here, I'll put on the TV," said Louise, thumbing the remote until the television buzzed and pinged to life. Theirs was an old set, the kind owned by those who make a point of telling you how little TV they watch. On the curved screen, another jetfighter was being launched into another clear blue sky.

"Crazy, isn't it?" said Louise.

Natalie concurred with a painful nod. Louise went to the kitchen and began making coffee.

"We would have put you in a cab," she said, her voice raised. "But you were asleep, and it's so far. Besides, if you'd had an accident…"

"An accident?"

"If you'd puked."

"Oh."

"Someone told me they fine you, like, a hundred dollars. So we thought it was better if you stayed here. And some of those drivers. I don't trust them."

"Thank you."

"I hope you slept okay."

"Yes. Thanks."

Other details of the party were coming back to her. Trying to get one of Louise's colleagues, a cellist, to dance, and him demurely turning her down. Knocking a woman's wineglass into her handbag. Standing on a chair shouting, "Toast! Toast!" And then the toast itself. Oh God.

"To those of us who didn't die!"

Awkward faces. Nervous laughter. Carol helping her to get down off the chair and asking Natalie if she would like a glass of water. Then, nothing. She must have passed out on the sofa. But had she really slept, or was she simply unconscious? Probably the latter. She felt exhausted.

This wasn't her. Or, at least, it hadn't been her. Not before. Before September she would never have done a thing like that. There had been parties before and she had got drunk before, but the memory of that "toast" made her want to implode with shame. She was only glad no-one present had lost anyone.

It was 8:15, and she had to get from Harlem to the Upper East Side by 9am. She thought about the subway. Going down, sliding her Metrocard through the reader; that trapped feeling as she passed through the turnstile. A crowded platform, a crowded carriage. She couldn't do it. The walk would take an hour. She was going to be late.

In the bathroom she carried out a routine inspection. Minimal damage to her make-up. Hair kind of shabby, though she could always pretend it was the look she was aiming for. She opened her mouth wide, poked out her wine-blackened tongue, pulled the flesh taut around her eyes. Her face felt like an unconvincing mask. *This can't be me.* She applied lip-liner, dabbed away the smudges of mascara, tamed the worst excesses of her hair and went back to the lounge.

"Here's your coffee. Black, one sugar, right?"

How did Louise remember a thing like that? How was she so organised, so alert after a late night? Typical. Natalie had always been a little envious of Carol and Louise, of everything they had, but lately it was getting worse. It was her problem, not theirs, but they were the light behind a window, and Natalie was the moth bashing its head against the glass. When she'd drunk only half of her coffee, she began preparing her exit.

"I feel like I should stick around, help you to tidy up..."

She had no intention of doing so.

"It's fine," said Louise. "You have work, and besides... I've got this."

The hallway was lined with framed photographs: Carol and Louise in Paris, Carol and Louise in Rome, Carol and Louise in Machu Picchu and in Marrakech and next to the Great Wall of China. Louise and the dogs followed Natalie to the door.

"Listen," Louise said. "You're Carol's friend, so it's probably not my place to say anything, but are you okay?"

This had all the makings of something heartfelt. Natalie cringed.

"Of course," she said, hoping it would end there.

"It's just. Last night... you seemed a little..."

Crazed? Desperate? Lacking in all sense of decorum?

"We're just worried about you, that's all."

"I'm fine."

"You sure?"

"I'm fine."

"Because... you know... these last few weeks have been crazy for everyone, and with Gino being away and you being home all by yourself –"

"I'm fine."

"– we just thought, you know, if you want to talk with

anyone. I mean, it doesn't have to be Carol. If you'd find it easier to talk with someone a little removed, I'd be more than happy to –"

"No, I'm fine. Really, I am."

"That's *so* English of you."

New Yorkers never missed an opportunity to tell her just how English she was, or compare her with some actress who was either ten years younger or twenty years older than her.

"I'm fine," Natalie said. "Honestly."

"Okay. Well. You know where we are."

It was a sunny morning, but it had been raining throughout the night, and the wet streets' glare was blinding. Natalie had a $5 umbrella in her bag but hadn't brought a pair of shades. She squinted her way down 121st Street and stuck to the shaded side of Frederick Douglass Boulevard until she reached the park.

It was almost a month since she had last used the subway. A childhood phobia of enclosed spaces had returned. Understandable, really. But was she the only one? There were faces she remembered from her old commute; the Korean woman with two small kids, the skinny guy with the pronounced Adam's apple, the old man who wore a cashmere coat even in summer. She'd passed none of them walking along Third Avenue each day, so perhaps it was just her. Perhaps everyone else was fine.

She reached the house on East 73rd Street an hour after setting out. Jamilah, Sol's carer, was leaving just as Natalie arrived. She paused at the bottom of the stoop to light a cigarette, saw Natalie and murmured a good morning. Jamilah never had much to say to her, and Natalie had the impression that the carer didn't like her. She had that impression with a lot of people.

There were four women in Sol Conrad's life, four women who tended to him daily: Natalie, Jamilah and the sisters, Rosa and Dolly De Leon. Their responsibilities often overlapped, but the De Leons kept the house clean and homely; no small task in a place this big. Rosa handled things most days, but that morning it was Dolly who leaned out into the hall, waving a soapy yellow glove at her, and calling out, "Good morning, Miss Natalie."

"Morning, Dolly. Where's Rosa?"

"Hospital. An operation. Her face."

"Her face?"

"She has a mole, here."

Dolly pointed to the place where her left nostril met her cheek and she slipped off the rubber gloves with a snap.

"You're late."

"I know. I'm sorry. I stayed at a friend's last night…"

"*Boy*friend?"

Every time. Every single time. They were like the elderly neighbours where Natalie had grown up, an English village where her mother still lived. Always asking if she was "courting", from the second she'd hit puberty. Courting!

"A *friend*," Natalie said. "I slept late. How's Mr C.? Is he okay?"

"Not so bad. He thought I was Rosa, but, you know…"

If Sol could remember Rosa's name, it was one of his better days. She would give anything for one of his better days.

"Where is he now?"

"In his study."

For a moment Dolly carried on putting away the plates and cutlery from breakfast.

"Oh yeah," she said. "There was a call. Eight o'clock, eight thirty. A man wanted to speak with Mr Conrad. He had a accent. I told him Mr Conrad was busy, so then he asked to speak to his secretary. So I told him Mr Conrad doesn't have a secretary, he has a *per-so-nal ass-is-tant*. Then he asked if he could speak to you, so I told him I would pass on his message."

"Which was?"

"Just to say he called."

"Did he leave a name?"

"I wrote it down."

Dolly shuffled out into the hallway, her plimsolled feet slapping against the parquet floor. She was wider in the hips than her sister and already had a fat woman's waddle. Rosa would have finished cleaning the house by now. Dolly had barely made a start.

She came back with a scrap of yellow notepaper on which she'd written "PAVEL GREKOV" and the address of a hotel on West 32nd.

"He's staying here?"

"No," Dolly huffed. "He's staying at Four Seasons in Jersey. Course he's staying here. Why you think I write it down?"

"Did he say what he was calling about?"

Dolly shook her head. "He wouldn't tell me. Very rude."

Chances are this Grekov was a fan. Unusual for a fan to get hold of Sol's telephone number, but stranger things had happened. Fans had been known to turn up on the stoop, asking for autographs, before now.

Natalie left the kitchen and went down the hall. The study door was open, and she heard music; one of the Fischer-Dieskau recordings of *Schwanengesang*. Sol was seated in the wing-backed chair nearest the window, awake but with his eyes closed; a copy of today's *Wall Street Journal* folded and unread in his lap. She couldn't remember the last time she had seen him actually reading the paper. It was probably for the best.

"Good morning."

The old man stirred, snuffled and opened his eyes. That morning they looked more grey than blue.

"Sorry. What? Yes. Good morning. Good morning."

"*Schwanengesang,*" she said, adding hopefully: "Because of Sunday?"

Two days ago they'd heard Christian Gerhaher perform the same pieces at the Frick; its first concert since the attacks. Lower Manhattan was still smouldering, and the mood in the concert hall that night was charged, bristling with something unsaid. Natalie saw more than one person crying, but Sol looked happier and more serene than she had seen him in months. Now, his expression was blank. He remembered nothing.

For a moment more they sat without speaking. The sunlight made constellations of the house dust and a corona of the stubble on his cheeks and chin. Later, in what was bound to be another brief exchange, she would ask Jamilah to shave him. From the kitchen, Dolly called out, asking Natalie if she would like more coffee, and she left Sol to his music and his unread paper.

When Dolly had finished for the day, Natalie called the hotel and asked for Pavel Grekov. There was a pause, hold music, and the receptionist told her Mr Grekov wasn't answering. Fine. At least she'd tried. Maybe this would be the end of it. Maybe he was just another fan of *Battle Station Alpha, Thunder Squad* or *The Man from Lamar*, trying his luck. Maybe, when all he got was a confused Filipino housemaid, he'd decided to quit. This suited Natalie just fine.

These hours, between the De Leons' exit and Jamilah's return, were her favourite part of the day, and each day at Sol's was much like any other. She spent her mornings going through whatever mail had arrived. On occasion, there would be fan mail, forwarded on by the network.

Dear Mr Conrad,
I am writing to tell you that I am an enormous fan of your work, and especially the theme from Battle Station Alpha. *I bought it on vinyl record when it was first released in 1979. I was 14 years of age and I still have that very copy in my collection, and in excellent condition. I had hoped to get it signed at Alpha-Con in 1995 but I was unable to attend. Perhaps, if you appear at another convention you would be so kind as to sign it for me.*
Yours gratefully,
Steven McGregor, Des Moines

She had saved a template reply to Sol's computer that she could then customise.

Dear Steven,
Thank you so much for your kind words. Though I have been retired for some time and make very few public appearances it gives me great pleasure knowing my work still brings joy to people. You have made an old man very happy!
Yours sincerely,
Sol Conrad, New York City

There were no fan letters that day; just a bill, two circulars and a notification from the Department of Planning, concerning a building on East 74th. She saw the words "rooftop bar" before she fed it, along with the circulars, into the shredder.

The fan convention invites were few and far between. Not that she minded. Going away provided a change from her daily routine, but little else. Sol had never much enjoyed them. The last he attended was at San Diego, two years ago. He appeared on a panel with some of the stars from *Battle Station Alpha*. Natalie hardly recognised them, with their toupees, girdled bellies, fake boobs and facelifts – familiar faces rendered strange by time and too much effort – and Sol remembered few of their names without prompting.

His dementia was referenced in the job description; she knew what she'd signed up for. Even so, they shouldn't have gone to San Diego. It was all too much for him. All that traipsing around a convention centre the size of an airport, an endless maze of walkways and escalators. There was a question, during the panel, about Sol's testimony before the HUAC. Fat guy, glasses, balding. His stretched grey t-shirt based on the Alpha Crew uniform. A living, heavy-breathing archetype. The room was full of them.

"Sir. Do you think your testimony before the House Un-American Activities Committee is why your movie career dried up? Is that why you moved into writing music for television?"

Either Sol didn't understand the question or he pretended not to. The panel's chair looked to Natalie for his cue. She shook her head, and the chair said they should stick to questions about *Battle Station Alpha*. In better days, Sol might have preferred a few questions about the hearing. He had never had much time for *Battle Station Alpha* or its fans. She hadn't told him that as a child she had watched all of its twenty-four episodes and watched them again, a decade later, when they were repeated on British television.

Like the radio signal on a long car journey, Sol came and went throughout the day, but after lunch she sensed that he was there, that he was with her, and so she asked if the name Pavel Grekov meant anything to him. It was a long shot.

"Who?"

"Grekov. Pavel Grekov."

He shook his head. It didn't mean anything to him right now; but then, he could have worked with Pavel Grekov for decades and still not recall his name.

Mid-afternoon, the phone rang. She picked it up instinctively. Occasionally, it might be an old friend of Sol's. Sometimes, it might be Dolly, Rosa or Jamilah. She answered and before she'd even finished saying her own name she guessed who it was.

"You are Mr Conrad's assistant?" he asked.

The accent Dolly had mentioned sounded Russian.

"That's right," Natalie said. "Is this Pavel Grekov?"

"I want to speak with him."

Didn't even answer her question. So Dolly was also right about him being rude.

"I'm afraid that won't be possible."

"Why not?"

"Mr Conrad is old and a little frail. But I'm sure I can answer any questions you have."

"We will meet."

Neither a question nor a request. What was this guy after? He didn't sound like a fan. A part of her wanted to hang up. The other part needed to know.

"Okay. We can meet, if you like. I'm free most evenings, or –"

"Tonight."

She laughed as if her diary was crammed with appointments. It was not. Meet him, humour him, and if it turns out he's a pervert or a psychopath, raise hell. But meet him somewhere public.

She went through a mental list of bars that might be busy on a Tuesday evening. If her roommate, Gino, was anything to go by, gay men rarely took a night off, and so she told him to meet her at Julius Bar, on West 10th Street and Waverly. When she'd hung up she wrote Grekov's name and the name of the bar on a Post-It note and stuck it to the kitchen notice board, where Dolly or Rosa would see it.

She spent the rest of the afternoon with Sol, reading him a review of *Idomeneo* at the Met and slipping *Sunset Boulevard* in the video, but she was distracted and paid little attention to the film.

There was no reason why she *had* to meet Pavel Grekov. She could go straight home, take a long bath, walk around the apartment naked for a while. Maybe get a couple of beers.

No beers. Her headache had cleared by lunchtime but her stomach was still uncertain. She saw her wineglass falling into that lady's handbag. Embarrassing in any circumstances, but the lady in question was someone senior from the Lincoln Center. She had gazed down into her wine-drenched bag with appal and Natalie apologised and tiptoed into another room as if making a stealthy getaway. She was still mischievous at that point; she hadn't yet crossed the line into the final phase, the mean phase. Somebody should have put her in a cab long before then. She would be surprised if Carol and Louise ever spoke to her again.

Jamilah returned shortly after five, her denim rucksack on her shoulder and a canvas book bag under her arm.

"He been good today?"

"So so."

"Hoping I'll get a little peace tonight."

"He should be fine."

Even as she left the house, Natalie still hadn't decided what she would do. She had always been this way. Capable of snap decisions or hours, days, weeks of deliberation, and nothing in between. Sometimes the snap decisions proved fruitful, like applying to NYU. Other times (the Dutch courage she'd had before Carol and Louise's party) less so. But these hours of pondering were the worst. Like a mental paralysis. The world became so much white noise. It had been so much worse this last month.

It took her an hour to reach East Village. Third Avenue was rush hour busy, and she had to elbow her way through legions of sightseers all across Midtown. Even after everything that happened, still so many tourists. Perhaps the flights were cheap.

Her hangover still hadn't entirely worn off. She wasn't sure she could face another drink. And still, the shame of it all. Getting up on that chair, getting everyone's attention by flicking her wine glass. "Toast! Toast!" The others laughing, thinking she was about to say something witty. The way their faces dropped when she didn't.

Hair of the dog. That was what she needed. A terrible excuse, really, but what else was she going to do? Go home and watch repeats of *Ally McBeal* on whichever channel wasn't showing rolling news?

There wasn't enough time for her to go home and freshen up, and so Natalie went straight to Julius Bar. She was on time, almost to the minute. She looked around, scanning the faces for any likely candidates, and saw none. She contemplated ordering a Coke. She asked the barman for a bottle of Sam Adams.

She was there for maybe a quarter of an hour before Grekov

appeared. The door opened, she felt the breeze on her back, heard the sound of traffic on West 10th Street, and footsteps. She looked across and saw a young man, younger than she'd anticipated, with short dark hair and blue eyes.

"You are Natalie."

She nodded.

"Pavel Grekov," he said, adding, as if she should know the name: "Sergey Grekov was my grandfather."

Natalie shrugged an apology. Never heard of him. She gestured to the bartender and ordered two more beers. Pavel Grekov took up the stool next to hers.

"So," she said. "How do you know Mr Conrad?"

"I don't know him. I only know what he did."

"And what was that?"

"Stole my grandfather's music."

That was a new one. Natalie laughed. She could guess where this was heading. Most likely, he was a grifter from no further afield than Brighton Beach. That's if his name and accent were even genuine.

"What music?" she asked.

"*Battle Station Alpha*. You know..." And he hummed the theme, almost tunelessly, but close enough for her to recognise it.

"You're telling me your grandfather wrote the theme from *Battle Station Alpha*?"

Grekov nodded. "He wrote it. For his ballet."

This guy was good. Ballet was a nice touch. Why would anyone make up a thing like that?

"Which ballet?"

"*Geroy nashego vremeni*. It's based on a novel."

"Never heard of it."

"*Hero of Our Time*. This is what you call it."

She knew of the novel, but not the ballet. If he was lying, he'd put some effort into it. But then, isn't that the nature of confidence tricksters? Don't they all go into this kind of laborious detail? She would hold strong. Humour him a little while longer, but only till she got bored.

"And where's your grandfather now?"

"He died when I was little."

"And where did he live?"

"Leningrad. St Petersburg."

"Was he famous?"

"In Russia, yes. As a young man."

"But only in Russia?"

Grekov nodded. Natalie was warming to this now. The first beer had levelled things out. She was at the sweet spot of alcohol-induced confidence.

"And his music... Was it performed in the States? Was it recorded?"

"Not this piece."

She began to laugh again, and Grekov shifted uncomfortably on his stool.

"You think this is funny," he said. "What your boss did?"

"No. What's funny is you walking in here and accusing him of plagiarism. Were you trying to blackmail him? Is that it?"

"Not blackmail," said Pavel. "I came to New York, to speak

with Sol Conrad."

"Well you can't. And you won't."

Pavel got up, his stool scraping against the floor, loud enough to make heads turn. "Fucking Americans," he said. She let it pass. "So arrogant. And you are wrong."

"So prove it."

He glowered at her and her body tensed, anticipating violence. Maybe she'd pushed this too far.

"There is proof," Pavel said. "I have the, ah, the *partitura*... the music written down in a book..."

"The score?"

"Yes. The score. I have it in my hotel. Exactly the same. Do you read music?"

"Yes."

"You read it, you will see. Exactly the same. But you don't read it, fine. I will take it to a lawyer."

"Be my guest. I'll wait for them to call."

Grekov stumbled out, clipping his shoulder against the doorframe as he left. Some of those sitting or standing along the bar looked at Natalie with condescending smiles. A lovers' tiff, they were thinking. What had they been arguing about?

Five minutes ago she'd found the whole thing hilarious, but now her hands began to shake. She ordered another bottle of beer, and chased it down with a shot of gin.

Chapter 2:
LENINGRAD, FEBRUARY 1950

Another time, another place; the city grey, the snowflakes falling in the street like ashes. Beneath the station's clock tower, two heavy doors swing open with a gasp, and Sergey Grekov steps out, his coat held around him and his gloveless hands clasped tightly in his armpits. Thirty-seven years old but prematurely grey and uncommonly thin, he looks at Leningrad as if it still might be a mirage.

From everything he has been told these last few years, he was anticipating ruins. Hollow buildings and charred timbers, streets strewn with rubble. Instead, he finds it repainted and rebuilt, and yet the place is different, as if everything has been moved around in his absence, as you might rearrange the furniture in an old room.

He's unaccustomed to choice. When he comes to a junction, he can go in any direction; left, right, straight ahead. The space is almost limitless. No perimeter fence, no watchtowers, no guard dogs. Yet this isn't complete freedom. His papers tell him where to go and when. The tenement, the factory. Disobey them, and there's every chance they could send him back.

The streets around the station are almost empty. The few people he passes look shabby, not how he remembers them. Moscow was always the peasant city, the place where people look as if they've just arrived from the country. Not Leningrad. Not *Piter*.

Moskovsky Prospect is busier, especially once he's crossed the bridge. There, he moves through a shuffling black mass of other people, winter coats and hats dusted with snow. A xylophone-ribbed dog shivers and keeps pace with him along the gutter. Red and white trams whisper through the slush, passengers pressed against windows opaque with steam. The bell of a nearby clock strikes one.

The last time he saw this street it was through the windows of a police car, in the early hours of a Tuesday morning. It was August then, the air already humid, and stuffier still inside the car. He remembers an agent, a lad barely older than twenty, lighting his cigarette for him – his own hands were cuffed – and the way the car was filled almost immediately with smoke.

As a young man, Leningrad's winters seemed so much colder than this – far too cold to consider walking very far – but the last leg of his journey was spent in a train compartment with ten others. They took it in turns to sit, but there was no room to lie down and sleep. Cold as it might be, it's good to be out in the open. Besides, he has known far colder.

His papers tell him to report to the tenement building no earlier than 3pm and so, to pass the time, he finds a café where he orders coffee, black bread and a bowl of *rassolnik*.

The secret police and their informants were everywhere in the north; guards spying on prisoners and even prisoners spying on guards. No-one trusted anyone. But what about here, in this café? The skinny lad behind the counter, perhaps. The old woman eating some indeterminate grey mush out of a chipped bowl. The crooked figure hunched over a newspaper in the far corner.

The soup, when it arrives, is mostly barley and carrots, little in the way of meat. Sergey dips his bread into the soup. He hasn't eaten in more than a day. The broth dances on his tongue. Its warmth spreads out, from his chest and through his limbs and into his fingers and toes. He closes his eyes, and when he opens them again he senses someone staring at him. The figure in the corner; the small man with stooped shoulders, his face drawn, pinched and beetle-browed. Though as threadbare and hungry-looking as everyone else in the city, this man *could* be secret service.

After studying him a moment longer, the stranger gets to his feet, tucks his newspaper into the inside of his overcoat, and crosses the café.

"Seryozha?" he says, his smile a gash of yellow teeth and greyish gums. "Sergey Andreievich?"

Sergey nods slowly, waiting for the stranger's smile to fade, and for him to say there's been a mistake, that Sergey should never have been released, that his rehabilitation is incomplete and that he will be placed on the very first train back to Komi, by orders of the MGB.

"Do I know you?" he asks.

The stranger laughs. "Know me? Sergey! Of course you know me! It's me! Vasily Nikolayevich. Sidorov! Vasya!"

Vasily Sidorov. A name he's neither said nor spoken nor even thought about in years. When did they last see one another? Perhaps the night of the premiere, or in the days that followed. No, his memory of that time is too clouded to picture the exact scene. When he *first* laid eyes on him, however… this he remembers clearly.

A rehearsal room, backstage at the Kirov. Secretary Remizov taking Sergey on a tour of the theatre, introducing him as "our latest genius". Echoing against a polished floor, the sound of a piano playing one of Chopin's nocturnes. In the studio, holding the bar, a young man, eighteen or nineteen, with dark, lightly curled hair, performing a series of *degage*, and stopping only when he noticed the presence of a stranger.

Now, in the café, Sergey's innards clench. He hardly recognises him.

"Vasya?"

The man draws out the facing chair and sits.

"I knew it was you!" he says. "I work nights at the children's hospital, and every day I come here for lunch, which is really supper, I suppose. But every day I come here, and I know everyone who comes in, if not by name then by face. I see them every day. But you, as soon as you walked in, I thought, 'Hold on, he's new.' And then I looked at you again, and I realised it was you."

"Yes," says Sergey, smiling almost painfully. "It's me."

"How long has it been? Ten years? Fifteen?"

"Twelve."

"Twelve years. Well. Can you imagine? Twelve years. Incredible. I heard you were up in Archangel, writing music for a theatre company. That's what everyone was saying. Is it true?"

Sergey shakes his head.

"Oh," says Vasily. "They must have got it wrong. But you're here now."

Sergey nods.

"And it's so good to see you! I hardly see anyone these days. We were, well, you know... One oughtn't say such things in public, but people like us, the artists, we weren't exactly front of the queue when the rations were being handed out. Were you here at all, during the blockade?"

Sergey shakes his head.

"Of course not. Silly question. But you were lucky. Say, are you going to eat all of that bread?"

"Yes."

"Only, if you weren't, I have some wood in my flat that I could swap. It's good, too. It's not damp and it won't burn too quickly, not like some of the cheap shit that's going around."

"No, I'm quite hungry, so –"

"Do you have a place to stay?"

Sergey tells him that yes, he has a place to stay, in Kirovskiy, near the Kirov plant.

"Nice, nice," says Vasily.

"Is it?"

"Oh, yes. And prestigious, too. You're lucky. Have you moved in yet?"

"Not yet, no," says Sergey. "I only got here an hour ago."

"Oh, well," says Vasily. "If you've not moved in yet, they might not have wood. In your rooms, I mean. They don't always give you fuel, when you move in. Some places, it takes weeks. So, you know, if you don't have any..."

Sergey draws his plate closer and dunks what's left of his bread into the *rassolnik*.

"You must be hungry," says Vasily. "I know they don't always have much bread on the trains. I've heard, a friend once told me, if you want a bigger ration of bread..." His voice drops to a whisper. "If you want a bigger ration of bread, you have to give the ticket inspector a blowjob. Is that true?"

Sergey smiles. "I wouldn't know."

"Oh, then you must be hungry," says Vasily, laughing and coughing at the same time. "Say, listen. I live near here. When you're finished, let's go to mine. I'm on the third floor, so it's not too cold, and I have some vodka."

A loaded invitation, but Sergey has nowhere else to go and two hours till he can report to his tenement. When the bill is settled he and Vasily walk the short distance to Vasily's building, just off Sennaya Square.

Twelve years ago Vasily Sidorov lived not so far from here, in an apartment complex on Sadovaya Street, and Sergey remembers summer parties when they would congregate on a small terrace overlooking the square, and they would drink champagne; Soviet champagne, of course, but ice cold, and sparkling and as crisp as a fresh apple.

Vasily's new building has no terrace. One of its two entrances is sealed shut by a frozen snowdrift, and the other opens only when Vasily barges into it with such force that Sergey worries he – and not the door – might break.

Once inside, they are taken up to Vasily's floor by a gloomy hallway and a flight of stairs that smells strongly of piss, while Vasily's room smells mustily of tobacco smoke, mildew and dust. Sergey recalls Vasily having a small collection of illicit

Persian rugs and a mantelpiece crammed with ornaments, but this new place – if it can be called new – is sparse, decorated only with a few pieces of old furniture. The floor and the walls are bare.

"Please, sit," says Vasily. "I'll get us some vodka. I only have one glass. Do you mind having yours in a teacup?"

"Not at all."

"What am I saying? You have the glass, I'll have the teacup. As you may be able to tell, I don't do much entertaining these days..."

Vasily opens a cupboard and takes out the vodka, a chipped teacup and a cloudy tumbler. He crosses the room with an awkward, scuttling motion; bug-like, a spider creeping along a skirting board. He was once the most graceful man Sergey had ever met. Small in build, but not feminine. Women and men alike considered him beautiful. Now he reminds Sergey of a gargoyle or some grinning demon, a *didko*, from an old folktale. He takes to the sagging armchair opposite, and for a moment they sit in silence; Vasily still smiling at him, scrutinising him.

"It's incredible," he says, at last. "That you came here. To Leningrad. It isn't often men come back. Usually, well, usually they're sent to some other place. Remember Remizov?"

As if the room has grown a degree or two colder, Sergey flinches. "Yes," he says. "I remember him."

Vasily goes on: "Ran into a spot of bother. Not long after you went away. Was trying to coerce some dancer into... well... you know. Didn't realise the lad's uncle was a party man in Moscow. Last thing I heard, he was teaching in Vladivostok."

"Is that so?"

"Well, that's what people said at the time. You know how it is. But no-one's seen him since before the war."

Secretary Remizov, joining the ranks of the disappeared. The news feels almost like a small, if pyrrhic, victory.

He and Vasily drink to "Peace and happiness for all men." They clink cup and glass together and they drink. The vodka bites; as unfiltered as white spirit.

"He knew about us, you know," says Vasily, through a succession of dry coughs. "Remizov."

Sergey nods. "I know."

"No idea who told him. One of the boys from the reserve troupe, I imagine. Bloody gossips. I hear he wasn't best pleased. Still... I suppose we should be grateful he didn't tell anyone. Well... He didn't have a chance. No sooner had you gone, than so had he. And then the war happened, and everyone was gone. At least, that's how it felt."

"You stayed here?" Sergey asks. "During the war?"

"You were lucky," Vasily says with a nod. "To be elsewhere."

"Was it so bad?"

Vasily begins to chuckle, his laughter bubbling up out of him uncontrollably. His eyes grow moist. "Was it so bad?" he says. "Was it so bad? Oh, Sergey Andreievich. Like you wouldn't believe. Everything... everything just fell apart. I don't remember the Civil War, I was too young at the time, but my father told me this was so much worse. The sense that everything was coming apart at the seams. He didn't have much time left. He died in the first January. We still had a little money to pay for his burial, and when we took his casket to the cemetery the corpses there were piled up on the roadside. Like so much refuse. There must have been hundreds of them. And the bodies on top of each pile had been stripped. First of their clothes. Then their flesh.

"They looked ridiculous, these corpses, with their oversized heads and bloated bodies. Arms and legs nothing but bones. Like marionettes."

Vasily laughs again, and Sergey experiences a wave of nausea.

"What happened to the place on Sadovaya Street?" he asks, wishing to hear no more about the blockade. "Why aren't you living there?"

"Oh, Sadovaya Street!" says Vasily. "Well. First, it was damaged. Mortar attack, or some such. Not a direct hit, you understand, but a shell landed in the square. Blew out every last window. They said I had to move, so they could fix it up. Moved me into this place. I think the previous tenants starved. Or perhaps it was typhoid. Anyway. The place was empty, so I moved in. And then, when the apartment on Sadovaya Street was all fixed up they told me I couldn't have it back. Some party member wanted it, after his house was destroyed. Charming. Anyway. I've been here ever since. I know it's not much, but it's cosy enough."

"And you don't see anyone else?" Sergey asks. "No-one from the Kirov?"

"They're all gone, I think. Either like you, or during the blockade. Tatiana Dmitrievna, well… the Little Barn Owl flapped her wings and flew off to Paris and then America. All very scandalous, of course. Seems the times finally caught up with her and that rancid little queen of hers. Even *she* couldn't get away with living like *that*, not even with all her Party friends. So she left. I don't think whatsisname was so lucky. Anyway… We don't talk about any of that."

"But you're still here."

Vasily grins, bearing ashen gums and the small black spaces where he's lost one or two teeth.

"Yes," he says. "I'm still here."

"And the dancing?"

Vasily begins to laugh again, a nervous giggle that escalates into something braying, almost hysterical.

"Dancing?" he says. "Oh, Sergey Andreievich! Do you remember a dancer called Vasily Sidorov? If you do, you have a better memory than me. No. I haven't danced in years. The Kirov was damaged during the war, so there was nowhere to dance. Then I was ill, pneumonia, that first winter. I pulled through, but I missed the season when they shipped everyone off to Kuybyshev and Perm. And then, to cap it all off, after we'd gone hungry for so long… well… look at me."

He sighs, waving one hand over a body that looks shrunken, consumptive.

"But do you remember how I danced?" he says, rising clumsily from his chair and taking another sip of vodka. "Remember your ballet?"

"I remember," says Sergey.

"I was Pechorin. The hero."

Vasily places his cup on an otherwise empty mantelpiece and performs an exaggerated march across the sitting room, humming a melody Sergey hasn't heard in several years. The dance is now an ugly parody of what it once was.

"It was a wonderful ballet," says Vasily. "Such a shame."

"It was a long time ago," says Sergey. "It doesn't matter."

Short of breath, Vasily braces himself against the back of his armchair and looks down at Sergey with that same appalling fascination with which he studied him in the café.

"I've just remembered!" he says. "I have it here somewhere."

He crosses the room to a small bureau and begins opening and closing its drawers, rifling through the papers in each one before producing a manuscript bound with a cover of purple card.

"Here!" he says.

"What is it?"

"Your ballet."

Vasily hands him the book, and Sergey begins thumbing through the pages, seeing, written in his own hand, snatches of melody both surprising and immediately familiar.

"You kept this?" he asks. "Even after everything that happened?"

"Yes," says Vasily, beaming. "Even then. I thought someone should. You left it here. After the party. Do you remember?"

Sergey offers the manuscript back, but Vasily tells him it's his, that he should keep it.

"I can't do that," says Sergey. "You've had it all this time, and besides..."

"Oh, I insist. Leave it here much longer and I may finally succumb to the temptation to burn it for a bit of warmth. And besides. I can't imagine they let you keep much of your work, where you were."

They hadn't. Not a page of it. There was little music in Komi. Sergey takes back his manuscript and holds it tightly against his chest.

"This could have got you in a lot of trouble."

"I didn't care. I thought that if I kept it here, one day you'd come back to collect it, and perhaps..."

"Perhaps what?"

Vasily shrugs with a disingenuous smile, and for a moment Sergey recognises the boy he first met in the Kirov's studio. There is that same wounded longing, edged with something calculating.

"How are you here?" says Vasily. "In Leningrad, I mean. The others, when they get out, they're sent elsewhere. They're never allowed *back*. What is it Akhmatova says about Dante? 'Even after death he did not return to his old Florence.' And yet here you are. How come?"

"I don't know," Sergey replies. "When I first got there, they said there'd been a mistake with the paperwork."

"A mistake? They don't make mistakes."

"Well, I don't know," says Sergey. "They said there was another Grekov. A thief. They thought perhaps he should have been sent north, and that I..." His voice trails off. He knows how to finish the sentence, but also knows some sentences should go unfinished. "You're right, though. Most people are sent east, or they're moved on to other cities."

"But you came back."

"I came back."

"Why? What was here for you in Leningrad? You have no family. And like I said, our friends, our old friends, are all gone. Why did you come back?"

Sergey drains the last vodka from his glass, and suppresses a brief, stomach-bracing heave.

"Leningrad is all I know," he says.

"Perhaps you thought you'd see some of your old friends?" says Vasily, folding his arms across the back of the chair. "Is that it?"

"I didn't know who would be here," says Sergey. "I didn't know if anyone was still alive."

"Did you think you would see me?"

"I didn't know who I would see."

"Did you miss me?"

Sergey rises and crosses the room to Vasily's coat stand. His was the second coat hanging there, and taking it away leaves it looking spindly and bare.

"Where are you going?" says Vasily. "I thought you might stay a while."

"I have to go," says Sergey. "But thank you for the vodka, and your hospitality."

Vasily follows him to the door and Sergey awaits an ultimatum, an offer caged inside a threat. Stay a while, or else.

Stay a while, or as soon as you step outside this building there will be men waiting for you, men who will put you on the first train back to Komi.

Instead, Vasily calls after him: "I'll see you around, yes?", and Sergey nods, descending the staircase quickly and without saying another word.

There are no men waiting outside the building, nor is he followed at any point between Vasily's street and the place where he catches the Kirovskiy tram. The tram is crowded and smells of damp coats and cheap booze. Standing beside him in the aisle, a young woman cradles her small boy, two or three years old, against her shoulder. The boy smiles at him, and Sergey smiles back. Sergey pokes out his tongue and crosses his eyes, and the boy laughs. The boy's mother scowls at Sergey and he turns away, blushing.

He had forgotten how much people changed, those last few years before he was sent away; the hardness they acquired. No sense of anything but proximity binding them together, and a kind of caustic animosity hanging in the air between each person, as if it would take very little for them to turn on one another like dogs.

Stepping off the tram, he's welcomed by a claggy, chemical stench that seems to cling to the back of his throat. Something heavy, industrial. A smell he can taste. His tenement building, situated opposite the factory, is old, dating back to before the Revolution. What it was before its rooms became *kommunalkas,* he couldn't say, but its cold lobby has a look of faded grandeur, a veneer of toffee-coloured paint covering its marble walls and pilasters. He's met there by the building's commandant, an older woman whose greying black hair is hacked close around her ears and sticks out from beneath a peaked cap.

A cursory glance at his paperwork. "You're Grekov?"

Sergey nods.

"And you came from Komi?"

"Yes. Komi."

"That's unusual. We don't get many from Komi. How long were you there?"

"Twelve years."

Her expression, previously so unflinching, softens. The force of resentment behind it, whatever it was that made her dislike him on some deep, fibrous level, begins to fade.

"And you were in Komi the whole time?"

"Not all of it," Sergey says. "During the war I was in Kotlas. I worked as a clerk, on the railroad. Then they sent me back."

"Still. Twelve years. Come. I'll show you to your room."

The elevator is "awaiting repair" – she doesn't tell him how long this has been the case – and so they climb four flights of stairs to his room. The steps are made of mottled stone; the walls painted a military shade of green. The commandant moves with the perfect rhythm of someone who has climbed these steps a thousand times, her head and shoulders stooping forward, as if she is being drawn along by some other force.

His room is small, partitioned off from its neighbours with walls of plywood that don't quite reach the ceilings. The kitchen, bathroom and toilet, a short way down the corridor, are shared with these rooms and several others on this floor.

"You'll report to the factory on Monday, at 8am," the commandant says, handing him a piece of paper printed with the factory's details and the name of his overseer. In a hushed and sympathetic voice, she adds, "Best make sure you're there on time. Don't give them any excuses."

Once she's gone, Sergey is truly alone for the first time since the day of his arrest. He takes the manuscript, the score to his ballet, out of his overcoat and places it beneath his bed, nudging it into the shadowy corner of the room.

Soon enough, exhausted by the journey, he falls asleep. He doesn't dream – or if he does, those dreams are instantly forgotten – but he wakes thinking of Vasily. He was rude to leave so suddenly. Few men are lucky enough to go back where they began, let alone be reacquainted with old friends. Most of the time, you must start over, somewhere new. He shouldn't have left him like that.

Vasily told him that he goes every day to the café where they met, and so Sergey takes the tram across town and heads straight to Moskovsky Prospect. There, he orders coffee and *rassolnik* and black bread, as if these things might make Vasily appear through sympathetic magic, and he waits. In the coming months, he will visit this café many times, always ordering the same thing, and as winter fades into spring he'll search the neighbouring streets for Vasily's building, but in vain. He will neither see nor hear from Vasily Sidorov again.

Chapter 3:
LOS ANGELES, MAY 1950

A low-ceilinged basement room on the edge of the Capitol lot. A ceiling fan whirs away full tilt but does nothing to clear the stale air. Two facing desks, two chairs, a filing cabinet and a wall calendar with a picture of somewhere tropical. Later in the day, the Venetian blinds will cast noirish shadows across the wall.

Sitting opposite you, Angela Daniels. Plaid shirt and blue jeans. Hair short and tousled, like Gloria DeHaven. She taps her pen against her teeth and sighs and your eyes meet hers across the desk.

You say, "What?"

She says, "What?"

"Why the big sigh?"

"I'm struggling," she says. "What's that you're working on?"

"Cowboys and Indians."

"Powwow or battle scene?"

"Battle scene. You?"

"Stuck on a duel. Wanna swap?"

You spent all last week writing duels. All those close-ups of squinting eyes and hands twitching near holsters.

"I'll pass."

There are eight rooms along this semi-subterranean corridor, each almost identical to this one, shared between sixteen composers; all working on stock music, stings and cues for the Capitol Pictures music department. Facing those offices, a row of ten smaller rooms nicknamed the Meat Lockers – soundproof cells, each containing an upright Steinway.

A knock at the door. Could be one of your neighbours, asking to borrow a pencil or some staff paper. Most likely, it's Henderson, the music department's very own vampire of mirth.

"Enter," says Angela, grandly, like a dowager countess in a costume flick, and Henderson enters the room: side parting, bow tie and sweater vest, holding a clipboard.

"Miss Daniels, Conrad," he says. Always calls men, the men who work under him, by their surnames, as if he believes it makes him sound more masculine. One of the guys.

"Hey, Henderson," you say. "I'm almost done on the circus stuff. I'll have it on Peggy's desk by lunchtime."

"I'm not here about the circus stuff," says Henderson. "What circus stuff?"

"Circus movie. Mature and Lamarr. He's the kind-hearted strongman, she's the acrobat with a secret."

"Oh. *That* circus movie. Sure. No. I'm not here about that. You hear anything about the Irving Gold picture, just got the green light? Lois Chandler and Chuck Logan?"

"Nope. Angie?"

"Chuck Logan," she says. "Remind me. Is that the prize-fighting pound of ham?"

"Sure as hell acts like one."

Henderson breathes loudly through his nose. "Neither of you are funny. But if you don't want the job…" He turns, a little theatrically, to the door.

"What job? You didn't mention a job. Which job?"

Henderson pauses, smiles.

"The Irving Gold picture," he says. "They're looking for a composer."

"Sole credit?"

"Sole credit."

"What's the picture?"

"*Scarlet Letter.*"

"The Hawthorne novel?"

"Correct."

"They're making a movie of *The Scarlet Letter* with b-actors?"

"Come now, Conrad. You know we –"

"…don't make b-movies. I know. But *The Scarlet Letter,* that's one of the… Angie? What's the word I'm looking for?"

"Cornerstones?"

"That's *exactly* the word. How do you *do* that? It's one of the cornerstones of American literature. And they're making it with *Chuck Logan*?"

"I know. What can I say? There wasn't much enthusiasm for it over in the West Block, but they owe Gold a favour, so…" Henderson shrugs.

"What made everyone so unenthusiastic?"

"The title. Scarlet. Red. You get the idea."

"You've got to be fucking kidding me."

"Could you not curse around the lady?"

"She swears like a sailor! Are you telling me there are people who think *The Scarlet Letter* is a communist tract?"

"I guess so. And look at the subtext."

"What subtext? It's a hundred years old."

"But if you tell that story *now*..."

"The book is a hundred years old."

"Be that as it may, it made some people nervous. So it's starring Chandler and Logan and the budget is one-point-four rather than two-point-eight and Laguna Beach will be standing in for Massachusetts Bay."

"Nice. Authentic. This town is full of idiots."

"No comment. Now, do you want the job or not?"

"Is that aimed at both of us?"

"Just you, Conrad."

"Gee, thanks," says Angela.

"No offence, Miss Daniels, but Mr Gold doesn't like women composers. So, Conrad, do you want me to put your name down?"

"It isn't mine for the taking?"

"Not yet. I'll have to run a few suggestions past Mr Walsh."

He's talking about Talbot Walsh, head of the music department. Henderson's boss. Everyone's boss. Collector of four Academy Awards, often for scores he neither wrote, arranged nor conducted. You've never met the man, but given his reputation you're more than happy to have Henderson act as intermediary.

"Which names are you running past him?"

"You. Jerome. Levine."

"Jerome? For a period piece? Isn't he a little screwball?"

"Walsh likes him."

"And Levine? Levine's good, but he's not that good."

"That's why I'm asking you. I think when Berg and Walsh hear some of the work you did on *Emerald Cutlass*, the job's as good as yours."

"Hear that, Angie? Job's as good as mine. Let me guess. Berg'll ask for Wagner with a touch of whimsy, because he wants Alfred Newman, but can't afford to borrow him from Fox. Am I right?"

"More or less."

"Okay. Put my name down. I'll start thinking 'Wagnerian Whimsy'. Or should that be 'Vimsy'? Nothing too Russian-sounding, of course. Wouldn't want to go scaring our friends in the West Block."

"You shouldn't joke about things like that."

"Who says I'm joking?"

"You're always joking. Anyway. I have better things to do than stand around all day listening to your smart-cracks. Conrad. Miss Daniels."

When Henderson has left the room, you and Angela exchange a look, both of you wide-eyed and grinning. Angela slaps her hand down on her notepad.

"Goddamn, Sol. Sole credit. That is good news."

"Don't. Don't jinx this."

"But Jesus, you must be happy."

"I'll be happy when the job's mine."

★★

Santa Monica Boulevard, roof down, a sassy version of

Duke Ellington's *Caravan* playing on the radio. You glance up at the rear view mirror and see the Hollywood sign in reverse. That thing was falling apart when you first moved out here; its letters a dusty shade of brown, the H caved in from where some drunk had crashed his car into it. Some of the studio old timers thought it was a portent, the end of an era, but since then it's been given a fresh lick of paint and sits gleaming up there on the hill.

This is a perfect Los Angeles evening. In New York it's snowing, and struggling to get above 25°. When you hear something like that, it's hard to miss the place.

The canyon is always a surprise. Never mind that it's been how long now? Nine months? Even after nine months you still take that right onto Laurel Canyon Boulevard, and the city is gone, replaced by brown slopes dotted with dark green. Italianate and art deco villas lining the hillsides, and the air rich with the almost overpowering fragrances of brickellbush and Jeffrey pine. You park up in front of the house, turn the ignition. The engine falls silent. The music cuts off.

Inside, you pour yourself a scotch. No ice, just a squirt of soda water. The way Ron used to take it. He looks at you, smiling, from a picture taken out near Patchogue in the summer of '47; the two of you in short-sleeved shirts. Both smiling, arms hooked around each other's shoulders.

Funny how deceptive a picture can be. You were happy that day, but the days and months surrounding it were miserable. Jobs were few and far between, and the little work you had – with *off*-off-Broadway theatre and a handful of TV networks

– was far from well-paid. Ron secured you a few days, here and there, transcribing pieces for sheet music, and there were a few session gigs, but you were hardly the talk of the town. You watched as men your age wrote ballets and symphonies and Broadway shows, and you were consumed with envy.

But that weekend in Patchogue was a happy one. The photo shows the Ron you knew, not the man who now gets written about by critics and academics. The man in the picture is the one whose voice you hear in letters you keep beneath your bed; smiling and carefree, at times almost boyish.

Good God, you miss him.

You sip your drink and look out through the window at the terrace and the lawn. Once again, it's been trashed. Clumps of earth all over the place, the trash can on its side and trash spilling out everywhere. Looks like a warzone. Third time this month.

"God… damn it."

The culprits nowhere to be seen, of course. Probably happened during the night. Didn't even notice it this morning. Got up, got dressed, made coffee. You were in the car and driving into Hollywood, and the whole time your back yard looked like *this*.

Out on the terrace, it gets worse. Whatever did this took a shit – or rather, a series of shits – all over the lawn, so that all you can see is shit.

"Told ya," says a voice from next door's garden. "Shoulda put bricks on your trash can."

Mary rests on the fence with folded arms, a cigarette

dangling from her lip in an ebony holder, the ash threatening to fall into her martini. Her eye shadow is a little heavy this evening, giving her look a touch of *Dio de los Muertos*. Other than that, her hair is as immaculately quaffed as ever, her gown – an oriental-style 1920s original, you'd guess – still fits. Garlands of orange and green costume jewellery hang around her neck.

"You think it's raccoons?" you ask.

"Gotta be. We had the same problem when we moved here, back in '36."

"I just don't get it. If they're after the trash, why don't they just go after the trash? Why this?"

"Because they're vermin. And they think this is their territory."

"Their territory? We're in LA, for Christ's sake."

"Don't let that fool ya. We're in the mountains here, Sol. About a month after we moved here my late husband – may he burn in hell – saw a cougar in the yard."

"A cougar?"

"Sure. There's cougars and coyotes all around here. Still, for my money raccoons are the worst. They'll just tear the place apart. As you can see. Say... What's your poison there?"

She takes the cigarette holder from her lower lip and points its stem at your drink.

"Scotch."

"Before six? A man after my own heart. Why don't you hop over the fence, and bring the hooch. If you like scotch I've got a bottle I picked up in England around here somewhere."

"I don't know, Mary. Shouldn't you be saving that for a special occasion?"

"Sol, I am fifty-one years old and haven't had a call-back in months. If I save that scotch for a special occasion I'll be cremated with it, and the explosion'll take out half of Southern California."

You join her on her terrace. Similar to your own – both houses were built by the same architect – but busy with dying pot plants. Above the mountains the sky is lilac, and you can hear cicadas chirruping in the scrub.

"I'm just not used to this," you say. "I mean, raccoons? Cougars? I grew up in New York. The only wildlife there is rats."

"Plenty of rats in this town, too."

"It's like living in a goddamn menagerie."

Mary laughs. She refills her glass and passes you the bottle.

"Reminds me of *Intolerance,*" she says. "Every day, that set was like a zoo. Jaguars, elephants, donkeys and doves. Every day there'd be a new animal on set. And one day these two stagehands, they're carrying a stone lion, except it isn't really made of stone. It's plaster of Paris, or some such. So they're carrying this stone lion and they almost drop it as they're walking past Seena Owen. She was one of the actresses. Had a bigger part than me, but we went way back. Well, Seena screams like you'd think it had crushed every bone in her foot."

You've heard the story before, but you don't tell her this. Instead, you top up your own glass and add a dash of soda from the syphon.

"And Mr Griffith, he just says, 'Seena, Seena, Seena. Calm yourself, woman. That thing couldn't have squashed a fly.'"

A brief pause. Cicadas. A twin-prop airplane yawns and putters its way across the sky towards Burbank.

"Is it true?" you ask. "What you said, about not having any call-backs?"

"I am going through a real dry spell, Sol. It ain't funny being fifty-one in this town. Too old to play the damsel in distress, too young to play *grandmaw* or mother superior. Besides, even when I *am* old enough to play mother superior, I don't think I'm exactly the habit-wearing type, do you? My only habit is this stuff."

She lifts her drink and swills it around, the ice cubes jangling against the glass.

"But you got it easy. Composers, I mean. Never past your prime. And the movies'll always need music, for as long as there's movies. And if that don't work out, there's always TV. You know, I auditioned for a TV show last year. Some *Buck Rogers* piece of crap called *Captain Video*. You know what they told me? They said I was 'too big for the small screen'. Gave the part to some radio actress. And now I hear they've cast Vivienne Leigh as Blanche in *Streetcar*. An Englishwoman playing Blanche DuBois! That said, same bitch went and got herself Scarlett O'Hara. Not that I'm bitter. *Everyone* auditioned for *that* part. I believe even Danny Kaye gave it his best.

"Anyway. I called them up at the studio, I called them and I said, 'I'm just checking my name is still on file', because these things happen. Your file gets misplaced, and suddenly you don't exist. So I called 'em, and I said, 'Am I still on file?' And they said, 'Sure you're still on file, Miss Lafayette.' And I said, 'Well, that's funny, because last time I checked I was a Louisiana-born actress of a certain age and yet I was not asked to audition for *Streetcar*."

"And what did they say?"

"They said Mr Feldman and Mr Kazan already had an actress in mind, and that open auditions were not held."

Mary throws another couple of ice cubes into her glass, and drenches them with scotch. The ice cracks.

"But they can all go to hell," she says, and somewhere in the mountains, as if agreeing with her, a coyote howls.

★★

You love Los Angeles at night. People on street corners. Music from bars. The air cooler, but never cold. The city's lights glide along the contours of the car, and you smile at your reflection in the mirror; a lopsided grin weighed down by whisky, though you're not too drunk to drive.

You park near Pershing Square and stroll across, trying to look like a man walking home or at least walking *somewhere*. There's a statue of Beethoven, incongruous in a square lined with palm trees, and around its base stands a group of men, none any older than twenty, twenty-one years of age. Preppy-looking, in their blue jeans and plaid shirts. Hair slicked back. Nearby, three beat cops who would rather be anywhere but

Pershing Square on a Friday night.

One of the young men glances your way. He says something to his friends before leaving them and strolling towards you.

"Hey! Bill!"

Not you. Someone else. Seemed too good to be true. He's very attractive.

"Bill!" the kid says again. He's looking right at you.

"I think you've mistaken me for someone else," you say, quietly so the cops won't hear. "My name's not Bill."

"Oh, I know that," says the kid, smiling and grabbing you by the hand, giving you a firm, manly, hey-there-old-buddy handshake. His accent sounds southern. "That's just for them," he adds, tilting his head towards the cops. "We start talking like we never met before and we'll end up in jail. This way, we're just two buddies who happened to see each other. So. What *is* your name?"

"Sol," you tell him. "Solomon."

"Like King Solomon! Well, hi, Sol. I'm Nick." And he shakes your hand a second time, as if you needed reintroducing. "You from LA?"

"New York."

"I love New York," says Nick. "I mean, I never been there, but I'm sure I'd love it if I did. I am from Wichita Falls, Texas. You ever been there?"

"I haven't."

"You ain't missing much."

He asks what you do, and you tell him you're a composer for the movies. Not too much of a stretch. You've written music that's been used in films. You just haven't seen your name in the credits.

"Well, ain't that a coincidence?" says Nick. "I'm an actor."

He grins, the smile of every kid who thinks this could be his big break, that you might be his ticket, because maybe you know someone who knows someone. You ask if you might have seen him in anything, and he tells you not yet, but you will one day. His confidence, his certainty, is appealing; the kind you only ever see in those who haven't been here very long. Give him another month and it won't run anywhere near as deep.

He asks where you live, and you tell him you live in Laurel Canyon. He says he lives in West Hollywood and asks if you have a ride.

"Because if you have, maybe you could take me home. If you're already going that way, I mean."

★★

The kid has a quiet intensity about him. Maybe not the sharpest tool in the box, and he has more swagger than you would normally find attractive, but there's something behind his eyes, a spark of something. You're just not yet sure what it is.

Remember the first guy you brought back here? You'd been in Los Angeles three weeks. Picked him up at that place on Sunset Strip where you press a buzzer to get in, like a speakeasy. He was a slab of beef; handsome enough, and square-jawed. He reminded you of somebody. You know who he reminded you of. It may have been a long time ago, but still. Did you think this guy would be the same? Did you think that night would be as special? Fat chance. This guy had nothing going on between the ears. Wouldn't have been so bad if he was any good in bed, but instead he just lay there, as if you should be grateful, as if your role was simply to worship him, and his was to bask in it.

Every chance this kid will be the same – they usually are, the ones aware of their own beauty – but right now you're too anxious to even think about what happens next. Instead, you pour the drinks, Nick staring at you from the doorway the whole time.

He tells you that you have a nice place, and you thank him, and he says, "You must be making a whole lot of money to have a place like this."

"Not really."

"Then how'd you afford it?"

"I had an inheritance."

"Your folks?"

"A friend."

"Well, it's a real nice house."

He talks about acting, and says he never really studied it, he just knows he'd be good at it. And they're making so many Westerns these days, why, they must be crying out for actors with a voice like his. He says there's a bunch of actors living at Sunset Towers, but they're New York types. Serious types. He lives in a shared duplex off Fountain Avenue. He asks if you ever met anyone famous, and you tell him you once met Edward G. Robinson.

"The gangster?"

"He plays gangsters, sure. My father and he grew up together on the Lower East Side. He took me to see him in a play when I was nine or ten. We went backstage and met him."

"What's he like?"

"I don't remember much. He wasn't so famous then. His dressing room smelled of pipe smoke."

"Gee," says the kid, genuinely impressed. "Say. You ever meet Montgomery Clift?"

You tell him you haven't.

"I have," says Nick. "This one time. He's the best. You ever see that movie of his, *The Heiress*?"

Of course you did. Copland's score is the favourite to win the Oscar, and if *he* can do it, if *he* can come out here and write movie music…

"That was a great movie," says Nick. "It had Montgomery Clift and what's-her-name from *Gone with the Wind*. Olivia DeHavilland. That was a great movie. And say, you kinda look like Montgomery Clift. Anyone ever tell you that?"

He's flattering you, though he isn't the first person to say so.

"Never," you say.

"Sure you do," says Nick, moving a step closer. He takes his drink from you, and with his free hand reaches out to touch your face. "Same eyes. Same nose. Same mouth."

He leans in close and kisses you, his mouth soft and fleshy

and a perfect fit with your own. When you part, he says, "Say. You even kiss like him. Do it again."

Chapter 4:
MANHATTAN, OCTOBER 2001

Three more beers. A cheeseburger from the counter near the window, served up on a paper plate. She carried on drinking. Everything was a little fuzzy now. When she placed her hands on the bar she couldn't tell whether it was her hands that were shaking or the bar. A guy in a Hawaiian shirt sat on the stool next to hers and delivered a rambling monologue about how Britney Spears was this century's answer to Billie Holiday.

"We need our icons to suffer," he said. "They die for us, if not literally then through their art. We need them to fail."

People like him had once seemed a part of the city's theatre; as if the authorities hired actors to play them. Now they were mostly a nuisance. Wasn't New York crazy enough? And no sooner had the guy in the Hawaiian shirt left her alone than another man – lilac pompadour, Burt Lancaster teeth – sat down and began filing his nails. He smiled at her without saying anything and when he was finished grooming himself he ordered a bowl of Wasabi nuts, picking at them daintily.

"You want one?" he asked. "I'm sure they're terrible for one's waistline, but I can't help myself." He popped another little green nut into his mouth. "They say you are what you eat, which I suppose must make me a bitter old rice queen."

A moment later his attention was drawn away by a young man in a snug grey t-shirt.

"Hugo, darling!"

Natalie was alone again. Just how she preferred it. It wasn't healthy, the way some people needed constant company; and if not in real life then in online chatrooms. Why did everyone have to be talking all the time? She couldn't understand it. Just leave me alone on this stool and I am Zen. I am the calm centre of the universe.

She finished her drink and walked across the Village to East 12th Street. It was night time now, and the apartment was dark. She turned on a few lights, opened a cupboard. Schnapps. Half a bottle. The bodega near Thompson Square Park would be open, but the man who ran the place always lingered when handing over the change, and she only had a ten dollar bill in her purse. Schnapps it is. She sighed and poured herself a glass. She heard muffled TV rockets and explosions coming from the apartment below.

Her roommate, Gino, had been away since early September, touring Europe with a dance company. Theirs wasn't the biggest apartment – four rooms wedged into one corner of their building – but it felt large and empty without him. Neither of her parents had ever seen the place. Her mother hadn't visited the States in over a year, and when last in New York she had stayed in a hotel.

What would they think of the apartment? Her father might look on it with a kind of rough admiration. Maybe he would be happier for a son to live in a building with rodent problems and damp, its staircases tilting with subsidence, but at least his daughter wasn't blowing all her income on a place she couldn't afford. Her mother, on the other hand, would have staged an intervention. The credit cards would soon be splayed across the chrome dining table. In the phonebook she would circle the names of nearby cleaners and interior decorators, and she would phone them, getting quotes. By the time Gino got back from Europe he wouldn't recognise the place. But in its present condition, even Natalie had to admit it wasn't what she'd ever imagined for herself.

She finished the schnapps and went to bed, hoping the booze might help her sleep. No chance. She lay there, in the dark, going over the same thoughts in a loop. Pavel Grekov was a scam artist, out to blackmail ageing writers and composers, accusing them of plagiarism. Pavel Grekov was a psychopath, obsessed with obscure figures from TV history. Pavel Grekov was delusional; his grandfather's music and the *Battle Station Alpha* theme sounded nothing alike.

She had never really met anyone like him. There were one or two Russians on the musicology course at NYU, and she'd met others since, but none like Pavel Grekov. He was rougher than the men she had known. In the village where she grew up the men – no, *boys* – wore rugby shirts, chinos and tan Oxfords. They went snowboarding in winter and slummed it around the nicer parts of India in their gap years. When she chose NYU, rather than the Guildhall or the Royal College, it was partly because of them, partly because everywhere in England – even London – felt so bloody parochial.

In New York the men she knew were pleasant, bookish types. They read Frank O'Hara poems and played guitar and knew the name of every vegetarian restaurant within a mile of Washington Square. They could speak intensely about

Schoenberg or Ginsberg or Leonard Cohen for hours on end. On the surface, they may have seemed entirely unlike the boys in rugby shirts and chinos, but they spent just as much time enjoying the sound of their own voices.

Pavel was like none of these men. If he was, she might have guessed what he was after. Money, prestige, honour. A combination of the three. But she couldn't place him, she didn't "know his sort". If he wasn't dishonest or insane, what could he possibly want?

She moved onto her side and closed her eyes. All she could hear, over and over, was that music. Not even the whole piece, just the first few bars; the part everybody knows. The part any child could hum along to, even now.

Did it *sound* Russian? Or rather, did it sound *uniquely* Russian? Could it have come from some other time and place than Sol Conrad's imagination in 1978? Shades of Stravinsky, maybe a dash or two of Holst. Was there something else?

If Grekov had the score, she'd know a fake the second she saw it. And by reading it, she would know if the two pieces were the same. Not just similar, but identical.

The sleepless night wore on, long enough for her to sober up. The nearest bars and bodegas were now closed, and besides, once that first drunken buzz had worn off, there was no point in chasing after a second.

She got up, went to the lounge, and for the first time in months took her cello out of its case. All this time, during everything that happened, it was there, hidden away in the dark. She sat near the window and placed a practice mute over the strings. She adjusted the tuning and began playing the prelude from the second of Bach's cello suites. Not immediately, of course. There were missteps and bum notes before muscle memory took over. Then it came back to her, and the room was filled with music.

When she'd tired of Bach, she opened the window and the city's noise burst in like the howl of a jet engine. She waited as it settled into separate sounds and then she played along with the chugging bass of helicopters, and the swooping glissandos of police sirens, and she improvised around the short, sharp blast of hip-hop as an open-topped car went past. The music vibrated through the edgework and into her thighs and through her fingertips as they pressed each string against the neck. That sound, like a feather or a dust mote suspended in the air. The purest expression of all the things she would never say. This was the closest she had come to creating music in years, and she played instinctively, without concentrating, till her fingers were sore and her eyes were tired, and the theme from *Battle Station Alpha* had faded into silence.

Chapter 5:
VORKUTA, AUGUST 1942

Dusk and dawn feel like the same thing. The sun sets around 9pm, rising again before 2am, and it never truly gets dark. It won't feel like night, true night again until September. As such, August is a month he associates with an approaching darkness. This month marks the fourth anniversary of his arrest.

At 8pm the sun still hovers over the low hills on the river's western banks. No snow on the ground. There hasn't been snow since April. In the few places not yet built upon the earth is covered in the dense black scrub that passes for vegetation in this part of the world.

Not that it's ever felt like a part of the world. Vorkuta is another planet, the kind of place you might read about in *Technology for Youth* magazine. A barren, alien world explored by brave, Soviet pioneers. Though in those stories the pioneers are always proud to be there.

Sergey spent over a year in a logging team before arriving in Vorkuta. It was followed by a short spell in the mines until the Camp Boss, Maltsev, learned that he was – or at least had been – a musician. The general is a young man, late thirties at most. There aren't many old men these days, at least not in the lower positions of authority. It's rare to see anyone older than forty in charge of anything.

"We have a band here," Maltsev said. "Did you know that?"

Sergey nodded. He'd heard them playing as they filed out

each day; a ragged band of players standing at the gates, playing a march or something similarly rousing. Something to raise their spirits as they set off for another twelve hours beneath the ground.

"We lost a few of our players in the winter," said Maltsev. "And they don't have a band leader. Do you conduct?"

Sergey nodded.

"Good. Well. That's decided. I've spoken with the *troika* and your brigadier and they agree that you can be excused from working in the mine for now. In the mornings you and the band will play at the gates. Then, when everyone has left, you can return to the barrack and do whatever needs to be done there. You can discuss all that with your brigadier. How are you with your fists?"

"I don't understand," said Sergey.

Maltsev let out a short, bleak laugh. "You're a young man," he said. "The others in your brigade may resent you staying home all day but getting the same rations. Can you take care of yourself? You look as if you've boxed."

Sergey shook his head. His flattened nose he acquired not in a boxing ring but an interrogation room.

Since that day in Maltsev's office, Sergey's routine has been more or less the same, with little variation. The alarm sounds at 5am. Thirty minutes later, once everyone has woken and washed, they congregate and are counted outside the cook-house before breakfast.

Sergey's fellow band mates are from other barracks: A Jewish trumpeter from Minsk, here for stealing wood from a warehouse; a young lad who plays snare drum, booted out of an army marching band for stealing bread. There are others, most of them thieves or petty criminals. None of them are fellow Fifty-Eighters, enemies of the state. For a Fifty-Eighter to play in the band is practically unheard of.

"Maltsev must like you," said the Jew. "Or else you'd have been kept in the mine or fed to the Urkas by now."

It was Maltsev who, on hearing it one morning, took a fancy to the *Pechorin March*. Sergey had only had the band play it out of restlessness. Each morning they played the same repertoire of standards, dreary old songs and marches. Perhaps if they played something he had written himself, he could forget where he was, if only for a moment.

"I like this one," said Maltsev. "What is it?"

"One of mine, comrade," Sergey replied, his voice raised as the band continued playing. "I wrote it."

"It's very good," said Maltsev. "You should play it every morning."

Once the last workers have left, the gates are closed. Sergey returns to his barrack and with some of the older inmates he sweeps the floor, lights the stove and empties the latrine tank. This will usually take up much of the day. The tank itself holds twenty gallons, and it takes several of them working in a team to carry it. The stench is unbearable, even in the coldest depths of winter. He'd thought he might get used to it eventually, in the way a farmer must grow accustomed to the smell of pigshit, but he never has.

If he finds himself with time to spare, spare minutes

unnoticed by the brigadier or the guards, he writes. Often the briefest passages of melody; never a whole piece. Paper and pencils are hard to come by. He'll write on anything. Maybe one day these fragments will coalesce into a single work – maybe even a symphony – but one that will never be performed.

Even if he gets through this alive, there will be no moment of absolution or redemption. The ones who enjoy that privilege are never those who were sent away. Look at Shostakovich. Sergey was there at the Philharmonic, the night they premiered Dmitri's Symphony No.5. The theatre was full, and at its end the audience cheered for a good hour, their applause lasting so much longer than the symphony. It was a powerful piece, alright. During the third movement, the largo, Sergey noticed people, men and women, weeping, and later that evening he heard men from the composers' union – Remizov, Dzerzhinsky and the others – talking about it so warmly.

Comrade Dmitri had more than atoned for his dreadful Formalism, they said, and for that disgusting opera at MALIGOT. (None of them even dared mention it by name.) It was a pleasure, hearing him abandon all that nonsense and stick to true, Soviet virtues.

But Sergey heard something else in the music, something that troubled him immensely. How could the others not have noticed? It was there, in the largo that made people weep; a despair so absolute, nothing that followed could contradict or overturn it. Now, in the piece – or rather, pieces – he's written,

Sergey hears a similar desolation, and it's not a *mea culpa.* It's a scream.

The days pass easier if he can forget where he is, or at least why he's here, and what brought him here. He wants to remember life before this, but each time he remembers it's unbearable.

At 8pm the brigades return. Sergey hides his paper and pencil beneath a floorboard near the bunk he shares with three others, and along with the old timers he sets about looking busy. It wouldn't do to have men come back from the mines and see them lying around on their bunks.

First to enter are the two Poles, Lubinski and Bajek. They hurry in, closing the door behind them, and glance furtively at Sergey and the old men before speaking to one another in German. Perhaps they think that nobody will understand them, but Sergey hears mention of a time – 10:30 – and a place; the eastern edge of the compound, far from the nearest guard dog and watchtower.

"Wird es dunkel genug sein?"

"Nicht sehr dunkel, aber dunkler als jetzt."

The old men watch them for a moment. When it becomes clear they won't understand a word, they carry on cleaning the room. Sergey feigns ignorance.

The Poles arrived in Vorkuta a few months after him, prisoners of war after the invasion of Poland. Both younger than Sergey – neither any older than twenty-five – but working in the mines is ageing them, the way it ages everyone. All of the men here look like corpses.

Lubinski is the older of the two, and stronger. Bajek is

attractive, almost boyish, and more timid than his friend. Sergey senses that Lubinski is the protector, but whether the relationship is sexual, he couldn't say. There could be a physical convenience to it, when the lights are out, but the same could be said of many others.

He can't remember the last time he thought of sex. For the first eighteen months he thought of little else, as a drowning man must think of nothing but drawing breath. In the barrack he masturbated almost constantly, often regardless of whether or not he had privacy, but it was no longer a pleasurable act. Rather, it was an effort, a physical need to expel something. Thoughts of sex, of tenderness and intimacy, are unhelpful in a place where neither tenderness nor intimacy exist. Remembering them would only make him ill. Better to work away at himself until he had let those thoughts go.

Dinner: A second ration of *balanda.* Oats, watery broth and fish bones. The same as every night. On a good day, there might be enough bread left over to mop it up. One of his bunkmates, Smirnov, tells him he may have got his hands on a chessboard and asks Sergey if he can play. Sergey replies with a noncommittal nod. Hasn't played in years, but anything to pass the time. Dinner over, they leave the canteen and return to the barracks.

Sergey's is home to a small, but growing, number of Old Believers; their leader an aged priest who arrived during the winter. In the towns and cities these men would be jeered at and beaten for their antique superstitions, but here they're tolerated, more or less. Most of the men ignore them, but they fill the barrack's brigadier, Charkov, with an almost comical unease. He's an old party man, convicted of fraud. Not old in years, but a party member since he was old enough to join, and despite everything he still balks at anything of which the party wouldn't approve.

Sergey listens to the Old Believers' prayers, but they may as well be praying in some obscure Siberian dialect. The individual words he understands, but the meaning of it all is lost to him. How, in a place like this, can they believe some benign, supernatural being is listening to their prayers? Is it hope, simple-mindedness, or desperation?

Lights out, and Sergey and three others – Smirnov, Koslov and Lebvedev – crawl into their bunk, beneath separate blankets. Limbs jostling for space. Short, frustrated sighs. Koslov's foot is too close to Sergey's face. Lebvedev sleeps shirtless and has his arm behind his head, so that if Sergey were to lie on his side he would have his face in Lebvedev's armpit. It's a nuisance, of course, but they're glad of it in winter. He can't imagine how it would be to sleep alone out here when it's at its coldest. The barrack becomes a chorus of snuffles, coughs and farts. Somebody mutters something from the far side of the room, and a handful of men laugh.

"Keep it down," says Charkov.

Sergey is the only one who notices that the Poles have already made their escape. They were crafty. They must have known exactly what time Charkov carries out his nightly headcount, and then crept out via the shallow alcove housing the latrine. Maybe they snuck out while the Old Believers were praying and everyone else was playing cards or reading. Crafty Polaks.

They chose the best time of year for it. Usually, when someone tries to escape, they do so in the dead of winter, thinking the darkness will help cover them. But if the searchlights don't pick them out against the snow, the cold kills them before they're a mile beyond the fence.

In spring, however, the twilight of the small hours renders searchlights all but useless, and it's no longer murderously cold.

They stand a chance, the two young Poles; a chance, at least, to get more than a mile away from the camp. But then what? A thousand miles of unforgiving waste in all directions. That is the secret, the incredible genius behind a place like this, and he admires it, in a way. Not only is Russia blessed with vastness, it contains within that vastness places so remote they may as well be other worlds, separated from the cities of the West by stretches of country no man, however strong, could survive.

And if the cold and hunger don't get to them, the Zyrians will. Every few months they come by, the local tribesmen, with a fresh cache of severed heads and hands, and they collect their reward from Maltsev, who never asks what happened to the rest of the bodies.

The Old Believers see these things – the darkness of the mines, the bitter cold of winter, the violence of the Zyrians, the Urkas, the secret service, of *everyone* – as proof that what they call the "End Times" are upon us. Unlikely. An end would be a relief, and time is meaningless here. One day, repeating itself, and in high summer or low winter even the hours just rolling around in circles, like the final moments of a spinning coin. Sergey doubts he will see Leningrad again, if Leningrad even exists as something more than a memory or an idea.

The trains no longer bring in people from the cities. Just other prisoners from other camps. Perhaps the camps are all that's left. Perhaps the rest of Russia is gone, burned to the ground.

Asleep in his shared bunk, Sergey stumbles through half-remembered rooms and along impossible streets, before finding himself clinging to the outer edge of an immense railway bridge. He believes it represents a bridge he once knew, but couldn't name, across the Neva, but in this dream the river is impossibly wide, more like a roiling sea. There are few places for him to hold on, too many trains clattering back and forth for him to walk along the tracks, and so he edges his way slowly along a reddish brown girder with cautious sidesteps.

Dogs are barking. Perhaps the railway men are after him. He's trespassing on their bridge. Then Koslov mutters something, and Lebedev replies with a whisper, and the dream unthreads itself, and Sergey stirs and asks them, "What's going on?"

"An escape," says Koslov. "Must be."

The camp's guard dogs are tethered to metal wires, strung up between the watchtowers, and as they run back and forth their leashes howl and screech against the cables. The barking he could stand, if only just, but the cold mechanical shriek of metal against metal makes him nauseous.

There's movement, something from the alcove. Breathing, short breaths, anxious. Someone crawling on his hands and knees across the room. One of the Poles, Lubinski or Bajek; he can't see which.

"Get into bed, you fool," someone hisses. "Before they turn on the lights."

A commotion, the crack of shin against bedframe, and the Pole, whichever one it is, swears loudly in Polish. Then the lights come on.

He'd expected some of the NKVD men, perhaps even a sleepily ill-tempered Maltsev in his overcoat and pyjamas. Instead, three Urkas enter the barrack, two armed with knives, the third a crowbar.

He's seen them before, these men. There aren't many Urkas in this camp, so they stand out. Impossible not to notice them, strutting around as if they were camp bosses. Bare-chested as soon as the temperature creeps above freezing. The two carrying knives look like brothers; tall and muscular but with narrow, vulpine faces. The one with the crowbar is short and fat, his arms and chest covered in tattoos.

They say nothing, the Urkas. They don't shout or yell, they simply walk across the barrack to where the Pole – Sergey sees that it was Bajek – is cowering beneath his blanket; trying, and failing, to make it look as if he has been there the whole time.

Charkov is out of his bed, a grey blanket over his shoulders. He shuffles across the room.

"Listen, here," he says. "What's going on? What's happening?"

The short, fat Urka with the crowbar turns and punches Charkov in the face, and Charkov hits the ground and doesn't move.

The taller pair drag Bajek from his bed and begin beating him, and Bajek takes the beating silently, with not so much as a whimper. Perhaps this is it. Perhaps this is all the punishment he'll get tonight. The Urkas know he tried to escape, but it's pointless going to town on him when a simple beating would suffice. Isn't it?

No such luck. When the boy is broken and bleeding they drag him out from the barrack; the short, fat Urka kicking Charkov in the stomach as they leave. Charkov grunts and retches but says nothing. Then it's lights out again.

It's an age before Sergey gets back to sleep. Not the first time he's seen someone dragged away, knowing he wouldn't see them again. This is how the world is now.

The *reveille* sounds. A quick wash with cold water. Dress and walk over to the canteen. Charkov isn't there. He was gone from his bed when everyone woke up and no-one has seen him since. No-one mentions the two Poles. The belongings they left behind – a pack of Belomor cigarettes and a box of tea – have already been divided between the two others sharing their bunk.

Sergey meets his bandmates at the stockroom, as they collect their instruments. The old Jew from Minsk asks if it was his barrack the two Polish lads escaped from. They file out to the gates. The rest of his barrack are marching out with a new brigadier. Still no sign of Charkov.

It's a moment before he notices the bodies either side of the gates, propped up against the fence and facing outwards, like stone lions guarding a tomb. Lubinski's skull has been bashed in. Bajek is naked and covered in too much black, congealed blood for them to know exactly how he died.

Sergey and the band play within yards of their corpses. *O Field, My Field* and *Farewell of Slavianka.* The workers file out past them, stopping only occasionally to glance down at the bodies beside the gates.

"Stop gawping!" a brigadier barks. "Nothing to see but a couple of dead Polaks."

Maltsev appears. He watches the brigades march out for a moment, absently smoking a cigarette, before addressing Sergey.

"I don't like this tune so much," he says. "Play the other one. The one you wrote."

The rest of the band look to Sergey and not Maltsev for their cue. After taking in a deep breath Sergey nods, and they begin playing the *Pechorin March.*

Hearing it this morning is like the experience of seeing, but not quite recognising, his reflection in a mirror. That momentary disconnect. *That can't be me. This can't be it.* He hears a melody, played as clumsily as ever, hears the same notes he remembers writing, but something has changed. Not its melody, but its intent. Gone are the knowing irony, the mock heroics. All that remains is bombast, and an ugly, empty void between the notes.

Later that afternoon, once the barrack chores are complete, he goes to Maltsev's office. The Camp Boss's secretary greets him with his customary peevishness.

"He's a busy man," he says. "And I'm sure you have work to do."

Sergey tells him that his work is done, and that he would very much like to speak with Maltsev.

The secretary sighs, drumming his pencil on the pages of an open ledger.

"He won't be pleased."

A minute later, and with simmering petulance, he shows Sergey through to Maltsev's office. Not his first time here, but he often forgets how out-of-place it feels; the walls decorated with framed photographs and watercolour paintings, the floor between the door and the desk covered almost entirely by an oriental rug. The shelves are crammed with books; encyclopaedias, a complete set of Tolstoy, a number of volumes about the German War.

Maltsev is smoking a cigarette, and as Sergey takes a seat he nudges the open pack of Prima across the desk.

"Please," he says. "Help yourself. Now, 237. How can I help you?"

Sergey bites his lower lip.

"I want to work in the mines, comrade," he says. "Starting tomorrow. When the others from my barrack go to the mines, I want to go with them."

Maltsev laughs until he starts coughing. "Are you mad?"

Sergey shakes his head.

"You know," says Maltsev, "I have men cutting off their own fingers and toes so they won't have to work in the mines, and you're asking to go there? When every day the toughest thing you do is pick up a violin?"

"I know," says Sergey. "But I don't want to do it anymore. I don't want to play music."

"Why not?"

"Because music is all I have, and playing it out here is killing it for me."

A mistake. One must never let them know what you think or how you feel, about *anything*.

Maltsev takes a long and final drag on his cigarette and stubs it out in the ashtray with a forceful twist.

"Is that so?" he says. "You say this as if, I don't know, as if you were still working at the Kirov. As if you had much of a choice."

"I know. But I think I'd be better placed in the mines."

"Listen, 237. I have thousands of men here, in this camp, at my disposal, and it's up to me and the *troika* to decide where you can be made useful. I want you playing violin on those gates, same time tomorrow."

"I would rather go down the mines."

Leaning back in his chair, Maltsev takes another cigarette from the pack and lights it.

"You know," he says, "I'm not an unreasonable man. Really, I'm not. Is this because of the Polish boys?"

Sergey says nothing.

"They were from your barrack, yes?"

"Yes."

"Then I understand. I'm not inhuman. It must have been

upsetting, seeing them there this morning. But you understand why they had to be made an example of, yes? If we didn't set an example there would be chaos. Now, chaos is all well and good in the city, with all the hustle and bustle that entails, but here? Out here, chaos endangers lives, and I can't let that happen. Please. Do one thing for me. Go back to your barrack and think long and hard about this. I won't tell your new brigadier about the conversation we've had. Is that fair?"

He hadn't expected Maltsev to be quite so reasonable. Not much ground gained, but little point in pleading his case, and so he leaves and returns to his barrack.

It's maybe twenty minutes before the Urkas arrive, the same three who took Bajek away last night. Their leader – the shorter one – tells the others to get out, and when they hesitate he says it again, but with greater force. The old men shuffle out of the barrack. The door closes behind them. A silence that seems to drain all colour from the room.

"What is this?" Sergey asks. He hates the Urkas, not just these three men, but all of them, and has done since the day he arrived. He hates their sadism and their swagger, but more than that he hates their warped code of conduct, the strict set of rules they live by, and will happily kill for. He's known them to cut a man's throat over a game of cards before now; the authorities more than happy to ignore it, to simply strike the man's name from the roster. One less mouth to feed. In the Urkas, there's something more terrifying than simple brute force. They are the distilled essence of man's worst traits, given free rein. They rarely speak at times like this. They never have to.

Two of them – the shorter one and one of the taller pair – rush across the room. Sergey swings at one of them, but they've got him by the arms. He tries to wriggle free, but they are so much stronger than he ever was. The third man hits him in the face. Sergey tastes blood. He hits Sergey again, this time in the stomach, and when he's limp in their arms the Urkas carry Sergey to a table and pin him, face down, on its surface.

Someone lowers Sergey's trousers and his underwear and tears off his shirt. The metal buttons scatter across the floor. One of the men, Sergey can't tell which, grabs him by the hair and slams his head against the table. Something hard is pressed against the cleft between his buttocks.

The pain of being violated is immediate. Like something hot tearing at his insides. He feels skin against his skin, a man's knees against his thighs. Almost a relief. If they had used a crowbar or a broom handle to do this, he'd be as good as dead. Not that this is much more dignified. One of them spits, and he feels something warm and wet land between his shoulder blades. One of them punches him in the back of the head and the room kaleidoscopes around him. He hopes no-one is outside, watching. He hopes all memory of this goes away. He hopes that no-one will ever speak of it.

The Urkas take turns, each one cheered on by his friends, and when they're finished they throw him to the ground, delivering a final volley of kicks before leaving the barrack.

The old timers file back in, but keep their distance. Sergey cleans himself up, washing the blood off his face and out of his mouth, washing the phlegm from his shoulders and the semen from his backside and from between his legs. When the brigade returns, no-one says anything to him, but it's obvious they all know. He's different now.

The following morning Sergey and the camp band are back at the gates. Wolves must have come here in the night, because the bodies of both Lubinski and Bajek have had large, ragged chunks taken out of them. In the mild warmth of the morning they're beginning to rot, and the stench of rancid meat hangs heavily in the air.

The band plays *We Are the Red Cavalry* and *There Marched the Soldiers* and *Farewell of Slavianka* and Sergey hears Maltsev before he can see him.

"Good morning, men."

The band carries on playing, and Maltsev smiles at each of them in turn, ending with Sergey.

"Say, 237," he says. "Why don't you play the one I like? The one you wrote. I'd like to hear that now, I think. It is so very stirring."

Chapter 6:
LOS ANGELES, JUNE 1950

An unfamiliar beach. The tide going out, each step you take blanching the damp sand around your feet. The ocean heaves back, towards the setting sun, leaving pebbles and ribbons of seaweed in its wake. The smell of smoke; a bonfire. The flames and the smell intensify, black clouds drifting towards you across the sand.

You're awake and something is burning. You slip into pyjama pants and hurry to the stairs. No signs of smoke, but you can still smell it. An electrical fault. A spark. A curtain on fire. A room. This house. You lose your footing, sliding down three steps before steadying yourself. No signs of fire in the hallway, the lounge, the kitchen. You step out onto the terrace and the smell of smoke gets stronger still. A continuous black cloud rolling across your yard and out over the mountain. In Mary's garden, a bonfire. Stacks of papers and photographs burning, the letters blackening and vanishing in seconds, the photographs blistering and twisting into knots.

"Mary?"

She comes out in a nightgown, barefooted and with her hair in curlers. She's carrying an armful of papers and photographs and she tips them into the flames before noticing you.

"Oh, hi, Sol," she says, as if you'd caught her in the act of mowing her lawn. "Beautiful morning, ain't it?"

A telephone rings and she runs back indoors, her pink satin nightgown billowing behind her. She answers the phone. There's a moment's pause before she starts talking to whoever's on the other end of the line.

"They're following me," she says. "I *am* fucking calm. And I'm not making this up. Don't you tell me not to panic, you son-of-a-bitch. You're not the one with agents outside his goddamn house."

She appears at the window, the phone's receiver cradled between her shoulder and cheek. She scowls at you and draws the curtain shut.

★★

"You're late," says Angela.

"What time is it?"

"Half nine."

"Really?"

"Really."

Like you'd stood her up on a date.

You sit behind your desk and begin arranging things for the day ahead. You've got your staff paper, all you need now is a pencil. Where the hell is that pencil?

"Weirdest thing," you tell her. "I think my neighbour, you know, the actress I was telling you about? I think she's gone crazy."

The pencil is precisely where you left it on Friday, in the old olive tin you use as a pen caddy.

"How so?"

"I'm sorry…?"

"I said how is she crazy?"

"Oh. Right. She was in her garden, burning stuff. Letters and photographs. Talking to someone on the phone. Sounded crazy. Paranoid. Something about being followed."

"Maybe someone's following her."

"She's an actress. Why would anyone follow her?"

Angela tilts her head to one side: *Don't you get it?* The penny drops.

"Mary? No way."

"All that happened this morning?"

"The smell of burning woke me up. Maybe 7am?"

"I take it you haven't seen the latest *Counterattack*."

"What's that?"

"Sol. Do you pay *any* attention to what's going on in the world?"

"Not if I can help it."

"It's a right-wing rag. Real John Birch stuff."

"Funnier than *Charley Jones*?"

"Hilarious. Latest issue has a list of 'suspected communists' working in the entertainment industry."

"This again?"

"What do you mean, 'again'?" says Angela. "It never went away."

★★

You can't recall ever seeing him before. A small guy, early forties. Grey-black hair slicked sideways, heavy eyebrows and a neatly groomed moustached. Taupe suit, single breasted. Straight point collared shirt. Black tie.

He approaches you in the shaded gully of Avenue L, near the corner of Stage 7, and stands in your way so that you have no choice but to stop walking.

"Mr Conrad?" he says with a broad smile.

"Yes?"

"Roy Carmichael." You shake hands with him. "I'm head of security. You done for the day?"

"I am."

"Then maybe I could trouble you for a little of your time?"

"Sure."

"Where you parked?"

"Near Melrose Gate."

"Good. We'll walk and talk."

What could security want with you? You've never so much as stolen paperclips from this place, let alone anything valuable. Unless. But how could they know about Mary? No, this is something else. They couldn't know everything, could they? Nobody knows *everything*.

Together you cross the lot, out from the sunless trenches between soundstages and into the bleaching light of a June afternoon. He walks at a brisk pace, and even though you're a few inches taller than him you struggle to keep up.

"You from New York?" he asks.

"That's right."

Carmichael prods his chest with his thumb.

"Chicago, born and bred. I was wondering, Mr Conrad, if you'd seen this."

He reaches inside his jacket and produces a pamphlet. The cover features the drawing of a bright red hand clutching a microphone. *Red Channels The Report of Communist Influence in Radio and Television*

"Heard of it," you tell him. "Hadn't seen it."

"But you know what it contains."

"A list of Reds."

"And you know who's on that list?"

"John Wayne?"

Carmichael smiles again but doesn't laugh.

"That's a good joke, Mr Conrad," he says. "Ronald Bernard is on that list."

"Ron?" you say. "But that's… listen… Ronald Bernard has been dead for over a year. And even when he was alive…"

"I was aware of Mr Bernard's passing," says Carmichael. "You were friends with him, were you not?"

You think you know where this is going.

"I studied under him at Juilliard. But yes. I was also his friend."

"And were you aware of any political beliefs he may have held?"

You're out in the parking lot now, black cars lined up like shellfish clinging to a rock. You're fumbling for your car keys long before you'll need them.

"Political beliefs?" you ask. "Not really, no. I know he didn't vote for Dewey, if that's what you mean. But other than that, I was not aware of his 'political beliefs'. When we spoke to one another it was about music."

You're at the Oldsmobile, the keys held tightly in your fist, the metal digging painfully into your skin.

"This is my car," you tell him. "Was there anything else I could help you with?"

"Mr Conrad," says Carmichael, still smiling. "With all due respect, if there is anything, and I mean *anything* you're keeping from me, because you think it'll protect Mr Bernard's reputation, or your own, now is the time to tell me."

"I don't know what you're talking about."

"Yes, Mr Conrad. You do."

How much could he know? If he knew everything, he'd just tell you, wouldn't he? He wouldn't play games with you like this.

"Ronald Bernard was not a communist," you tell him. "And neither am I. If he's on that list, it's bullshit."

"No call for profanity. I'm just doing my job."

"Yeah. Just following orders. We've heard that before. Is that all, Mr… I'm sorry, what was your name?"

You remember his name. His name is Carmichael. Though, from his complexion and his build and that rat-a-tat accent, you'd guess it ended with a vowel before he moved out to the Coast.

"Roy Carmichael," he says.

"Okay, Mr Carmichael. Are we done?"

"We're done. Thank you for your time."

With a gentle tug, Carmichael takes the pamphlet from you, rolls it up and slides it back inside his jacket. He leaves you with a smile and a nod and walks back towards the studio, whistling as he goes.

★★

There's a Buick parked up in the road at the end of Mary's drive. In the front seats, two men in snap-brim hats. You can't see their faces, only their silhouettes, and they hardly move, except to smoke.

Aren't they meant to disguise themselves as mailmen or maintenance men? Their presence is so obvious, so deliberate. They want Mary to know she's being watched. That's assuming, of course, it's her they're watching.

You shower and change your clothes and you call on her, jumping over the fence with a half bottle of Scotch and two clean glasses. She's already on the terrace, wearing a floral kaftan, a green silk headscarf and furred slippers. Though it's only 6pm you can smell the alcohol on her breath as you lean in to kiss her on the cheek.

"You know," she says. "I ought to have quit Los Angeles a long time ago."

"What do you mean?"

"This place. The industry. It's changed so much since I first came out here. Back then it was run by *artists*. Oh, sure, there were money men, but they knew art when they saw it, most of them. And they knew when to keep their distance. When to sign a cheque, and when to let the artists do their work. But now? Now it feels like the movies are being made by suits and politicians."

"Tell me about it."

"Well, exactly. You must know this already, working down there every day. Sometimes I think out here on the Coast is where this country of ours goes mad."

"What do you mean?"

"Think about it. The frontier. All those pioneers heading west. All America's momentum pushing in this direction. But that drive, to head off into the wilderness, not knowing what was on the other side of the next mountain range, the next ridge… It must have taken some kind of madness."

"Or bravery?"

"Oh no. Bravery has a nobility to it. Doing the right thing, even when you're scared of the outcome. The pioneers, they were just crazy. They could have stayed at home and got along just fine, most of them, but they had to keep going. Driven by madness, or greed. Looking for gold, looking for oil. And by the time they reached the Pacific all they had left was madness."

She knocks back what's left of her whisky and reaches for the bottle.

"The trouble with this madness," she continues, "is that it hits the coast and has nowhere to go but backwards, rolling over the country till it reaches Washington. And there it sits, and stagnates. Just you mark my words, Sol. We have become a people scared. Look at what's happening in New York, with this Rosenberg character. They'll crucify him for what he's done. For what he's *alleged* to have done. And they won't stop there. One sacrifice begets another. They'll crucify us all."

"But if you've done nothing wrong..."

"You don't have to do something wrong, Sol. You know, during the war I was a part of something called Bundles for Britain. You know what it was? A *knitting circle*. Sending clothes over to kids in London when they were getting all hell bombed out of them. Now they say it was a Red organisation, a Communist front. Can you believe that?"

Is now the right time to tell her? Though she's been drinking all day, or at least all afternoon, she sounds collected enough to understand.

"There were men outside your house tonight."

"Oh, I know about *them*," she says. "They been there all day."

"They looked so out-of-place."

"It was the hats, wasn't it? You never see men wearing that style of hat out here. And they're meant to be 'undercover'. You know their best trick? They tie a white rag to your bumper so they can follow you through heavy traffic."

"You're kidding."

"Wish I was. Did it to me, one of the last times I drove into Hollywood. I was meeting an old friend for lunch. Katy Rogers. You remember her? *Hopalong Gals of '36?*"

You remember it. You and your brother saw that movie at the Sunshine on Houston. Every boy in the cinema wolf-whistled whenever Katy Rogers appeared onscreen.

"Well, it was Katy who saw it. And she said, 'Laffy…' That's what she calls me. That's what they all used to call me. She said, 'Laffy, you got a white rag on the back of your car.' I thought I must have just picked it up some place, just some rag left in the street got caught up in the bumper somehow. But no. That thing was tied on real tight. And they've been bugging my telephone calls."

"How do you know that?"

"Tapping sound. Beginning of every call. Tap tap tap. Not exactly cloak and dagger."

"Jesus. What's happening to the world?"

"You know what I don't understand? During the war I believed, I truly believed, we were fighting against the Fascists. I thought that was the whole reason we went to war. Now I think we just took Fascism and gave it another name. Cleaned it up a little. But you think about it. These Feds, and that goddamn Committee… who are they chasing after? Oh, they may *say* they're going after Reds, but look at the names, look at the people on that list. Jews, queers and unionists. Every last one of them."

★★

There's little chance you'll get much sleep tonight, and so you're back behind the wheel, driving down the Canyon and into the city. Ella Fitzgerald singing *Stairway to the Stars* and the engine purring low beneath the music.

No late night movies this time. No sitting at a bar making

a single beer last an hour while you make up your mind about what it is you want. You drive straight to Pershing Square, coming in on the northwest corner, and you perform a single clockwise lap, slowing as you pass along Hill Street.

He's there. Nick. Talking to his friends. And as you slow the car he waves at someone – not you – and calls out, "Hey! Bill!"

Impeccable timing. Was everything tonight timed just so you could witness this? Perhaps the night you met there was another man, like you, driving around the square or looking on from the side lines. And now Nick and this other 'Bill' are walking away towards the public restroom. In your stomach, a knot of envy and disgust. In your eyes, the vinegar sting of tears. You clear your throat.

How does the poem go? Ron read it to you once. You read it and re-read it after he died. How did it go?

For the world, which lies before us like a land of dreams

Has really neither joy, nor love, nor light…

It's gone. Couldn't even remember a single poem. You slam the ball of your hand against the steering wheel. As the immediate pain subsides you hit it three more times in quick succession. The lights of Downtown blur into coloured snowflakes. You wipe away the tears, wipe your nose with your wrist, and drive back towards Hollywood and Laurel Canyon.

Chapter 7:
MANHATTAN, OCTOBER 2001

Rosa was back at her post that morning, with a small white dressing in the place where they'd removed her mole.

"It was very quick," she said. "I barely feel a thing. They say in five days they take this off and in a few weeks you will never know I had a mole."

She went back to the utility room and began loading laundry into the dryer. Natalie stayed at the kitchen's breakfast bar, drinking coffee. From the laundry room, Rosa called, "Dolly tell me you were late yesterday."

Natalie made a face Rosa couldn't see.

"I slept late."

"With a boyfriend, she tell me."

"It wasn't a *boy*friend. I stayed at a *friend's*."

"You should find yourself boyfriend."

"Why would I want to do a thing like that?"

"Pretty girl your age should have boyfriend. Should have *husband*. But start with boyfriend. When was last time you have a boyfriend?"

Natalie took a deep breath as if it might help her to remember.

"Not that long ago."

"How long?"

"Does it matter?"

Three years. That's how long it had been. Tyler. Lovely Tyler.

Even now, three years on, a twinge of remorse whenever she thought of him. There had been no good reason to let it fizzle out, and as time passed she found it harder to remember why she had.

Sol was unusually mobile that day, shuffling from one room to the next, going through old papers and books, taking them down from their shelves and dropping them to the floor. Natalie spent much of her time chasing after him, picking things up and putting them back where they belonged. It became a kind of game between them. She sensed the mischief in him. When, finally, he rested, Natalie went through his mail; a royalties statement ($0.75) for a film she'd never heard of, an update from one of his charities. The box file of old paperwork was almost full. She would have to go through it someday soon, pick out the stuff no accountant would ever ask to see, and shred it all. The only thing holding her back was the worry that she might destroy something important.

Sol began humming along to some piece of music in his head, and Natalie paused a moment to watch and listen to him. She felt an overwhelming desire to take him somewhere. Just bundle him into a hire car, swaddled in blankets. Drive him across the country. Never looking back.

He knew – or, at least, *had* known – about the attacks. He and Rosa watched it all happening on TV, and he and Natalie spoke about it the following day. Four weeks on it was still all anyone could talk about, but Sol no longer mentioned it. She almost envied him.

Pavel Grekov's timing couldn't have been much worse. First

the attacks, now this. Sol needed routine. He needed calm. And every week seemed to bring with it more rupture. Perhaps it would have made more sense to ignore Pavel's message. Tear up Dolly's note, forget the conversation, pretend it never happened. If he was serious, let him pursue it through a lawyer. Yet all she could think of was the score. He had it with him in New York. And if she saw it, she would know. So she had to see it.

She called the hotel and the receptionist put her through to Grekov's room. He asked why she was calling and she told him that perhaps they'd got off on the wrong foot. Maybe they could meet again. Maybe this time he could bring along the score.

"Then you come here. To my hotel."

"I'd be happier meeting somewhere more public."

"I won't bring the score outside. You could take it, or your friend could take it for you. Run away. Steal it."

What was he picturing, exactly? That they'd meet somewhere outdoors and that some accomplice of Natalie's would swipe the score from his hands and make off into the subway? Absurd. But still, she had to see it.

"Alright," she said. "We'll meet in your hotel."

It was unseasonably warm; one of those early autumn evenings when summer splutters its last. The sunlight struggled its way through a thick haze and every city block seemed to have doubled in length.

He met her on the ground floor of his hotel. Typical for Midtown. Fake marble lobby, beige corridors. He was on the fifth floor, so they had to take the elevator. She hadn't used an elevator in weeks. Her hands grew clammy. The world dropped away beneath her, like a rollercoaster's sudden descent. She breathed as deeply and as quietly as she could and closed her eyes. An automated voice said, "Doors closing" and the doors closed. She went through everything that might happen. Fire. Snapped cable. Both.

"Floor 5. Doors opening."

She sprang out into the corridor, breathing in for the first time since the lobby. Another deep breath. The corridor went off in two directions, and Grekov gestured to the left. As they walked to his room she asked him how long he had been in New York.

"Four days," he said. "Before then, I was one month in Los Angeles. I knew Mr Conrad worked in Hollywood, so I went there. Sounds stupid, no? I wasted so much time in LA. And my visa was about to expire." He lowered his voice. "It expired yesterday. So I come here."

His room was small, with a view of an adjacent car park and the grey-brown flank of the Empire State; too close to be immediately familiar, too immense to be anything else. He told her to sit, and Natalie took a chair next to the dressing table. The only other place to sit was his bed.

Grekov opened the wardrobe and lifted out a suitcase in a washed-out shade of olive green. He laid it flat on the bed, opened it, and from beneath a layer of shirts and socks produced a manuscript; its cover made of faded purple card, the paper inside yellow with age. It looked authentic enough. At the very least, it looked old.

"Here," Grekov said, opening it on a particular page. "*Marsh Pechorin*. The Pechorin March."

"What does that mean?"

"Pechorin is the hero. He duels with his enemy, but before the duel there is a march. This piece."

She gestured to the score. "Mind if I…?"

"No. You read it. That's why you're here, no?"

He smiled. His manner, now that she was here and about to read the score, was transformed. She glanced at him just briefly before she began. His gaze was fixed on her and not the score. There was a lively, attractive mischief in his eyes. She looked away. She had come here to see the manuscript.

And here it was, open in her lap. The paper, though stained by cigarette smoke and spilt coffee, was delicate and smooth to the touch. The ink had faded from black to a rusty shade of brown, but was still legible. Some of the notation was unclear, she didn't recognise the Cyrillic script, but she could follow it well enough. She ran her finger gently across the first few bars and hummed the melody beneath her breath.

There it was. The same tune that had kept her awake the night before. A melody any child could hum, if you asked them to. But not only that, not just the melody. The same intervallic progression on the same beats; the same starting note moving up to the same fifth. Identical.

"You see?" said Grekov.

Don't nod.

"The same, yes? Exactly the same."

"They're very similar."

Don't nod.

"It's the *same*."

She asked how he came to notice the similarity, and he told her it was his father who had noticed it first.

"Ten years ago," he said. "We start getting American television, and we have *Battle Station Alpha. Boyevye Stantsi Alpha,* we call it. And when the show begins they play the music. My father, he pointed at the television and said, 'That is your *dedushka*… your grandfather's music.'"

Pavel's father had only ever heard the *Pechorin March* played on a piano. Even so, he was convinced these two pieces were one and the same, and he passed on to Pavel the desire to prove it.

"My father died six months ago," said Pavel. "Cancer."

"I'm sorry."

"It is okay." He smiled sadly. "But I make a promise that I would come here and find Sol Conrad and speak to him."

Natalie looked again at the score.

"There's no way Mr Conrad could have seen this. This is the first time it's been to the States, yes?"

Pavel nodded.

"And was it ever recorded?"

"No."

"Then it's impossible. Or a coincidence. They say there are only so many melodies, only so many possible combinations…"

"But you read it. You know it's the same."

"Then how do you explain this?"

"He must have heard it."

"Where?"

"Russia."

"And I told you, he's never been."

"I have to meet him."

"You can't."

"I won't upset him. I just want to speak with him."

Natalie laughed, a little more cruelly than she intended.

"He struggles to remember what he had for breakfast most days, let alone events that happened fifty, sixty years ago."

"Then what harm is there?"

Perhaps, all the harm in the world. Sol's life was one of patterns, routine. But they could meet, Pavel and Sol. They could meet, and either it would be a Good Day or a Bad Day. And if it was a Good Day, Sol would have all the answers. And if it was a Bad Day Sol would have nothing and Pavel would leave empty handed, mystery unsolved. Natalie didn't know which outcome she would prefer. Give Grekov the answers he was looking for and who knows how it would end? Deny him those answers, and he would just keep trying. But she had seen the score now. There might only be so many melodies, so many combinations, but this was something else. She had to know.

"Okay," she said. "But if he gets upset, or angry, you'll have to leave."

Pavel smiled again; another half-sad, uneven smile. With her on the chair and him on the bed their legs were interlocked and almost touching, like the teeth of a zip.

Chapter 8:
LOS ANGELES, SEPTEMBER 1950

Arthur J. Henderson, Assistant Producer of Music, is finishing a phone call; apologising for something that can't possibly be his fault, and then apologising, it would seem, for his apology. He wasn't expecting you, and for a moment after he's hung up he just sits there, blinking.

"Conrad? I didn't ask to see you. Did I ask to see you? I didn't ask to see you, did I?"

"No."

"Then why… what are you… why are you here?"

"*Scarlet Letter*."

"What about it?"

"Did I get the job?"

"Oh, well. Gee. Truthfully, I don't know. I believe Mr Walsh is still weighing up all the options."

"It's been three months."

"I know, but Mr Walsh is a very busy man."

"Oh, come on, Henderson. Everyone's treating it like a b-picture, so what's taking so long?"

"From what I hear, Gold is busting the studio's you-know-whats trying to get another half million, so it's been delayed. But, listen. Conrad. I'll call Janice, find out if Mr Walsh made a decision yet, and as soon as I know anything I'll come a-knocking. How does that sound?"

"Sure. Okay. I guess."

"Well, what do you want me to do? Ring him up and say, 'Why haven't you made up your gosh-darn mind yet?' He's a busy man, Conrad. A very busy man. Don't tie yourself up in knots. Like I said, you're the best name on the list. I can't see him picking Jerome or any of the others."

"Others? I thought there were only three of us. Me, Jerome, Levine."

"And Steinman."

"You didn't mention Steinman."

"I asked him after I asked you. Look, don't sweat about it. Steinman was only half interested, and he's chasing after some pirate movie right now."

"Okay. Well. Just keep me informed."

"I will. Was there anything else?"

There is not, and so you leave the office. Angela is waiting for you in the corridor, eyebrows strained as if she's been holding that expression the whole time you were in there.

"Well?"

"*'Mr Walsh is a very busy man'*," you tell her.

"I thought the job was yours."

"Me too. Who takes three months to choose a composer for a boobs and bonnets picture?"

"Boobs and bonnets. You just make that up?"

"Well, that's all those movies are. Take some highbrow book off the shelf, stick Jane Russell in a low-cut top, and if the MPAA complain, tell them it's art. Boobs and bonnets."

You hear the click and clack of heels behind you, and a voice says, "Mr Conrad?"

"Yes?"

One of the girls from reception.

"There's a lady here to see you."

"Does she have a name?"

"Wait. I wrote it down." She flips through her notebook. "Bernard. Margaret Bernard."

Angie's eyes almost pop out of their sockets. She knows you studied under Ron, even if she doesn't know *everything*. She'll have made the connection. Ronald Bernard's wife, here at Capitol, asking to see *you*. She's thinking this must be a good thing. You know it probably isn't.

Last time you saw her was Lawn Cemetery, East Hampton. Miles away from any place Ron considered home. It took you three hours to drive there, and another three to drive back.

You follow the receptionist across the square to the place where visitors check in. Margaret Bernard is waiting for you in a low, black leather chair, her knees together and a handbag in her lap. Still remarkably handsome for a woman of fifty; she's wearing a high-necked cream dress and has a lace-trimmed fascinator clipped or pinned into her auburn hair. As you enter the room she stands and holds out her hand, which you take, remembering the correct way to shake a lady's hand. (Ron taught you that.) You ask what brings her to LA.

"I'm visiting friends," she says, her accent mid-Atlantic; Katherine Hepburn with an even higher register. "And my doctor recommended I spend a few days in the sun. This is your place of work?"

You tell her it is.

"And you write the scores?"

"Some of them, yes."

"Ronald enjoyed the motion pictures. Never could stand them myself." A pause. She's waiting for you to jump in, tell her she's wrong, but you say nothing. She goes on: "My car is waiting outside. Perhaps we might go somewhere for iced tea. That is if you have the time, of course."

It's late afternoon. You spent much of today planning your trip to Henderson's office, giving him hourly deadlines to tell you the job was yours. Extending the deadline each time he didn't. If he knew you'd clocked off early, he'd probably bust a capillary, but fuck him.

"Sure," you say. "I have plenty of time."

There's a white Packard waiting in the visitors' parking lot near the DeMille building. A Negro driver in peaked cap and gloves stands beside it, holding open the door. You pass the journey across Hollywood in silence, and Margaret fills the limousine, not physically but with her presence and her perfume.

She's staying at the Chateau Marmont, and it's the first time you've ever visited the hotel. You try not to look too impressed. Its high arches and vaulted ceilings are pitched somewhere between gothic and arabesque. Your footsteps echo crisply on the marble floors. From the saloon bar, you hear a pianist give a good account of Chopin's *Raindrop* prelude.

Margaret tells the receptionist you'll be taking afternoon tea in the garden, and a member of staff leads you through to a secluded oasis of green. You sit beneath a parasol and

Margaret orders iced tea for two without asking what you'd like, only speaking again as the waiter leaves with her order.

"You've settled into the Los Angeles way of life?"

She pronounces 'Angeles' with a hard 'G'.

"Very much so," you tell her.

"Different to New York, I imagine."

"Yes."

"And the Lower East Side in particular."

"Very."

"I hear you bought a house with the money Ronald left you."

"I did."

"Very sensible. Many young men would have squandered it in a month. Ronald would be pleased to know you spent it wisely."

Margaret seems content to let silences last. Silences are when the mask begins to slip. Yours, not hers. And which mask are you wearing today? Successful young composer? She would have seen through it the moment she entered the reception at Capitol. She could have guessed then the kind of shoebox office where they have you tucked away.

"You must be wondering why I called on you in particular?" she asks. "Well. I suppose working out here you will have heard about that list which appeared in some god-awful magazine some months back."

"I heard something about it."

"So you know my husband's name was on that list?"

"Yes."

"Ridiculous, of course. How much harm do they think he can do now? That's assuming, of course, he could have done any harm while he was alive."

"Exactly."

"I worry, Mr Conrad, that this nonsense will damage his reputation. I'm not talking about his reputation as a man, or as a 'patriotic American', whatever that's supposed to mean. I'm talking about his music. Great music survives when it is played and listened to. I remember Ronald telling me – he must have been working on *Jason and Medea* at the time – but I remember him telling me how Aristotle makes no mention of Euripides, whose plays are still performed today, but he *does* talk about Agathon, whose entire body of work is now lost. Now what does this tell us? Well, first it tells us that perhaps Aristotle preferred Agathon to Euripides. But it also tells us that great works, revered works, can be forgotten and lost. The artists who slip into obscurity do so because people stop discussing them. Aristotle may have held a flame for Agathon, but the generations to follow felt differently. I wouldn't want that to happen with Ronald."

"Me neither."

"I worry that in this ridiculous climate my husband's work may become taboo; that mediocrities will take his place while he's forgotten."

"I hardly think that's likely."

"Tell that to poor Agathon. No. I don't want that to happen with Ronald's work. His work is all I have of him now."

She smiles insipidly.

"It was all I had of him a long time before he died."

Where you grew up, a woman in Margaret's shoes would have opened all the windows and cursed your name out loud for all to hear. She would have come to your apartment the minute she knew what was happening between you and her husband, and rung the buzzer, and screamed and bawled till everyone was listening. She wouldn't have stopped until the pair of you had been tarred and feathered. Margaret Bernard is not one of those women.

"If people stop playing him," you tell her, "they'll just stop playing. If people want to stop listening, they'll just stop. We can't force them."

"Perhaps not. But we can remind them of what he achieved. A concert. His major works, performed in a single evening. Preferably in New York, though it could be repeated elsewhere. I was thinking perhaps *Mill Neck, Giudecca*. Perhaps the overture from *Jason and Medea*."

"All great pieces."

"And you to conduct."

"Me?" She has to be joking. This has to be a game.

"Why not?"

"Because there must be a hundred conductors who'd bite off an arm to conduct Ron's… *Ronald's* music. Koussevitzky. Bernstein. Leinsdorf."

"Bernstein? With all that thrashing about and perspiring? Oh, good grief, no. I wouldn't ask him. And Koussevitzky has become very frail lately. Besides, if these others bit off their arms they wouldn't be much use, now, would they? You knew my husband how long?"

"Thirteen years."

"And is there a piece of music he wrote that you haven't heard?"

"I've heard everything. Read everything. Played most of it."

"You studied conducting under Stoessel, yes?"

"I did."

"Then it's settled. I would like you to conduct."

"No."

"I'm sorry?"

"I said no."

"Why not?"

"Because this is Hollywood. This is where I work. I can't risk that. I wish I could, but I can't. I'm sorry."

You're out of there before the iced tea arrives. Back through the lobby and out onto Sunset. A vanishing point of billboards and palm trees. Down Sunset, down Fairfax and Santa Monica Boulevard.

Why would she ask a thing like that? And why would you say no? All those times when people, Ron's friends, hardly noticed you were there. They would have noticed you now. But you said no.

You're walking back to Capitol. You could have left the car there overnight, got a cab back to Laurel Canyon, but that was unthinkable, and so you're walking, and you can feel the heat of the sidewalk through the soles of your shoes, and the city's grid makes every street seem infinite.

What made you say no?

It could have been a trick. She must know what the climate is like here, what it would mean if you conducted a concert of her husband's music. Blackballed, maybe fired. The whole thing could be a set-up, a test. But would she really go to such lengths for revenge? That's the stuff of opera, not real life. And that isn't why you said no. You said no because you can't fail out here. Whatever it takes, you have to make this work.

The Capitol car lot is almost empty by the time you get there; yours one of the few cars remaining. Without even thinking, you check its rear bumper. No white rag. That's something, at least.

You drive out onto Melrose and take a right, flicking down the visor to shield your eyes from the sun. Billboards and telephone wires and palm trees stretch on and on until they merge. Along the way you stop at a liquor store on North Fairfax. These places always make you feel like a hop-head, looking for a fix. The formal ritual of it. The brown paper bag. The sooner you can get out of this one the better, but there's a queue. From a radio behind the counter, a news report. There's been a train crash somewhere in Ohio. Multiple fatalities. The queue inches forward. You're close enough to feel the breeze from a small desk fan next to the cash register. You ask for a bottle of Johnnie Walker, pay for it and leave.

As you park up in your driveway there's movement in one of Mary's windows, the slightest twitch of a curtain. You haven't seen her in weeks. You could always ring the doorbell, hop over the fence. Share the whisky and put the world to rights. It's been a while since the agents in the Buick showed up. Why is she hiding away in there?

Best leave her alone. Maybe she prefers it that way. And besides. If she's still in trouble, Mary's the last person you need to be talking to.

★★

The needle touches down with a familiar crackle and you count the revolutions before it begins: The sudden strings, like an intake of breath; a heart frozen between beats. You're in another place. The classroom at Juilliard. Ron telling you how the symphony, Shostakovich's fifth, was meant to describe a journey from darkness to light, but even he had to admit that the brightness of its allegro was forced, too energetic to be taken on face value. And here, in its opening, there is simply too much raw sadness to be overcome by all that veneer-thin bombast.

The doorbell rings and you almost spring out of your chair, spilling scotch onto the rug. You weren't expecting anyone, so perhaps it's Mary – she saw you, saw the bottle, thought she'd say 'Hi' – but the shape behind the reeded glass isn't hers.

Nick looks as if he hasn't slept in a month; his hair a mess, dark bags beneath his eyes. Still young and arrogant enough for it to make him only more attractive.

"Can I come in?"

You reply with a question. "Are you alone?"

Too easy to imagine him turning up with two or three friends, promising they'll stay only a few nights, before nights turn into weeks and months. You've seen it before. Producers and casting agents with young men who turn up one night and don't leave. The kind of boys who do little more than hang out by the pool, getting drunk or getting high.

"Course I'm alone," says Nick. "So can I come in?"

In the lounge you offer him a drink, and he asks if you have bourbon.

"I have scotch."

"Scotch'll do just fine."

You pour the drinks and take him through to the lounge.

"Are you okay?" you ask. "I just… I wasn't expecting anyone. What happened?"

"Got kicked out of the place where I was staying, had nowhere else to go, and…"

He's running out of breath. You tell him to sit. He takes a moment to settle and he continues.

"So I was on Sunset, and I figured your place wasn't too far. Hope you don't mind."

"Not at all," you say, hunching forward in the armchair, your glass held between both hands.

"Say, what is this?" Nick asks, gesturing toward the record player with a nod.

"Shostakovich."

"Shosta-who?"

"Dmitry Shostakovich."

"Never heard of him. He sounds foreign. Or Polish or something."

"He's Russian."

"Is he a Commie?"

"I guess so."

"It sounds kinda sad."

"It's meant to. Why did you come here?"

"I didn't know where else to go."

"But why here? Why me?"

"If you want me to leave…"

"No. It's just… we hardly know one another. Don't you have any friends?"

"You lose friends quickly in this town," says Nick. Then, with another tilt of his head: "Say, I kinda like this."

"I heard him play some of it, on the piano," you tell him. "Last year. Madison Square Garden. Must have been fifteen, maybe twenty thousand people there."

"To hear one guy play a piano?"

You both fall silent for a moment. The symphony has moved on to one of its passages of strained jollity; all timpani, snare drums and dizzying swagger. It doesn't seem like the right kind of music for the moment, but to change the record would be too obvious. And what kind of music does a moment like this demand? Besides, it soon reaches the largo, the movement in which everything changes, its profound melancholy almost too much to bear. Everything here is so delicate, caught between the sweep and the chaos of the other movements.

Nick stares into an upper corner of the room. His jaw trembles and his eyes glisten. He lowers his head with a desperate laugh.

"I'm sorry," he says. "I guess I'm kinda tired."

Without acknowledging whatever it was that just passed between Nick and the music, you ask if he's had any auditions lately.

"Not one," he says. "I thought it would be easy. So many studios, so many movies being made. But every busboy and bellboy wants to be in the movies."

"Everyone has rent to pay."

"Oh, I know that, but there are so many people like me. I got here thinking I'd be a movie star. But everyone looks like a star, and acts like a star. How does anyone stand out? How is anyone any different to anyone else?"

"Sounds like you're having an existential crisis."

"I don't even know what that means."

"Probably a good thing."

"You're making fun of me."

"Wouldn't dream of it." You pause to take a mouthful of scotch. "You know, I saw you in Pershing Square a few months ago."

"Really?"

"I hadn't been there in a while. I was busy with work, and... I don't know. Sometimes just going there, just gathering the strength to go there, makes me blue."

"How so?"

"Do you ever stop and ask yourself what it is you're looking for? When you're in the square and you see another guy you like the look of. Do you ever think to yourself, 'Why am I here?'"

"Never."

"Honestly?"

"Never. Why? You?"

"Always. What am I doing here? What am I looking for? Is it love? Company? What?"

"Maybe you just want a blow job."

You fall back into the chair, trying to put into words a thought, an idea that's been hanging around your neck for weeks, maybe months, like a deadweight. The wretchedness and emptiness of mornings after, any morning of waking alone or with the prospect of saying goodbye to someone and never seeing them again. Or, worse still, of the liaisons that last minutes, not even hours. Pick-ups at the Richfield gas station. Dank restrooms. Shady parks.

"It isn't just that," you tell him. "It can't be just that. I hate it when people even talk that way."

"Why? It's true, ain't it?"

"Well, if it's true, it's the saddest thing I ever heard."

"But *why*?"

"Because it's sad if that's all anyone is looking for. If we're all just looking for someone to…"

"Fuck?"

"Don't say that."

Nick laughs. You flinch.

"So you went to the square," he says. "And then what?"

"Nothing. Drove around the square. Saw you. But you were talking to someone. You called him 'Bill'. Just like you did the night we met."

"I did? What night was this?"

"I don't know. It was three, maybe four months ago now. Do you even remember?"

"No."

"And that's what I'm talking about. You don't remember. Did you go with him? Did he come home with you? Did you drive up into the hills, find some place to park?"

"I don't remember."

"Of course you don't."

"I was probably high."

"And the night we met?"

"Not then."

"So you remembered me?"

"I came here, didn't I?"

"When you had no other place to go. Cheaper to do this, I guess, than check into Sunset Towers. Come here, offer yourself to me, get a place to stay for the night. Is that it?"

"No."

"Then why now? Why me?"

"Because I liked you. You're different from the others."

"You make it sound like there are so many. Well. Are there?" You close your eyes. "I'm sorry. You don't have to answer that."

"I know what you think of me," says Nick. "The kind of person you think I am. And you're probably right. I don't remember what happened with that guy. I don't recall his name. Did I fuck him? Who knows? Who *cares?* This is a lonely world, Sol. I don't think I knew that until I came here. Back home, oh boy, it might be a bad place for people like you and me, but people there know each other. Here, you're just another grain of sand. And with you… I don't know. I thought I mattered. You didn't just throw me down on the couch and tell me to drop 'em. Some guys, they ain't even that polite. They'll cum and then they'll kick you out of the car. Stick a five dollar bill in your hand for the cab ride home. You weren't like that. But I'm here now, and if you want to treat me that way, you can."

"I don't want to."

"But you could. I ain't going nowhere."

Nick rises from the couch, blocking the light from a corner lamp. His shadow falls over you, covering you. Your pulse quickens, the familiar stir of fear and lust. The sense that anything could happen.

"You don't have to do that," you say, your voice catching in your throat as if the words were dry.

"Well, I'm here now," he says, removing his jacket and throwing it to the floor. He lifts off his t-shirt. Against the dim light his body looks like something chiselled into being.

"Please, don't," you tell him.

You want him more than anything in the world.

"And if I want to?" he says, taking another step closer and unbuckling his belt. "Because I want to."

★★

You wake alone. The mattress cold and a dented pillow in the place where Nick slept. Every chance he ransacked the place and left. Anything of value, anything on display, gone. The Franz Kline sketch or Ron's Rolex or the Dutch vase Ron brought back from Amsterdam. That's if the kid even knows how much those things are worth.

You hurry downstairs and everything is where it was last night. You find Nick on the terrace, wearing only his shorts; gazing up at the mountains with his back to the house, like something from a painting by Caspar David Friedrich.

"Good morning," you say, ironing out the last traces of worry from your voice.

Nick turns, and for a moment it's as if he's looking at a stranger.

"Nick?"

He snaps out of it and says, "Good morning."

"You okay?"

"Sure, I guess." He looks back at the mountain. "I tell you what… I never realised how far away this is."

"It's not so far. You *walked* here, remember?"

"Not distance."

"What do you mean?"

"I thought I heard something, when I came out here, like a wildcat."

"Probably a cougar."

"In Los Angeles?"

You stand next to him and point to the lawn, or what's left of it.

"See that? Raccoons. We're not far from the city, but we are on the edge of wilderness."

"We're on the edge of something, alright."

He has that look again, the same expression as when he listened to the music and experienced something. A kind of fearful ecstasy, overcome by the vastness of the world. If you could only read his thoughts.

"Don't pay me any notice," Nick says. "I talk bullshit sometimes."

"What do you mean?"

"My thoughts. These thoughts I have. It's like they're someone else's. And my dreams. They're just crazy."

"Everyone has crazy dreams."

"Not like these. Did I wake you?"

"I had to get up, anyway. I have to go to work."

"Okay."

"Where will you go?"

"Downtown, I guess. I have folks I can call. People I couldn't call on last night. I'll probably find a place to stay. Might be a little easier, now the sun's up."

You tell him he could always come here, if he needs to, and he smiles with genuine surprise. He kisses you on the mouth, tenderly at first, but with a growing urgency, as if to stop would mean the end of something vital.

★★

You drop him off on Melrose; the parking lot of a hardware store that hasn't yet opened for the day. You get out with him, as if to hug or kiss him goodbye, though you both know this can't happen.

You reach for your wallet and he grabs you by the wrist.

"Please, don't."

"I insist."

"I'd rather you didn't. Not this time."

The space between you becomes taut. You hate this sort of goodbye. You always have. Always that hope, often beyond reason, beyond experience, that you might see him again. Whoever that "him" might be.

"I guess I'll see you around," he says, and you tell him you'd like that, and remind him that if he needs somewhere to stay…

He cuts you off: "Say, what's that?"

He's pointing to the car's rear bumper, and to the white rag fastened to its chrome. The sensation is like a half-dream in the first moments of sleep, when it feels as if you're falling.

Crouching, you begin untangling rag from chrome, but it's held on tight. No mistaking the intention behind it. It didn't just get picked up, caught on a breeze and stuck. This thing was tied on with purpose.

"It's nothing," you tell him. "Probably some kid's idea of a prank."

"Kind of a dumb prank."

"You're telling me."

Breathlessly, you search the parking lot and Melrose, searching, searching…

Nick knows something is wrong but says nothing more except a final goodbye. Then you're back in the car and driving along Melrose, and it's a bright and sunny day, but the city looks somehow different. A menace behind the cream walls; every building a façade, another movie set. Los Angeles feels impossible. A temporary town set up in the desert, the kind of place that could be levelled by a stiff breeze.

You spend the day in Room 01B waiting for Henderson, but he doesn't come. The pile of work you'd hoped to finish by 5pm remains untouched by the day's end. Someday soon they'll invent a machine that can write these cues and stings to order. You want sinister? I'll give you sinister. Just key in the code for "sinister", and out it comes. Sinister. Slapstick. Haunting. Romantic. Just pull the arm down and see what you get, like a slot machine.

What is music if it means nothing to you, if the melody is something you could have written in your sleep? If all you're doing is taking somebody else's melody and moulding it into something only slightly different? If you write like a machine, churning out short pieces on demand, can you still call yourself a composer?

Ron once played you the andantino from Shostakovich's piano suite; the one written when he was just sixteen. This was at Juilliard. Ron asked what state of mind you thought the composer was in when he wrote it.

"Agony," you replied, blurting it out, forgetting for one moment that Ron was your tutor, then worrying that your answer was too sentimental, too subjective. You half expected him to clip you around the head with the score, but instead he smiled.

"Exactly right," he said. "His father had died a few months before it was written. Now, it may be a little obvious in places, and it's clearly a sophomore piece, but the emotion is all there, isn't it? There's nothing false, nothing deceptive about it. This is a sixteen-year-old boy who, so far as I'm aware, spoke no English, telling you, a lad more or less the same age as him, who speaks no Russian, exactly how he feels. Through sound alone. Don't you find that remarkable?"

And you *did* find it remarkable. He played it for you again, asking that this time you think about a boy who'd lost his father, at a time when people were literally starving to death all around him.

"Music is a magic trick," Ron said. "But one to which no-one, not even the magician, knows the secret. I can't explain why something in a minor key makes one feel sad, or why something in a major key makes one happy. And I don't trust anyone – any musicologist or psychologist or neurologist – who says otherwise. It's magic, Sol. Alchemy. It's that line which gets attributed to everyone, from Debussy to an old Zen proverb. Music is the space between the notes. It's like Mahler said. If one could say it with language, one wouldn't write music."

What would Ron say about the music you're writing now? If he listened to your most recent work – provisionally titled *2m3 (Ship Enters Harbor)* – would he find something meaningful in those silences between the notes? Does the music say anything you couldn't say in words?

It says a ship has entered the harbour. But then, so does the image of a ship (albeit a model) entering the harbour (the Capitol water tank and its painted backdrop of sky). The words in the script describe a ship entering a harbour just as successfully. Your music is little more than a ribbon on the gift wrap.

In the absence of good news from Henderson you sit and stew in your own thoughts. There's a white rag on the front passenger seat of your car, a torn strip of soiled white cotton that served no purpose other than to mark your car out in traffic. How long was it there? How often did they follow you? Are they following you still?

You would have noticed it, if it had been placed there any earlier. You always park right up behind the tall hedge facing out onto Melrose, the car's tail end facing the studio. If someone put it there yesterday afternoon, you would have seen it when you got back from the Chateau Marmont. You even checked for a rag. You know you did. Those sneaky sons-of-bitches must have come up the driveway in the middle of the night and tied it on while you and Nick were together.

Some coincidence, for it to happen last night. Months with no sign of them, the men in the Buick, and in one night the kid shows up and there's a rag tied to your car. You were distracted long enough for them to do this. Some coincidence.

You drive home in a mood, listening to no more than a few seconds of radio – Teresa Brewer singing *Music, Music, Music* – before turning it off again. Funny how a song that was just background noise for so long can turn into something so aggravating, like a piece of grit in your shoe.

Once home you pour yourself a scotch – you're nearing the end of the bottle – and you sit in silence. It takes a moment for the residual noise, the pools of melodies unfinished, to evaporate like the last puddles after a June rainstorm, and for your mind to clear.

Blank canvas. Empty concert hall.

When the doorbell rings it takes a second for you to react. You must have been sitting in silence for an hour, maybe two. The shadows in the lounge are waxing, swallowing up the room, but you hadn't noticed.

You step out into the hall. A familiar shape on the other side of the glass. The doorbell rings again.

"Hey, Sol. It's Nick. Remember what you said, about me coming here, if I needed to? Well. I came."

Of course he did. This morning it was all ifs and maybes. Said he'd find somewhere to stay. That was before he spoke to them, of course. His handlers. Before they sat him down in some diner off Melrose, scolding him for pointing out the white rag before they gave him his next orders.

"Go to him again. Ask him questions."

"What kind of questions?"

"About his friends. Get him talking about politics."

How did the kid get himself mixed up in this kind of mess? And when did they get to him? Perhaps after that first night. You drove him back into town in the morning, left him on the corner of Sunset and Fairfax, and as he was walking back to wherever he was staying they pulled up in that Buick of theirs and called him over.

"Hey. Hey, kid. How'd you like to make a few bucks?"

He hesitated. It wasn't even half eight, and here were a couple of johns in funny-looking hats inviting him to go where exactly? And do what? Maybe they said something to put him at ease. Maybe they just came out with it, told him they were agents and showed him their badges. Then they took him to a diner, bought him breakfast. And while he was wolfing down his pancakes they told him you were the very worst kind of person. The kind who endangers American values, American lives.

"Sol. Please. I know you're there."

And now he's back with his rehearsed questions and his distractions and tomorrow there may not be another white rag tied to the bumper, but there'll be *something*.

"Sol? Listen. I don't know anyone else in Laurel Canyon, so could you please let me in?"

He raps his fist against the door three times, as if maybe you didn't hear him. He holds down the door bell, so that it keeps ringing.

You can't move.

"Sol, please. Don't be like this. You got someone else in there? Is that it? Your *boyfriend* come home from the Navy? Well. Thanks for nothing. I guess I'll just have to walk all the way back to Sunset. Fucking asshole."

The shape of him melts away behind the reeded glass, but you still can't move. You wait for something to happen, for a rock to come crashing through the window, or for Nick to return, begging and pleading you to let him in, but he's gone.

Chapter 9:
INTA, NOVEMBER 1940

Even at midday the taiga is dark, darker still when they're far from base camp and the more well-trodden paths. By the time Sergey joined the railroad the more accessible areas had already been felled. To find fresh supplies of wood, they are sent out in pairs to search the uncharted stretches in the east.

Today he's been partnered with Orlov, a petty criminal from Novgorod. Even after months of working out here, Orlov is still a plodding barrel of a man, and this makes him a slow partner when trekking through the hills and forests. He stops regularly to catch his breath and complains, almost incessantly, about his clothes chafing or his boots letting in snowmelt. He doesn't complain much about the cold, but perhaps that's because he's so much fatter than anyone else.

For Sergey, and for most of the men on the logging teams, the cold is the most unbearable thing of all, and it will only get worse as they sink further into winter. He has never known a cold like it. Even as a boy, during those bitter winters of the Civil War, when there was never much fuel, he doesn't remember a cold this relentless; a cold that seems intentional, malevolent.

Orlov's resistance to it only makes the man more annoying. And he never complains about having been sent here in the first place, not like the others. The other prisoners make sarcastic toasts to "that bastard in the Kremlin", and either the guards don't care or they pretend not to have heard. The other prisoners become wistful, talking about life back home, wondering aloud if they'll ever see their families again, but never Orlov. To Orlov, this is just a job, not so different to those he had in Novgorod, whenever there was work. If anything, the railroad has been kinder to him than home.

"There were times when I didn't know if I would earn enough to survive," he once told Sergey. "That never happens out here. Here, there's always work to do, and a roof over my head, all year round."

Orlov said those words a while ago, but lately he's begun complaining about the rations. They're giving him less than the next man, he'll say, pointing to a line on the inside of his soup can which only he can make out.

"See? The *balanda* used to come up to there, and now it comes up to here. Do you see?"

Sergey told him they all get the same, more or less; two ladles of *balanda* from the vat.

"Then they must be using smaller ladles," Orlov said. "That's it. Moscow have sent up smaller ladles. Smaller ladles means smaller rations. Smaller rations means less money being spent on the likes of us."

At least when they're hiking Orlov doesn't speak quite so often – he's too short of breath for proper conversation – but whenever he does it's another complaint.

"This left boot is letting in water again. I only had it fixed last week. That bastard Koplowitz is a lying, cheating Jew bastard. I gave him five cigarettes to fix these and he didn't fucking fix them."

"Maybe they broke again," says Sergey.

"Then he didn't fix them *properly*."

Sergey wishes Orlov would shut up. Still, if there's any justice in the world, Koplowitz will have done a substandard job on purpose, just to spite the fat bastard.

By rights Orlov should be the one carrying most of this stuff; the felling saws and the ropes and so on. That's just about all he's good for, as a human pack mule. Strong and dumb, just how the camp chiefs like them.

It still grates that out here men like Orlov are treated with greater respect. It makes no sense. Orlov is a cretin, but a cretin follows orders and he never strikes. Not that striking does much good. There is a trail, stretching back hundreds of miles, of bodies buried beneath the crossties. And not just those who strike, but almost everyone who steps out of line. The Kotlas-Vorkuta railway, scheduled for completion in the coming year, is built on a foundation of dead strikers, thieves, malcontents and *masterschyks* – the self-maimers. Better to keep your mouth shut and your head down.

Every so often, even in these remote places, they come across evidence that there were people here once; the brick shells of buildings, roofless and without windows. Impossible to say how old they are; they look like ancient ruins, but could have been abandoned only a few years ago. Always far apart, no two buildings in close proximity. On a previous jaunt Sergey saw an old Orthodox chapel, hours away from anywhere, and when it began to rain he and his partner for the day took shelter inside it. It was so remote, it hadn't even been ransacked, but there were bullet holes in its outer stonework. The interior, though soiled with bat droppings and crawling with bugs, was more or less intact, even the icons. The people who lived in this region must have thought the rest of the world would leave them alone. They were wrong.

Sergey and Orlov are two hours' trek from the basecamp when it begins to snow. Only a few small, bitty flakes at first, becoming gradually heavier, until the blizzard fills even the denser parts of the forest and they can see barely ten metres ahead. There is no provision for men who get lost in snowstorms. If they don't return to basecamp this evening, no-one will come looking for them. The tools they have are ancient and cheap, easily replaceable, and there's no chance of escape, nowhere for them to escape to. There's little point in walking any further, and so Sergey suggests they stop and rest for a while. The snow looks as if it will eventually pass.

It is one o'clock in the afternoon and already dark by the time they – or rather, Sergey – begins building a fire. Orlov watches him with mild curiosity.

"It needs more kindling," he says. "Smaller twigs at the bottom. That's what my uncle used to tell me. I'd help you, but I have no feeling in my hands. Not the cold. It's a condition. No sensitivity at all. I could seriously burn myself and I wouldn't know."

When the fire is lit he and Orlov sit by it and toast some of their bread.

"If we had butter," says Orlov. "If they gave us butter! Oh, think of that, Grekov! Hot buttered toast."

Sergey says nothing. He looks at Orlov with an expression that says: Don't talk about the things we *don't* have. Don't tell me about hot buttered toast or the meals your *babushka* made you when you were a boy. Just don't.

"These rations they give us are getting smaller," Orlov says. "I swear, they're getting smaller."

"I've told you before, everyone gets the same."

"We'll starve to death on these rations."

"*You* won't."

"What's that supposed to mean?"

"I mean fat men never starve to death. Not quickly, anyway."

"How dare you, Grekov? How fucking dare you?"

Orlov lifts his toast away from the fire and takes it from the end of his fork, sniffing at it like a pig.

"Mmm, toast," he says. "I wonder why toast doesn't smell anything like bread."

Sergey could bash his head in. He could take his mallet from the canvas bag still strapped to his back, and smash the fucker's head right in.

Instead, he says, "Because it's toast. It is different."

"But it's still bread, though."

"Shut the fuck up," Sergey says through clenched teeth.

"Don't you tell me to shut the fuck up," says Orlov. "Tell me to shut up once more and I'll cut your fucking throat. And don't think I wouldn't."

Orlov has made plenty of threats before – "I'll give you a black eye", "I'll break your arm" – but everyone laughs at him.

He's a clown. He's that boy you went to school with who lied about everything and anything. How his father was a decorated war hero. How he once flew in a biplane. How he's related, on his mother's side, to Lenin. But this time his tone, his expression… it's as if he hears himself saying he could cut Sergey's throat and realises he might do it.

"You wouldn't dare," Sergey says.

"No?" says Orlov. "Two hours from basecamp. I go back there, tell everyone you fell into a ravine…"

"There are no fucking ravines."

"A hill, then. Or into a stream. 'He fell into an icy stream… I did everything I could to rescue him, but the water was too fast. He went under the ice and I couldn't get him out.' You think they'd come all the way out here, looking for you? Just to find out if I was telling the truth?"

"Fuck you, Orlov."

"Fuck *you*."

Orlov looks at him from the other side of the fire. His eyes narrow. That big, red-cheeked face of his seems to sag. The emotion draining out of him. A dead look falls across his eyes. Orlov was never violent, was he? Never gets into fights. Tried telling the men in his barrack, before Sergey's time, that he'd been a prize-fighter back in Novgorod. It became a recurring joke and he never mentioned it again. But then, he's never threatened to cut anyone's throat.

His chubby hand moves towards his belt and his pick axe; the only tool he ever carries.

"What're you doing?" Sergey asks.

"I don't know you," says Orlov. "You're nothing to me."

Never could Orlov have moved so quickly. He launches himself across the fire, kicking up a storm of orange sparks, and swings the axe, missing Sergey and jamming it into the trunk of a nearby tree.

Sergey scrambles to his feet and with his arms outstretched he begins clawing his way blindly through the forest. He hears the axe being wrenched from the tree and the crunch of snow beneath heavy feet.

"Don't run," Orlov yells. "I'll make it quick, I promise."

This is absurd. Like a cartoon or a puppet show. He can hear his own heartbeat thudding in his ears. His foot catches on something – a rock or an exposed root – and the cold, dark ground rushes up to meet him. Snow and dirt in his mouth. His hands grazed and tingling. The wind knocked right out of him.

Get up. For God's sake, get up.

Orlov lunges and Sergey kicks out, his boot connecting heavily with Orlov's crotch. The fat man doubles over and Sergey kicks again, this time hitting him squarely in the face with a hollow crack. Orlov's hand moves to his face. Even in this light, Sergey can see the blood pouring from his nose.

Sergey gets to his feet, his ankle sore beneath his weight, and he runs off into an even darker part of the forest. It's still snowing, and away from the fire the cold is absolute, burning his lungs each time he breathes. He scans the area for a hiding place, but sees nothing. He feels his way around the nearest trees until he finds one that might hold his weight. He begins to climb. His limbs ache and his head spins and his breath tastes of copper. Frozen chunks of dead bark come away in his fingers, but still he climbs, his feet slipping against exposed wood before finding each new branch or stub that takes him further. He's perhaps fifteen feet off the ground when Orlov reaches him.

"You can't stay up there forever," Orlov says. "We may as well get this over and done with. Why are you drawing this out? It must be agony for you."

"I won't come down," says Sergey. "Not till you've gone."

"I'm going nowhere," says Orlov. "Where would I go?"

"Listen. Even if you tell them I slipped and fell or drowned, they'll still punish you. Put you on pumping duty. Cut your rations in half."

"Rations?" says Orlov. "I'd have my own rations."

It takes a second for Sergey to understand. His stomach clenches. He puts one hand over his mouth. A sour mix of bile and half-digested toast spills up onto his tongue, burning his throat. He's heard the stories. Escapees who take along an extra person for when their food supplies run out. Bones found in the woods.

"Then I won't come down," he says. "You'll have to wait until I fall or die of thirst."

Orlov begins pacing around the tree, stamping his feet and clapping his hands together to keep warm. He sits for a while, his head craned back, staring up at Sergey with an imbecilic grin, like some village idiot, occasionally laughing to himself. Something in him has snapped, that much is clear. Perhaps he's stuck like this; a murderous, overgrown child. Plenty of men go mad out here, but never like this.

In the distance their fire grows dim, eventually dying out altogether. The grey smoke drifts across the forest through the falling snow. Orlov remains beneath the tree. Sergey could jump. Leap off the branch and onto Orlov, and while Orlov is dazed he could take away his axe and give him a swift blow to the top of the head. Dead in an instant. Does he have it in him to kill a man? Does he even have it in him to take the axe from him? And what if he missed Orlov altogether and hit the ground feet first? He'd break his legs. No running away then.

Time passes. Holding on to the tree is hard work. The snow melts around his body, making the branches slippery. If Orlov could just fall asleep, if only for a moment, it might give him enough time to run. He can remember his way back to the path, he's certain of it.

Movement below. Orlov getting to his feet, still chuckling to himself. He holds up his axe for Sergey to see.

"Idiot!" he says. "I've been an idiot."

His first blow makes barely a dent in the tree, but the second is powerful enough for Sergey to feel it.

"Please," he says. "Orlov. You don't have to do this."

Orlov swings again, taking another sliver from the trunk, and Sergey closes his eyes and clings on more tightly than before. What a ridiculous way to die. Hacked to death by the camp clown, the butt of everyone's jokes. And they would even joke about this, the other prisoners. Orlov would come back alone and they would say to him, "What happened to Grekov? Did you eat him?"

The shadows of the forest floor play tricks with him; myriad colours dancing in the dark till the blackness seems to swirl and move of its own accord. Orlov takes another swing and something splinters.

If the tree falls, let it fall on Orlov. Even if it kills me too. Let us both die out here.

Orlov is readying himself to strike the tree again when something heavy crunches down into the snow behind him. He pauses, each silvery breath drifting towards something massive and dark only a few feet away. Another powdery whump as the immense dark form takes another lumbering step towards him.

"Oh God," Orlov mutters, almost too quietly for Sergey to hear.

The bear moves slowly – it should be hibernating – but is still too fast for Orlov. In two short bounds it has him, charging into him and slamming him into the snow. The tree shakes and Orlov screams – unguarded, shrill – silenced only when the bear bites down and tears away his head. Blood splashes against the tree, and the snow around it turns black. Orlov's body flails about beneath the bear; the flesh stripped from its arms and legs, a steaming cavity opened up in the torso. Sergey wants to look away, but he can't. Orlov's head remains almost unscathed, and his dead eyes glare skyward as the rest of him gets eaten. Nearby, sharp teeth connect with hollow-sounding bones. The bear grunts and paws at something wet. It heaves its massive bulk around and licks the blood from Orlov's face before dissolving almost silently into the night.

For three more hours Sergey waits in the tree. The bear may have had its fill, but it could still be lurking nearby. His hands burn with the cold. He's straddling a branch, his chest and stomach flat against the tree, and he wraps his arms around the trunk, stuffing each hand into the opposite sleeve to warm them and to form a kind of clasp. He can just about reach. It wouldn't have taken very long for Orlov to cut it down. Melting snow has begun to seep in through his trousers, freezing again in shards of ice that are moulded around his legs. He rests his head against the damp bark. If he were to doze off, even for a second, there's a chance he would fall, hitting every branch on the way down. His feet are beginning to tingle and his arms are beginning to ache. He can't stay here all night.

Above the trees, the sky grows darker still. The snow stops falling and the clouds part to reveal a dense spray of stars. Out of nowhere, a thin green ribbon of light trails across the sky, widening and pulsing with life till it resembles a vast, flowing curtain, suspended over the taiga. Presently it lights up the whole forest, and the shadows of the trees wheel giddily on the forest floor, like compass needles.

He never imagined he would see this with his own eyes. There is something miraculous in those lights, transcending this cold, dark forest, and Orlov's butchered corpse, and the knapsack of tools and grubby soup tins now buried in the snow. The material things of this world no longer matter to him, and he hardly dares to make a sound, afraid that by doing so he could break the spell and stop the coloured lights from happening.

This is the most beautiful thing he has ever seen.

Mahler's *Urlicht*. That's what he can hear. A piece he hasn't listened to in so long, yet he remembers it entirely. Every note. Every nuance. Kept pristine, complete, in a place the camp guards can't get to it. Perhaps there will be a life after this.

The walk back to the base camp takes him three hours. In places, the snow is two feet deeper than it was this morning. His body feels raw; his lips and knuckles are beginning to crack. He wonders what on Earth he is going back to, and whether it could possibly be worth it. The instinct to survive was never rational.

He returns to the camp and his brigadier empty handed but for his tools. He tells him that Orlov was killed by a bear, and that he spent much of the day hiding in a tree. He doesn't tell him the exact circumstances of Orlov's death, or the green lights that he saw. The brigadier strikes Orlov's name from his ledger, and tells Sergey he'll receive only a half ration of bread tomorrow and the day after.

It will be another fourteen months before they reach Vorkuta.

Chapter 10: LOS ANGELES, SEPTEMBER 1950

A bar on Larchmont Boulevard. Misty blue and grey with smoke. Empty but for the barman, two pool players, Angela, and you. The two of you sit together in a booth near the window. The jukebox is playing Dinah Shore.

"I don't even know why I'm still here."

"Not this again," Angela sighs. She looks out through the window, past the skeleton of an unlit neon sign. Across the street, an ugly, squat apartment building with narrow balconies; a Latina housemaid hanging laundry from a washing line. The sky above the building is a dusty shade of pink.

You didn't get *The Scarlet Letter.* Walsh chose Steinman. Steinman who wasn't interested, except suddenly he was, and now he's the one getting sole credit on *The Scarlet Letter.*

You hope it bombs.

No reason was given. Only the bare details. You didn't get it. Steinman did. When Henderson told you, it was like he thought you might leap up and sock him across the jaw. You almost did. It took a lot of willpower to stay where you were, and not go marching over to Walsh's office to call him a *Yekke* son-of-a-bitch.

You know why they didn't choose you.

"You're always threatening to leave LA," says Angela. "We all do it. But does anyone ever leave?"

"I might."

"You won't. I haven't, and I've lost count of how many times I've threatened to."

"You must love the place."

"Are you kidding? I hate it. I only came here to piss off my folks."

"How old are you, exactly?"

"You know exactly how old I am."

She's thirty-two, though she'll never say it aloud in a bar, not even one this quiet.

"Aren't you a little old to be pissing off your parents?"

"Cut me some slack. That was ten years ago."

You know the story. Rich parents, by your standards. Not Ronald Bernard rich, but wealthy. Dad sold real estate. The family lived in an upmarket Chicago suburb. Angela was an only child. Piano lessons paid for by cash or by cheque, unlike yours, which were paid for in veal cutlets and chicken livers. Her parents expected her to go into teaching, or to relegate music to a hobby. She got engaged to the son of her father's business partner ("We'd known one another since kindergarten"), but broke it off when he came back from the war with a leg in plaster and an unrelated case of the clap. After an unsuccessful pep talk from her mother – who used the phrase "Boys will be boys" – Angela boarded a Greyhound bus. She once told you that she came to LA only because she was ten minutes late for the bus to New York.

"You know what you need?" she says.

"Don't tell me. Another pitcher of margarita."

"A girlfriend."

"Are you serious?"

"Of course I'm serious. You need someone in your life. At the very least, you need to go out and get laid."

"But a girlfriend?"

"Why not? You need someone."

"Who?"

"Anyone."

"I don't want just 'anyone'."

"Well, who *do* you want?"

"Who says I want anyone, period?"

"Everyone wants someone. It's the way of the world."

"Not my world. Not right now."

You've seen that expression before. She's waiting for you to say something, as if she's given you enough cues to say whatever it is she wants to hear, but you won't say it. Instead, you pour the last of the margarita into your glasses and light another cigarette. On the balcony across the street the Latina housemaid rests against the balustrade with folded arms, letting out a sigh so heavy you can feel it from here.

★★

At night the city is limitless, a jewelled web that shimmers silently. The slightest breeze passing over the hillside mutes the drone of distant traffic.

In these dark and secret places, away from the crowds, you remember a park on the Lower East Side. Heavy, autumn fog. Walking home alone. Couldn't have been any older than fourteen, fifteen years old. You could barely see ten feet in front of you, but there were figures, shadows in the mist, all men. You walked with purpose, eyes fixed on the path, though a part of you wanted to stop. There was something intensely erotic about those half-hidden strangers.

You take a final drag on your cigarette and crush it beneath your heel. From somewhere nearby, the crunch of gravel and the soft murmur of a car's engine. Little point in feigning surprise. You know why you came here. The car parks up a short distance from the Griffith Observatory. The engine cuts out. Its lights go dark.

The sudden flame of a match, the tip of a cigarette flaring orange. The car fills with smoke and the driver opens the window an inch or two. He takes another drag.

This is why you came here. Not for the drive, or the view, but for this; the suspense and the thrill of anonymity. It's always in places like this, near yet far. Hidden from the public, yet exposed to the heavens.

You play through every possible scenario: A walk down into the park and a search for somewhere more shaded, or a car ride out across Glendale to somewhere shamefully remote. These men are shadows. All you remember of them are their voices – if they speak – or the way they smell and taste; almost always of drink. Dutch courage. Occasionally you'll catch one of them taking off his wedding ring.

He's waiting in the car, perhaps expecting you to make the approach. He'll open the passenger side door, ask you to get in. Maybe it'll happen there on the front seat. He'll open his flies, hold you by the hair and force you down. He'll be aggressive, maybe unkind. He will hurt you. You want him to do all of these things. You only wish you could see his face a little clearer. If you could only see his eyes.

The car is a Buick. Same colour, same model, as the one that was parked outside Mary's house. There were two men that time, but you couldn't see their faces, couldn't see their eyes.

What would have happened, that foggy night on the Lower East Side, if you'd stopped walking? If you'd stood near a tree and just waited there? Would someone have stopped and talked to you? Would you have gone somewhere with him, back to an apartment, or maybe a restroom? Would that moment have cancelled out others yet to happen? This was a choice, a fork in the road. You carried on walking. Maybe even quickened your step. When you got home your mother still asked what had kept you out so late.

Now here we are again. Another fork. And he's still waiting there, the Buick's driver; still smoking his cigarette. You start walking towards the car and he pauses; one hand on the steering wheel, the cigarette tilting between his knuckles. You get nearer and he takes another drag, but you keep walking, past the Buick and across the otherwise empty lot, away from everything that might have happened.

★★

Margaret Bernard is at the same table in the same garden of

the Chateau Marmont where you saw her last. If she wasn't wearing a different dress and a different hat you could be forgiven for thinking she'd been waiting here the whole time.

"Mr Conrad. Please, sit."

You arranged this. Called the hotel and passed on the message that you would like to meet with her again.

"I've ordered iced tea," she says. "Perhaps this time you'll stay long enough to try it."

On cue, the waiter returns with a jug and two glasses, filling each in turn. Margaret tells him that'll be all and he walks away, called to another table by the click of someone's fingers.

"I hadn't expected to hear from you again," Margaret says. "Not after our last meeting. Have you reconsidered?"

"I have."

"But you seemed so adamant. You made it sound as if conducting a concert of Ronald's music would harm your career."

"It still could."

"Then what brought about this change of mind?"

"I no longer care if it does."

"That sounds rather rash."

"Do you want me to conduct the damn concert or not?"

"Mr Conrad. I'd thank you kindly not to adopt that tone of voice with me. Yes, I would still like you to conduct the *'damn'* concert. But you're a young man with his career ahead of him. I understand your reluctance. And now, now it seems you've changed your mind out of wilful self-destruction. Is that it?"

"Not at all."

"I should hope not. Did Ronald ever tell you I studied psychology at Brown? Not as my major, you understand. But psychology was all the rage back then. Not many young women wanted to study it, but I was fascinated. Still am. So when a young man declares himself unafraid to risk his career, I have to ask myself why."

"Call it a matter of principle."

"You'll excuse me, Mr Conrad, but I never had you down as a man of principle. Given the circumstances of how we are… *acquainted…*"

She pauses, taking a sip of her tea.

"That was unkind," she says. "I apologise. If you say it is a matter of principle, we shall leave it at that. And I *am* grateful, really I am. I want you to know that. I didn't ask you out of spite."

"Why would anyone ask it out of *spite*?"

"You underestimate human nature. There is an emotional sadism in most women and homosexuals. The men, I mean, not the lesbians."

Nearby, a mature woman in red cat-eye glasses and a pancake hat hears the word "lesbians" and glances over in horror. Margaret pauses only to sip her iced tea and continues.

"We dress revenge up as a favour, take pleasure in seeing others heartbroken. We play games with those we should care about, and claw at them when they are weak. Oh, I'd no more trust another woman or a man of *your* inclinations with my wellbeing than I'd leave a cat to look after the canary. But you… perhaps you're different. Perhaps you are a man of principle.

How does a man of principle survive in a town like this?"

"With great difficulty."

"I can imagine. It's a city of philistines. Present company excepted, of course. I often told Ronald this is where you'd all end up."

"Meaning?"

"Composers. The moment Copland came out here and began writing scores, I knew what would happen. You see, there is a gulf opening up in music, Mr Conrad. A great abyss between the sort of music listened to by the social elite and that listened to by the masses. Music – the decent sort, I mean – is migrating away from the concert hall and into the motion pictures, where no-one really notices it. No-one listens to it for its own sake. Oh, I suppose there is the *other* sort of music, written by those Europeans who fancy themselves as scientists and mathematicians. An awful racket. But I'm not talking about *them*, I'm talking about *classical* music. It still exists, but only in the motion pictures."

"Well. It's a living."

"But not a very dignified one, I'll wager. Ronald was born into the luckiest generation of all, that brief moment when we recognised the true value of art. We saw it as something more than just a commodity to be bought and sold. It isn't fashionable to say so, I'm sure, but the Soviet system is far better than our own. Oh, I know they have their excesses, and their behaviour before the war was simply inexcusable, but there, at least, the state *supports* its artists, gives them prestige, honour.

"Here, in the so-called *free world*, we subject a thing of beauty to market forces, ask that it stands up to commercial scrutiny, and if not we toss it aside as if it were worthless. What's worse, we take young artists, who fifty years ago would have composed symphonies, operas, and we funnel them into an industry like the motion pictures."

"Ron didn't hate movies so much."

"I know he didn't. Except when it came to music, I was always so much more of a snob than him. But on this, I agree with Toscanini. 'In life, one should be a democrat; in art, an aristocrat.' And which would you rather, Mr Conrad? That we divide society, like the British, along lines of birth-right, or lines of taste?"

Chapter 11: LENINGRAD, AUGUST 1938

The curtains have gone unopened for three days. He prefers to sit in the dark, only occasionally lighting his lamp. There is a small suitcase beside the door, containing a pair of shoes, two pairs of socks, two pairs of underpants, two clean shirts and a pair of trousers. Though it's August, his heavy winter coat hangs on a nearby hook. Just in case.

He's tried reading, but finds his concentration drifts when he's barely halfway through a sentence. His thoughts are like a dull, obtrusive noise from a neighbouring room.

On the third day of darkness, late in the afternoon, he gives in and opens a curtain. He sits in the window and looks down into the square. No sign of the men who have been following him these last few weeks.

It's a gloriously sunny day. There are children playing "Reds and Whites". He cracks the window open a few inches so that he can hear their mock battles more clearly.

It was a day much like this when he left Otmichi, the village where he was raised. Late summer and sweltering. His brother, Misha, was playing *salochki* in the village square. Their father called him in, so that they could sit together a moment before Sergey set off for the city; an old custom still observed in their house. Andrei Grekov sat with his hands on his knees, looking stoically through the window. Knowing that if he met his father's gaze one or both of them might cry, Sergey stared down at his own feet. Misha, meanwhile, kicked his legs back and forth, his shoes scuffing against the wooden floor. Then it was time for Sergey to go. His brother went running back out into the square. Andrei Grekov carried his son's trunk out onto the front step. The carriage was waiting, the driver idly picking his nose and taking a moment to study whatever he found. The horses nickered impatiently and pawed the muddy ground with their hooves.

Sergey and his father embraced, his father's beard rough against his cheek. Andrei Grekov handed his son the brown leather trunk containing his belongings, Sergey climbed into the carriage, and with two loud cracks of the whip they pulled away.

As they neared the edge of the square, Sergey leaned out and called his brother's name, and Misha turned and nodded but he didn't wave. Did he understand the moment's gravity? Perhaps he was putting on a brave face, feigning indifference in front of his friends. Neither brother knew that it was the last time they would see one another.

He remembers the day clearly enough, could probably find his way around the old village blindfolded, but their faces – Misha's and his father's – have grown vague with time. He no longer has any photographs of them. He burned them all when it seemed the only sensible thing to do.

Dusk falls over the city. The children in the square are called in one by one – some by their mothers, many more by their grandmothers – and the place falls empty and silent. It is that moment when the city becomes a stage cleared between acts;

the painted backdrop hoisted up, the dancers in their dressing rooms. The boards are bare, the stage is lifeless and dark.

The lamps light up in sequence when the sky is a shade somewhere between red and gold. A moment later, men enter the square. Not uniformed, but everything about them – the way they walk, the way they're dressed – seems official. An unmarked black Ford comes puttering from the far corner of the square, drawing to a halt directly outside Sergey's building.

It won't happen yet, it's still too early. But it will happen.

Sergey closes the curtain again and crosses the room to his gramophone. He takes a record, Mahler's second symphony, and lowers it carefully onto the turntable. He cranks the handle several times and lowers the stylus. He sits in the nearest chair and closes his eyes. When the fourth movement, the *Urlicht*, is done he moves the stylus back to the beginning and listens to it again, and he repeats this three more times. There are places they could take him where there'll be no more music. If he can memorise just one piece, it should be this.

He recalls the purges of a year ago, though even remembering them feels forbidden. Entire floors emptied of their inhabitants. Vans lined up, dozens of them, in the street outside. Gunshots echoing in the night. He felt safe then, perhaps one of the few men in Leningrad who did. He was the toast of the Kirov. Their rising star. No-one had a bad word to say about him. So what had changed? It couldn't just be his music. This felt like something else, something random, as if his name had appeared in some morbid lottery. He felt sick.

He will apologise. He will do everything Secretary Remizov asked him to. The anonymous reviewer in *Pravda* was right. "Vulgar individualism". "Pretentious Formalism". His music *is* "a self-centred racket", an "egregious rejection of Socialist Realism". He will admit to all of these things and perhaps then they will let him go.

But when have they ever let anyone go? That isn't how things happen anymore. If he's lucky, they'll send him away. If he isn't, he'll receive a bullet in the back of his neck as they frogmarch him along some corridor. There won't even be a proper grave. He's heard the stories. Everyone has.

He rolls and lights another cigarette. The first puff makes him gag. He takes another draw and listens to the paper and tobacco crackle and burn. The room around him seems to take on a greenish hue.

He won't sleep. He wants to be awake and alert when they knock. There'll be questions, and he needs to give the right answers. Why haven't they knocked already? How long are they willing to wait? Aren't there other doors for them to knock at? He contemplates putting on the Mahler one last time, but no. He has it now. If he listened to it again, it might dull the effect.

Despite his efforts, he drifts asleep. He doesn't even feel it happen. He sinks into sleep as an unconscious man might drown. He wakes to a heavy, insistent knocking at the door. This is it.

"Open up, Grekov. We know you're in there."

He answers the door, still drowsy. Two men, the building's

commandant and a younger man, almost a boy, dressed in the uniform of a GUGB agent.

"Sergey Andreievich Grekov," the boy agent says, his voice flat, emotionless. "I am Sergeant Merkulov of the Main Directorate of State Security. I am arresting you under Article 58 of the penal code. Do not try and make a run for it. There are more agents downstairs. Is that understood?"

Sergey nods, and Merkulov pushes past him. The commandant is more sheepish, offering a shrug.

"I'm sorry," he whispers. "I have to be here. It's the rules."

"I know," says Sergey. "It's okay."

In the sitting room, Merkulov has begun rifling through his books, taking them from the shelves, flicking through the pages and dropping them to the floor. He walks over to the gramophone, lifts the needle and takes the record from its turntable. He holds it up to the light, squinting at its label.

"Ma..."

"Mahler," Sergey explains.

"Mahler... Auf... Aufer..."

"*Auferstehungssinfonie*. It means *Resurrection Symphony*."

"Resurrection? A *religious* work?"

"It was written before the Revolution, comrade, and besides, Mahler was Austrian."

"Hmm. We may need to look into that."

Sergey has the strangest urge to laugh, but if he began there's a chance he wouldn't stop. *We may need to look into that,* the boy said. As if they might have to investigate whether or not Mahler was Austrian. The absurdity is intense, dreamlike. A complete stranger going through his belongings, eyeing him with disdain, turning over books and records and now making his way around the edges of the room, rapping the wall with his knuckles. Merkulov walks back and forth in straight lines, stopping occasionally to stamp his heels. The search continues in the bedroom, where he takes a brace of letters from Sergey's bedside table and pockets them.

"Some of these look like English," he says. "We'll get them translated at the station."

Sergey has no idea what hour it is, but by the time they leave the building and drive across the city it's beginning to get light. It's a short drive, only a few minutes, and the streets are empty. Four of them inside the black Ford, the same car he saw parked outside his building. Sergey, Merkulov and two plainclothes men, whose names he isn't told. Sergey's wrists are bound with handcuffs. Merkulov offers him a cigarette, which he takes, and helps him to light it. Soon the car fills with a pale grey smoke, and Merkulov winds the window down to clear the air.

"My wife would kill me if she knows I'm still smoking," he says. "She hates the smell of it on me."

At the DPZ headquarters Sergey is signed in by a tired-looking desk sergeant at the end of his nightshift. In a side room, away from the desk, the agents make Sergey strip, and they search him, ruffling his hair and making him touch his toes. They trim the metal buttons from his jacket, unthread the laces from his boots, and confiscate his belt. Then they take him through into the prison.

The corridors here reek heavily of disinfectant, with a suggestion of ammonia. The building is cleaner than he had expected. The corridors look, smell and feel sterilised.

He's heard about the prisons. Thirty, forty men to a cell, they say. Hardly any room to lie down. Bugs everywhere. But this place is clean, and he's the sole occupant of his cell. A narrow bed, hard mattress. A small toilet without a proper seat. A roll of toilet paper with visible bits of wood pulp. They tell him to get some sleep. Early start. They lock the door, but leave on the light.

How long since they were in his flat, with Merkulov going through his music and his books? Twenty minutes? Thirty? Certainly no more than half an hour. How long since he was asleep in his armchair? An hour, maybe less.

This is how the world works. A life changed in minutes, seconds.

He can't sleep. The room is too bright and there doesn't seem any point, now that it must be daytime. Not that he can see any daylight. Every window is boarded up. It could be any time of day or night, and those in custody would be none the wiser.

He waits for an unknown length of time; it could be minutes or hours. He tries counting the seconds but gives up when he reaches two thousand. The cell door opens and the NKVD men enter, accompanied by another, older agent. Intelligent, aquiline face. A small, pouting mouth and sad eyes that droop in their corners.

"Comrade Grekov," he says. "I am Colonel Kaverin."

Kaverin shakes his hand and offers a smile that lasts a fraction of a second, before walking Sergey along another corridor. The agents walk ahead, while Kaverin stays behind him. Sergey waits for the feeling of cold metal against his nape. This is how it's done. A long walk down a corridor and a bullet in the back of the neck. It must be sudden. The prisoner probably wouldn't know what had happened. No wonder the place smells so strongly of disinfectant.

He's taken to an interview room. No windows. In one corner, a wash basin; in the other, a toolbox. In the centre of the room is a small brown desk and two wooden chairs, and Kaverin and Sergey sit either side while the agents remain at the door. Kaverin offers Sergey a cigarette and pours some water from a tin jug into a cup, pushing it gently across the desk.

"Please, drink."

Sergey gulps most of it down in one.

"I think there's been a mistake," he says.

"Do you know," says Kaverin, "I've literally lost count of how many people I've interviewed in this room. There have been so many. And they all say the same thing. *'There's been some sort of mistake.'*"

"But I don't know why I'm here."

"Is that so?"

Kaverin reaches beneath the desk and lifts a black leather briefcase onto his lap. He opens it, releasing the twin locks with a double-barrelled thud, and from it produces the sheaf of letters taken by Merkulov, and a handful of photographs.

"Here," he says, pointing to one of the images. "This was

taken in April, yes? At the Kirov?"

Sergey nods.

"This is you. And these are… who are these people?"

"Our guests."

"Guests of whom? The Kirov?"

"The state."

"Guests of the state. I see. You seem very friendly with these 'Guests of the state'."

"They came to my ballet."

"Ah, yes. The one based on the novel by Lermontov. Not the most *Soviet* of subjects…"

"I know that," says Sergey. "I realise that now. It was a mistake. I shouldn't have written it."

"And on the opening night of this ballet there were guests. American guests?"

"American. British. Some from France."

"Spies."

Sergey laughs nervously. "I'm sorry?"

"You heard me. Your guests were spies."

"They weren't *my* guests, comrade. They were guests of the state. They were as much your guests as they were mine."

"*My* guests? I didn't meet any of these people." Kaverin waves his hand over the photographs. "I put it to you that they were *your* guests. And that you stayed in contact with them, passing across classified information, in order to undermine the power of the workers' and peasants' Soviets."

"That's ridiculous," says Sergey.

"Is it?"

Kaverin moves the photographs to one side. He takes one of the letters and lays it out on the desk. It's not one of those that Merkulov found in Sergey's rooms; it's one that Sergey wrote himself, and posted months ago. Now he understands why there was no reply. Intercepted and kept on file. Not even censored with black ink and sent on.

"This is your handwriting, yes?"

Sergey nods.

"And written in English. Now, I don't read English myself, but we've had it translated."

"They're just letters to a friend."

"A friend?"

"Yes."

"Comrade Grekov. You need to understand the seriousness of your situation. We know that you have been working to undermine the workers' Soviets. We believe you may have been doing this in collaboration with outside forces. Americans, and perhaps the British. The sooner you confess, the more understanding the court will be."

He feels the anger welling inside him. He leans forward, his hands gripping the edge of the desk.

"I have nothing to confess," he says, his face only inches from Kaverin's.

In a second, one of the agents crosses the room and strikes Sergey across the face, hard enough to knock him to the floor. Seconds are lost. When he comes around he is back in his chair. He can taste blood.

"Comrade Grekov," says Kaverin. "We would rather not do

things this way, but if you insist on being so stubborn, you'll give us no choice. Here…" He opens his briefcase again and produces a single page of typescript. "Your confession."

"I've confessed nothing."

"These things are a formality. One confession is as good as the next. Will you sign?"

"How can I sign if it isn't true?"

He's been here before. Another piece of paper, waiting for his signature. Above that empty line, a lengthy denunciation of his father and brother, written by someone else. He signed it then. He won't do it a second time.

Kaverin sighs, massaging the bridge of his nose with his forefinger and thumb. To the agents, he says, "Take him away. He isn't to be fed."

They return Sergey to his cell. Time dissolves. Minutes. Hours. He's hungry and thirsty. Sign the confession, and they would feed him, give him water. But then what? No-one gets out of this. Not right away. But he won't put his name on that line.

They come back for him, cuffing his wrists and nudging him in the ribs with a baton, and they march him back to the interrogation room. Kaverin is waiting for them. He looks bored, as if he wants to be here no more than Sergey. As if this is all so very tiresome.

"Again," he says, turning the page so that Sergey can read it. "Your confession. Will you sign?"

"I can't."

"Can't, or won't?"

"What's the difference? I can't sign it, so I won't."

Kaverin gestures to the agents with a nod, and one of them steps forward and holds Sergey in a bear grip, pinning down his left hand by the wrist. The other takes his truncheon and slams it against Sergey's knuckles. The pain is incredible, passing through his body in waves. They know what they're doing, going for his left hand. They know he plays the violin.

"I'll ask again," says Kaverin. "Will you sign it?"

Sergey shakes his head. The pain is beginning to subside. What more can they do to him but this? Sign the confession and he'll be guilty, and they can do anything to him then.

Kaverin nods again to the agents, and again Sergey's hand is held against the desk and the truncheon smashes down, this time breaking through the skin. Dark blood pours from his knuckles. Sergey cries out and the first agent puts his arm around his throat, squeezing till he can no longer make a sound. Kaverin holds up the confession and a pen.

"Will you sign?"

Another choice. Give them names. From the Kirov. From the union. But whose? Every person he named would end up in a room like this, and perhaps that person would give names, and those names would give names, spreading out like a pandemic. This is how the world ends.

"Really, comrade," Kaverin sighs. "You're only causing more trouble for yourself."

He gestures to the second agent, who crosses over to the toolbox in the corner.

"Pliers, I think," says Kaverin. "He may have lost the feeling in his hand, so start with his toenails."

Chapter 12:
MANHATTAN, OCTOBER 2001

Pavel stepped into the house and scraped his shoes against the frayed doormat. He took a look around, his mouth gaping, as if he was standing in a cathedral or a vast cave.

"This place. Incredible."

She knew exactly how he felt. There couldn't be many houses still like this on the Upper East Side. Hallways and staircases lined with mahogany; heavy, brass-handled doors as old as the house itself. Most of these places had been swept through by interior decorators in the '80s and '90s. All that dark, old stuff torn out and walls and even floors knocked through to make them feel like warehouses. Sol's was certainly the only old-fashioned brownstone Natalie had ever set foot in. But there was so much space for one person; too much even when you factored in each day's visitors. There were rooms he used solely for storage and other, sparsely decorated rooms he didn't use at all.

When she began making plans to study at NYU, Natalie pictured herself living in a place like this. Not even a whole house, just an apartment, but one which looked exactly the same. She envisioned autumn leaves falling in the street outside. Walking down the stoop in a matching hat, gloves and scarf. A brisk morning trip to the Met to spend a moment looking at the Caillebotte painting of Paris in the rain. Good grief, it was all so much bullshit; a fantasy cobbled together from TV shows and fashion spreads. Yet still, a part of her held on to it, because in this house she saw that it was still possible, that New York could still be the place she imagined it might be. She held on to the hope that Sol would one day ask her to move in.

At the top of the house was a roof terrace with mossy furniture and fading pots of dry earth and dead twigs. Natalie and Sol had spent some time up there over the summer. Even though it was only a few storeys up, the view was magnificent. Rooftops and water towers. In the south, beyond the park's green wedge, the skyscrapers of Midtown. She hadn't gone up there in over a month. Not that you could see Lower Manhattan from there, but the skyline still had a hazy, smoky quality, and just sitting beneath a wide open sky was suddenly oppressive.

Sol once told her that he'd passed this house many times as a boy. His father had customers who lived nearby, a well-to-do doctor and his wife, who wouldn't dream of sending even a servant down to Houston Street to collect. Each Friday, before Shabbat, his father would drive up to make the delivery, and during school breaks he would take Sol with him.

"And these streets," Sol said. "They seemed so much wider, so much cleaner than ours. On our street, there were crates and wagons and even horses – people still had horses in those days – which meant horse-crap everywhere. But we'd come down this street, on our way to Doctor Lowe's, and I remember thinking, couldn't have been any older than ten, but I remember looking at these houses and thinking, 'One day I'm gonna live in one of these.'"

She understood completely, and Pavel, like everyone else

who saw the house, was impressed.

"I think you could fit my whole apartment in just one room," he said.

From the study they heard Sol stirring, his backside squeaking against the chair's leather as he peered out into the hallway.

"Who is that? Angie? Do we have visitors?"

"It's Natalie, Mr Conrad. And yes. Just a friend of mine. You can meet him in a moment."

What had she done? A mistake to invite Pavel here. At least before now he hadn't known the address. He could keep phoning, but that didn't mean anyone had to answer. They could even change the number if they had to. But now he was inside the house, and Sol was only a few rooms away. What had she done?

Pavel stared in through the study's open door.

"I want to speak with him."

"And you will. In a moment."

They went to the kitchen, where Natalie made them both coffee and went once more over the ground rules. If he's upset, we leave. If he's confused, we leave. If he knows nothing, we leave. Don't shout at him. Don't make fun of him. Don't talk down to him, as if he was a child. Pavel leaned against the work surface and drummed his fingertips against the cupboard door beneath. She tried to read his expression. Almost a smile. He looked impatient, but not bored. She was trying to delay the meeting, and he must have known it, but he no longer seemed to mind.

"Your English is excellent," she said. If they could talk a while it might give her time to think.

"I learned from movies," said Pavel. "They started showing American movies on television when I was a boy. Not on any official channels. This was before the end of Communism. Sometimes, a man would dub them. Just one man, doing all the voices, even the women. And sometimes they wouldn't be dubbed, so you had to work out what everyone was saying. I watched *Robocop* and *Die Hard* and I think there was one called *Planes and Trains*. There is a fat man and a man with grey hair and they are on a journey and everything goes wrong. It is very funny."

Natalie laughed, placing her hand over her mouth as if to hide her smile. If he was a con artist then charm was bound to be one of his tools. Fall for that, and you'll fall for anything. She couldn't look him in the eye. Each time she did she felt something waking up inside her.

"We should go in," she said.

Get this over with. Like wax strips. Like sticking plasters. Brief pain, and then it's finished, done.

She took him through to Sol's study and turned down the music. Sol stirred and shifted in his chair till he was sitting straight.

"Mr Conrad, I'd like you to meet a friend of mine. His name is Pavel. He's from Russia."

Sol looked up and smiled. He went to ease himself out of his chair, but Pavel leaned over, offering him his hand.

"A pleasure to meet you, sir," he said, flashing Natalie a

sideways glance. "I am a very big fan of your work."

"Oh, yes?" said Sol. He turned to Natalie, eyes wide, and in a stage whisper he said, "He's handsome, don't you think?"

Natalie blushed. She knew Pavel was looking at her but she wouldn't look back.

"And you're from Russia?" Sol asked.

"Yes, sir."

"Pavel's grandfather was a composer," said Natalie, gesturing to Pavel that he should take up the footstool, while she rested on the windowsill, her back against the cool glass.

"Is that so?" said Sol.

"Yes, sir," said Pavel. "You may have heard of him."

Sol nodded, shook his head, and nodded again.

"What was his… what… his name? What was his name?"

"Sergey Grekov."

"Say again?"

"Grekov. Sergey Grekov."

"No, I… I don't know. Natalie?"

The same voice he used whenever he was helpless. I spilled a drink. I dropped something on the floor. I wet myself. Natalie? She had to stop this.

"It's alright, Mr Conrad. This was all a very long time ago."

"I… I don't recall…" he said, his voice reduced to an almost inaudible croak.

"He wrote a ballet," said Pavel. "*Geroy Nashego Vremeni. A Hero of Our Time.* There is a novel…"

Sol lowered his chin till it was touching his chest and he shook his head.

"I don't..." he said. "It doesn't..."

"That's okay, Mr Conrad," said Natalie, turning his music back up. "We'll leave you in peace. Call me if you need anything."

They left the study, Pavel glancing back at the open door as they walked along the hall. In the kitchen he began pacing back and forth, his hands restless at his sides. What had he hoped for? What was it he wanted? If she could only summon up the nerve to ask him.

"I'm sorry," she said. "I did warn you."

"I want to speak with him again. I want to ask him if he went to Russia."

"And I'm telling you he didn't. When was your grandfather's ballet performed?"

"April 1938. At the Kirov. It's called the Mariinsky now."

"Okay. 1938. Well, that year he spent four months in hospital. A sanatorium down in Florida. I don't recall the exact dates, but I'm pretty sure he wouldn't have been well enough to travel..."

"How do you know this?"

"He told me the story a thousand times," she said. "And it came up at his hearing."

She felt something click into place, an almost physical sensation. The hearing. Sol's testimony. She got up with a start, the feet of her chair scraping noisily against the kitchen floor.

"What is it?" Pavel asked.

She was already out of the kitchen and half way down the hall. Pavel followed, past the study and into Sol's library. Her mind raced. The hearing. Ronald Bernard.

"What are you doing?"

She didn't answer him, but began searching every bookcase, shelf and alcove. He asked again.

"His teacher at Juilliard," she said. "He was a composer. Ronald Bernard. I think he visited Russia. I can't remember the details. But there was something mentioned at a hearing, like a court case, years later..."

There was, or had been, a biography of Ronald Bernard somewhere in this room. She'd read it not long after she began working for Sol. She knew of their relationship. Everyone now knew. It was no longer referred to as a "friendship" or "companionship". They were lovers. By reading this book she'd thought perhaps she might get to know Sol a little better, and – to a certain extent – she had.

She scanned each corner of the library, but found nothing. Maybe someone had borrowed it or Sol had given it away. When had she last seen it? She couldn't remember. And why was she even looking for it in the first place? She could end this now. Tell Pavel she couldn't find the book, that it was only a fancy, a half-baked idea she'd had. Sorry I couldn't help you. Goodnight and good luck. But she wouldn't. Now that he was here, now that it seemed they might have found some truth beneath time's clutter, she needed to know more.

They went to the study, where Sol was still listening to his music. Pavel waited in the doorway while Natalie logged in to the computer. Sol leaned to one side so that he could see the screen.

"Say. What're you doing there?"

"Just checking your emails. It won't take very long."

The modem coughed and spluttered and squealed its way online.

"Damn thing makes a hell of a racket."

"I know, and I'm sorry. I'll only be five minutes. I promise."

It was running slowly. Everything took an age to load. A short biography of Bernard on some music student's personal website and a few paragraphs on Wikipedia. Neither mentioned the events of 1938.

"Well?" Pavel said.

"Nothing. We need to get a copy of that book."

"A bookshop?"

"It's out of print."

Pavel sighed, his shoulders slumped. If she told him she'd done everything she could, he would have to believe her, and maybe he would go and that would be the end of it. He looked so defeated.

"But I know where we'll find one," she said.

Pavel's expression brightened and he beamed at her and Natalie gasped, almost a nervous laugh. This is happening, she thought, and for a moment she felt as if she might levitate out of her chair and keep going until she was touching the ceiling. Something is happening.

Chapter 13:
LENINGRAD, AUGUST 1938

The man staring at him on the crosstown tram does so indiscreetly, never bothering to mask his intent. It's the middle of summer, a hot, sticky day, and he's wearing a grey overcoat that reaches down to his knees. He must be melting inside that thing. And why is he following Sergey in the first place?

If Sergey was hiding something, involved in something, he might understand, but he's a composer.

Remizov. It started with him. The grubbiest kind of ultimatum. But it can't be that. Does Remizov really have that much influence?

They had a meeting at the Kirov yesterday to discuss next year's Spring season. Sergey wasn't invited. He hasn't received a phone call or a message in weeks. They're taking it too far. It's one thing to have work criticised on the grounds of political failings but no-one ever said he was a terrible composer. Quite the opposite. Political failings are more powerful when the music is good. But why shouldn't he be involved next year? And in the meantime, a man has to eat. The money from *Hero* ran out quickly. One too many parties. One too many lavish meals.

"Feeling flush are we, Sergey Andreievich?"

"Look at Comrade Moneybags, here."

"If this is the shape of things to come, I hope the Kirov perform nothing but Grekov ballets from now on."

They were good times, but if he'd cancelled a single supper he might have another hundred roubles in his pocket, rather than a handful of kopecks, barely enough to cover his tram fare.

He steps off near the Alexander Garden and walks the rest of the way, to a pale blue building overlooking the canal. He doesn't have an appointment, and so there's every chance this will have been a wasted journey – not to mention a waste of money – and that he'll return home with even less than when he set out.

The building's concierge is young. Plump and red-cheeked with a shapeless mouth and oily hair. Sergey's arrival sends the lad into a fluster, as if he is the building's first visitor in months.

"I'm visiting Tatiana Ivanova," says Sergey.

"Right. Yes. Comrade Ivanova. Of course… I… do you have an appointment?"

"I'm an old friend of hers."

The boy looks at him and an uncomfortable quiet spreads itself between them. The lad is like an actor bumbling a line. Hasn't been in the job very long. Promoted, perhaps following a predecessor's sudden, unmentionable absence.

"You could call her," Sergey suggests. "Speak with her assistant. Josef."

"Yes," the concierge snaps. "I know that. And I shall."

He lifts the receiver, dials three numbers quickly, and waits.

"It's Alexei, on reception. I have a man here. Says he's a friend of Comrade Ivanova's."

A pause. He places his chubby hand over the receiver.

"Name?"

"Sergey Grekov."

"He says his name is Sergey Grekov."

What does Tatiana Dmitrievna make of the boy? That's if she ever has to deal with him. She probably delegates these conversations to Josef. Any contact, even the briefest exchange, with someone like this would leave her feeling grubby.

"You can go up," the concierge says. "Fifth floor, third door to the –"

"I know where it is," says Sergey.

Josef is waiting for him on the fifth floor, holding open the door to the apartment. He gives Sergey the same look he gives anyone and everyone except his mistress – a glance of sneering contempt – and takes him through.

"This way, please. Mademoiselle Ivanova has company. An interview with *Ogoniok*. You'll have to wait until they're finished."

Sergey sits in the reception room, next to Tatiana's salon. This place always feels like a relic. Grand, opulent, but in a way that's strangely threadbare, as if it could disintegrate at any moment; paint peeling away from the walls, rugs consumed by mould, electric lightbulbs flickering their last. From the next room, voices; Tatiana's and another woman's, much younger.

"And do you think you'll ever retire?"

"Retire!" Tatiana spits it out. "I hate this word, 'retire'. Why should I retire? Why should I even consider retiring, when I feel as young today as I did when I was twenty-one? I shall retire only when I am unable to dance, and today I am able to dance."

He'd almost forgotten how melodramatic she can sound in full flow. Even with the wall between them, he can see the sweeping gestures of her arms, her pencil-thin eyebrows arching ever higher, her forehead furrowing. The way her make-up gathers in the lines around her eyes and mouth with each theatrical grimace.

The interview carries on in much the same vein; the young interviewer's flippant questions, Tatiana's flamboyant answers. Josef passes nimbly along the hall and enters the next room, telling the young woman her time is up, and a moment later he shows her out of the apartment. Sergey catches a glimpse of them as they pass by in the hall. The journalist can't be any older than twenty-two. She looks shaken. An experience never forgotten, that first encounter with the woman nicknamed the Little Barn-Owl by the press, by her fans, by those at the Kirov. But is it because of those big, expressive eyes, or her ability to pick off smaller prey without compunction?

"You may now see Mademoiselle Ivanova," Josef says, and Sergey follows him into the salon. As they enter the room, Josef announces, "Monsieur Grekov, mademoiselle."

Typical Tsarist old queen. One foot firmly in the past. Josef would have been a young man during the Revolution, yet still he acts like some 19th Century footman out of *Anna Karenina*. And calling Tatiana 'mademoiselle', as if she were still a mere slip of a girl. If she weren't so famous the pair of them could be arrested, perhaps worse, carrying on this way.

"Sergey Andreievich!" she says, rising from the chaise longue and gliding toward him in an invisible cloud of her own perfume, her fur-lined dressing gown trailing behind her. She kisses him on both cheeks and invites him to sit. "Josef. Would you be so kind as to bring us some tea? Or perhaps Monsieur Grekov would prefer something stronger?"

"Tea will be fine", Sergey says, and Josef leaves them, pausing at the door to flash him one last withering look.

"Well," says Tatiana. "This *is* a pleasant surprise. I'm sorry if you had to wait very long. I was talking to *Ogoniok*. Can you believe it's five years since I was last interviewed by them? Five years! Outrageous. So..." She sits back, pulling her dressing gown across her knees. "What brings you here?"

He hadn't planned what he would say, didn't even know if he would get this far. And now he's here, what next? Every chance she'll laugh him out of the apartment. And once he's out of the door, everyone at the Kirov will know. He'll be a laughing stock. Indignity heaped upon indignity. He glances down and notices a single crooked blue vein beneath her otherwise alabaster skin.

"Well?" says Tatiana, her smile saying: *I saw you looking, you naughty boy*.

"I wanted to see you," he says. "That's all."

"Really?"

"And..." He pauses. Deep breath. He should have gone elsewhere. Remizov, perhaps. All this started with him, after all.

"Well?" she says, her smile not breaking for a moment. "Spit it out. Come on."

"Listen," he says. "Tanyoshka… I know last time we spoke, it didn't… What I mean to say is I know we haven't always seen eye to eye."

"'Eye to eye'? A touch cliché, even for a farm boy like you. And it really doesn't do justice to what happened, now, does it?"

He's dizzy, nauseous. Two days since his last substantial meal, the larder in his rooms all but empty, what little money he has spent on tobacco and vodka.

"Have you seen Vasily Nikolayevich lately?" she asks. "Little Vasya?"

"I haven't."

"He speaks of you quite often. I'm convinced he does it to upset me. Which means he doesn't really know me at all. But I think, despite our little drama, he remains very fond of you."

Her expression hardens. She breathes in sharply through her nose and turns her gaze to the far corner of the room.

"I'd thought," she begins. A sigh. She faces him again. "I'd thought perhaps you might have come here to apologise."

"Apologise?"

"Am I being unreasonable?"

He lowers his head.

"You can't even look at me, Seryozha. So stubborn. I can see why you and Remizov had your little falling out."

"What do you know about that?" Sergey asks. "What did he tell you?"

"He told me nothing. But I have the impression that you're no longer this month's favourite. Little Vasya was devastated. He thought we might get tangled up in your notoriety. I told him. 'Vasya,' I said. 'You shouldn't worry about such things. No-one ever blames the dancers. They believe we're all quite brainless. Little more than marionettes.' Is that what you believe, Seryozha? That dancers are stupid?"

"No."

"You could have fooled me. And for a moment, you almost did."

There are few things more shaming than pride remembered after a fall. It makes him blush to recall how he acted, those first few months at the Kirov. So many people telling him how wonderful it was to work with fresh talent. Easy to believe the myth of his own potency. All eyes were on him, and he understood the power that gave him.

Vasya was first. It was the night after they announced *A Hero of Our Time*. They were, as Remizov put it, "celebrating the launch of a great endeavour"; a new Soviet ballet that would be the envy of Europe. Let the bourgeois composers of Vienna or Paris experiment with ugly noise. Sergey Grekov's ballet, based on the novel by Lermontov, would prove for once and for all the primacy of Soviet culture. This was not an age for understatement.

In the theatre, the cast and crew assembled on an otherwise empty stage, lit with spotlights, the auditorium's empty seats lost in the dark. They drank Soviet champagne, and all agreed that Sergey's music was sublime. The "next Mussorgsky", they said. It was always Mussorgsky, the only composer who stayed in fashion, who was never deemed unacceptable. There had been many "next Mussorgkys". He should have known what to expect.

After leaving the theatre, a group of them went on to a nearby café where they drank Georgian wine well into the early hours. When the café closed, Sergey and Vasily found themselves staggering in the vague direction of Vasily's rooms. Sergey lived on the other side of town and so Vasily invited him in, offering his couch as a bed.

They talked about Sergey's music, and how Vasily should portray the role of Pechorin. He's a hero only in the ironic sense, Sergey told him, and as for the title, well, that was Lermontov's most cutting joke of all. The author looked upon his age as one of vanity. He saw in his generation only self-serving arrogance and hubris. Sergey tried explaining this using language which had been drilled into him at the academy. Wicked individualism. The nihilism of the bourgeoisie. He and Vasily talked and drank vodka until it began to get light, and with increasing frequency their conversation turned to the subject of sex.

"It's been so long for me," said Vasily. "I can't remember the last time I was fucked."

Sergey coughed and spluttered and told Vasily not to be so scandalous.

"What's scandalous about that? It's the *truth*."

"But you shouldn't say such things," said Sergey. "Not at your age. Not at all, in fact. You don't know who's listening.

Say 'fucked', and people know exactly what you are. Men *fuck*. Men aren't *fucked*."

"Some are."

"You know what I mean. And you can be jailed for that."

"Locked up with lots of other sex-starved men. Sounds like a strange punishment, if you ask me."

"Well, that's as maybe, but you should be more careful."

Somehow, words became actions. A hand lowered onto someone's thigh, lingering there. Eyes locked. Every second seemed to vibrate. Vasily opened Sergey's trousers button by button, and looked to him for approval with each button undone. Within moments, he was fucking the youth with an aggression that frightened him; though what disturbed him even more was Vasily's breathless "thank you" when the act was done.

Sergey believed what had happened that night – or rather, in the early hours of the morning – remained a secret between them. He left before the first workers took to the streets, and crossed the city in a mood that shifted from pride to shame and back again. It was several weeks before he received an invitation to join Tatiana in her dressing room.

There, she told him she had heard "simply wonderful things" about *A Hero of Our Time*. "But of course," she said, "it's based on such an enchanting novel. A true Russian masterpiece."

She insisted they toast Sergey's burgeoning success with champagne, and not Soviet champagne but the real thing. He asked where she got it, and Tatiana tapped the side of her nose.

"I have my ways."

And so they drank champagne, and several times Tatiana mentioned the role of Princess Mary; how she had discussed this with their choreographer, how she felt the young princess's movements should be brittle and awkward, like a child's clockwork toy, particularly toward the ballet's end.

"And you have killed her, yes?" she asked, making it sound almost like an accusation of murder.

"I have," said Sergey.

"Quite right, too. I never understood why Lermontov lets her live. What's the point of her if she *lives?*"

Sergey said he agreed, and that he had asked their choreographer to select a young dancer for the part, fresh from matriculation. Tatiana gave him a look – part bemused, part appalled – and reared back.

"A *new* dancer? For Princess Mary? And he agreed? That's absurd. Pick some girl from the *reserve troupe* and she'll be all over the place."

With the greatest of tact, Sergey said he felt inexperience might suit the Princess better; that a little naivety could bring something unique to the role.

Still reeling, Tatiana asked, "So who am I to play?"

"I thought Vera," he said, relieved he hadn't suggested the part of Princess Mary's mother.

"That harridan?"

"She's not a harridan," Sergey laughed. "She's the love of Pechorin's life. What's more, a character like Princess Mary demands a girl's passion. Awkward. Naïve. Vera calls for something deeper, more sophisticated. A woman's passion."

"And which do you prefer, Sergey Andreievich? A girl's passion, or a woman's?"

Again, he laughed. "A woman's, definitely."

He watched her, waiting for a smile or even a blink, something inviting, but Tatiana remained impassive. She would never openly give him the license to have her. That would be vulgar. Instead, she expected him to come to her, to take what he wanted. He placed his glass on her dressing table and crossed the room to where she lay on an ornate couch; an antique that must have belonged to the theatre since long before the Revolution. Sitting beside her he placed his hand on her thigh, sliding it beneath her skirts. He had never before kissed a woman of Tatiana's age. Her lips, though full, were curiously rigid, and the kiss was too mannered, too practised. When he looked into her eyes, searching for reflected desire, he saw only a performance staged for an audience of one.

Through the weeks and months that followed he continued visiting Vasily at his apartment and Tatiana in her dressing room. Sex with Tatiana remained as passionless as that first encounter, while with Vasya each coupling was more aggressive than the last. Neither made him truly happy, but the duplicity of it contained a thrill of its own. It was only a matter of time before one or both of them would find out. Little surprise how Tatiana reacted. The sound of a shattered vase from the far end of the corridor. A shrill, anguished roar. The reserve troupe girls gathered outside, leaning as close to Tatiana's door as they dared.

Now, in her salon, Tatiana is more composed. Almost glacial. She regards him with an amused expression. There's nothing of the barn-owl about her. A barn-owl kills for food, and as quickly as it can. Only humans and cats ever seem to draw the process out as entertainment.

"So why *did* you come here?" she asks.

"Because no-one else will speak to me. No-one calls me, no-one has written. They have meetings at the Kirov to which I'm not invited..."

"Ah, yes. I was there. I thought it curious that you weren't."

"And I have no work. Nobody will commission me to write another piece, nobody will employ me." He reaches into his pocket, producing his last handful of kopecks. "This is all I have left."

"So it's money?" says Tatiana. "Oh, Seryozha. That is rather gauche of you, don't you think?"

"It isn't just money," says Sergey, helplessly. "I feel like my strings are being cut."

"Which strings?"

"You said yourself. We're marionettes."

"I was talking about *dancers*, darling."

"But it's not just the dancers. We're all puppets, in one way or another."

"Then who are our puppeteers?"

He glowers at her, but can't bring himself to answer.

Presently, Josef returns, carrying a silver tray with a teapot and two glasses in ornate *podstakanniks*, and a plate of chocolate covered *bouchées*. He pours them each a glass of tea, handing one to Sergey with the briefest of nods before taking Tatiana hers with a graceful, sweeping gesture.

"Mademoiselle," he says, leaving the room in reverse with another bow.

"Josef is such a sweetie," says Tatiana, pausing to stir two lumps of sugar into her tea. "So loyal. I'll have him write you out a cheque for… shall we say five hundred roubles?"

He bites his lip. Best not show any emotion. He won't give her the satisfaction. There's a cynicism behind her offer, and yet still it moves him almost to tears.

"Splendid," says Tatiana. "And please don't think of it as a loan. It's a gift, from a dear friend."

For a moment, her mask appears to slip; the gap between one performance and the next. Her face becomes expressionless, her eyebrows drop back into place and the lines become less pronounced. Behind her eyes, a flicker of something almost like sympathy or sorrow. For once, he can't quite read her. If something is communicated by this look, it's a chime of regret that seems to echo around the room long after they move on to other topics of conversation; Tatiana regaling him with the latest news about one of the *sujets*, or the recent scandal involving the *répétiteur's* wife and a certain high-ranking member of the party.

"Please," she says, gesturing to the plate. "Help yourself to the sweets. They're delicious. From Eliseev. I mustn't eat too many of them myself. They're terrible for the figure."

When Josef has cleared away the tea tray, Tatiana announces that she must begin dressing for the evening. She's having dinner with some "Moscow men" – generals, commissars and the like – at the Astoria.

"Wasn't that where we had the party for your ballet?"

Sergey nods.

"Funny… I hardly saw you that night."

Sergey thanks her, and Josef shows him out, all the way to the elevators, giving him his cheque just as the elevator doors open with a single chime.

"I shan't imagine we'll be seeing you for a while, monsieur," he says, folding the cheque and sliding it into Sergey's shirt pocket. "Shall we?"

Chapter 14: LOS ANGELES, OCTOBER 1950

He's sitting across the table before you even notice him enter the canteen. Flannel suit. Blue tie. Smiling as if he brings glad tidings, though there's little chance of that. Capitol Pictures' Head of Security. Roy Carmichael.

"Mind if I…?" he says, as if he hadn't already sat down.

"Not at all."

He points to your lunch.

"What's that?"

"Meatloaf."

"Any good?"

"Same as usual."

"I never ate it before. Not here, anyhow."

"Friday is meatloaf day."

"Mrs Carmichael always makes my lunch. Has done ever since we was newlyweds. Except when I was in Europe. You serve during the war?"

You shake your head.

"Had a hunch you didn't. Objector?"

"4F."

"Well. Can't be helped, I guess. But like I was saying… Mrs Carmichael makes my lunch. The only day I don't like is Thursday. Thursday is tuna sandwich day, and I don't like canned tuna. I just don't have the heart to tell her."

You wait a second to make sure he's finished and you ask

him what he wants.

"I was just wondering," says Carmichael, "if you could offer me some information. Illumination."

"Illumination?"

"Sure. You see, a little birdy tells me you're conducting a concert, sometime next year."

"Who'd you hear that from?"

"Doesn't matter. Little birdy. But they said you was conducting a concert of Ronald Bernard's music in New York. Is that correct?"

"Yes."

"I see. Now, I won't bother asking if you was aware that Mr Bernard's name appeared on the Red Channels list. I know you was, because I told you. So I guess, if I have a question it's this: Why are you conducting a concert of Ronald Bernard's music?"

"Mr Carmichael. As I told you back… whenever it was we had our meeting… Mr Bernard and I were friends. I studied under him. I know his music very well. His widow asked if I could conduct the concert, and I said yes."

"Interesting. Interesting. You see, I asked around and somebody told me you and Mr Bernard lived together, in New York."

"Who told you that?"

"Again. Little Birdy. Different birdy this time, but… y'know. Anyway. They said you had an apartment overlooking Central Park. Sounded impressive."

"Your point being…?"

"Were Mr and Mrs Bernard divorced at that time?"

"You should find a more well-informed birdy. They never got divorced."

"But she didn't live in the apartment with you?"

"No, she did not."

"And how many bedrooms were there, in this apartment?"

"Three."

"A three bedroom apartment overlooking Central Park? Jeez. That must have cost a few bucks. Were you sharing the rent?"

"Mr Bernard owned the place."

"I see. But it's funny, because when I mentioned Mr Bernard to you the first time, you said you studied under him at Juilliard, that you were friends, but you didn't mention anything about living with him."

"Why is that funny?"

"I don't mean funny 'ha-ha'. I mean funny curious."

"Why is it curious?"

"How long did you and Mr Bernard live in that apartment?"

"Six years."

"Six years? Six years you lived with Mr Bernard and you didn't mention it the last time we spoke? That's… that's curious."

"Where is this leading, Mr Carmichael?"

Carmichael lowers his voice almost to a whisper. The smile doesn't fade.

"Mr Conrad. As you know, it is my job to protect this

company. Most of the time that involves making sure no-one breaks in, no-one steals nothing, that the press can't take unflattering pictures of Mona Freeman. That kind of thing. But it also means protecting the studio's reputation. Now, to do that, I must be the Argus of Capitol Pictures. I got a hundred eyes. I know everything. Which actress had a backstreet abortion. Which actor is liaising with which busboy from the Cocoanut Grove. Keep secrets from your friends and family, by all means, but while you are an employee of Capitol Pictures you do not keep them from me. A secret kept from me is, well… it's like the little lump you keep hidden from your doctor. You're embarrassed and a little scared, so you hide it from him, and then it kills you stone dead. Am I making myself clear?"

"Crystal."

"Good. That's good. Well, I'll leave you to get on with your meatloaf. Can't say I'd swap it for one of Mrs Carmichael's sandwiches. Unless it was a Thursday, you know. Think on what we spoke about, Mr Conrad. I'll see you around."

He goes, taking your appetite with him, and you abandon your lunch half-eaten. You go back to Room 01B. Angela is standing over an open score, humming a melody, something bright and cheerful, conducting an invisible orchestra with a pencil. She keeps humming and conducting long after you enter. An exasperated sigh. She drops the pencil onto her desk.

"Sorry, I knew I couldn't work this out in my head, and all the meat lockers are taken. So I'm afraid you're stuck with my humming."

"It's fine," you tell her. "I like your humming."

Angela smiles, holding your gaze a moment before sitting down and scribbling some notes. Those first few months of working with her, she'd fill every silence with chatter. Lately, when neither of you has anything to say she'll just smile, all doe-eyed. You can't pretend you haven't noticed, and what's more, she knows you have.

★★

Again, the canyon road. It's late, but the last traces of sunlight are still fading over the ridge. You see this road as the spring launcher of a pinball machine, the city its vast playfield. Each location you might go to is another paddle, sending you off across the city at night. Pershing Square, or Griffith Park? Richfield gas station or another bar or club on the Sunset Strip?

Oh, city of possibilities! Even at this late hour, the night air is still desert hot with no sign of cooling, and rich with the scent of eucalyptus.

Half a mile down the road, a woman is ambling along the roadside. Barefoot and wearing a nightgown. Looks like a ghost. You slow to a crawl but you already know who it is.

"Mary?"

She looks at you askance, as if you're a perfect stranger.

"Mary? Are you okay?"

She scowls and shakes her head. She won't be answering any of your damn questions. She carries on walking.

"Mary."

She looks terrible. You can't remember the last time you saw her, but she looks as if she hasn't eaten anything or bathed or brushed her hair in weeks. You ease off the brake and allow the car to roll at her speed.

"What're you doing out here? It's late."

"I need to get to Goose Creek," she says. "Momma needs twine."

"What're you talking about? Mary. Do you want me to drive you home?"

"U-huh. Ain't s'pposed to talk to strangers. Gotta get to Goose Creek."

"Mary, please. It's late. Will you get in the car?"

She keeps walking, and when she's a couple of yards ahead of you she starts to sing.

"In the Big Rock Candy Mountains,
There's a land that's fair and bright;
Where the hand-outs grow on bushes,
And you sleep out every night."

You let go of the brake again and drive on, pulling up in front of her and blocking her path. You're out of the car before she has a chance to walk around it. Around each eye there are heavy smudges of eye shadow. Her hair is like straw. Her skin is just hanging off her.

"C'mon, Mary."

You place an arm around her shoulders and guide her gently towards the car. She's still singing.

Where the boxcars all are empty,
And the sun shines every day.
And the birds and the bees and the cigarette trees,
The lemonade springs where the bluebird sings
In the Big Rock Candy Mountains.

You ease her into the passenger seat. She isn't injured, she isn't bleeding. She's damaged, but in ways you can't possibly fathom. You have to do something. You fumble with the buckle of her seat belt and when she's safely strapped in you get behind the wheel and keep driving down the canyon.

At Cedars of Lebanon they give Mary a shot of sedative, and you're quizzed by a doctor while a Negro orderly pushes Mary through into a private room.

The doctor asks how well you know her, and if she's displayed any symptoms of mental disorder in the past. Mental disorder. Like an unkempt room. Drawers open and books and papers scattered everywhere. You tell him you're not sure, you don't think so. She's been under a lot of stress lately. She was being investigated. He seems to understand exactly what this means.

"That would suggest some kind of nervous breakdown," he says. "You were right to bring her in. This isn't the kind of thing that'll go away with tea and sympathy, I'm afraid. Does she have any family at all?"

"No family. Her husband died. They never had any kids."

"And does she work?"

"She's an actress. Was an actress. At Warner."

"I thought the name sounded familiar. Say, wasn't she in *Playboy of Paris*?"

"I don't know."

"I'm sure that was her. Shucks. My wife loves that movie."

★★

This isn't the fleapit on Broadway; you wouldn't dream of taking Angela to a place like that. Besides, the only reason you ever go there is its proximity to Pershing Square. No, this is one of the grand old oriental theatres that sprang up in the 1920s, made to look like some Far Eastern palace. Gold leaf – or at the very least, gold *paint* – and murals everywhere.

You wait for the movie to begin. The rustle of popcorn bags. Silhouettes edging their way along each row. Onscreen, a newsreel. Soldiers scrambling across craggy landscapes, between the charred remains of trees. Two soldiers in a machine gun nest; one firing the gun, the other feeding it with ammunition.

"In Korea, United Nations troops push on in their cautious advance against the communists; an advance whose purpose General Ridgeway states is not to seize ground but to wipe out the enemy!"

Angela whispers, "You think this could get worse?"

"I don't think so," you whisper back. "Something like this… it's just sabre-rattling. Us and the Chinese using this tiny little place to prove a point."

"What point could they possibly prove?"

"Damned if I know."

After the movie you head to a diner across the way, and drink milkshakes at a table facing out onto the corner of Hollywood and Orange. You're unsure about the device of a dead narrator; Angie thinks that was the best thing in the whole movie. She thinks Gloria Swanson was playing it too broadly. You wish she could have met Mary.

"That's the whole point of the character," you tell her. "What is it she says? 'I *am* big. It's the pictures that got small.'"

"Okay. That line was great. I'll give you that."

You exchange a smile. Elsewhere in the diner, a young couple hold hands across the table as they share one towering milkshake, and an older couple, out-of-towners by the look of them, eat stacked pancakes without speaking. Out on Orange, two police officers are helping a hobo into the back of a police van. If you look at Angie again, you know she'll still be smiling at you, that she won't have taken her eyes off you. She wants you to look at her.

★★

The house never felt this empty before. Each sound is amplified. Its rooms seem bigger. Maybe you should go back. Go east. LA bores you. You miss the seasons. Even the occasional tremor doesn't spice things up enough to make this place interesting. You'd swap the Village for West Hollywood any day. Wouldn't you?

Easy to get nostalgic, now it's over a year since you were in New York. Those final months feel fuzzier, less distinct. Easy to forget what it was really like when Ron was ill, when he was dying, and in the days and weeks after he was gone. Naïve to think you'd be allowed any part in all that; the pageant of a Great Man's death. Margaret Bernard was centre stage: The Widow. At the funeral she was seated with Ron's sisters and brothers, nieces and nephews, at the front of the church, while you sat three rows back, with his colleagues from Juilliard.

'Friend' was a euphemism you could just about bear, but when someone referred to you as Ron's 'amanuensis' you thought you might spit blood.

LA made sense. Copland was writing scores. Stravinsky was living here. Even Schoenberg – of all people – was teaching at UCLA. And then there was Bernstein, the *wunderkind*, hot off the success of *On the Town*, and blessed with matinee idol good looks. Didn't you hear a rumour they once asked him to screen test for a picture?

Bernstein. If you were to develop a malignant tumour and give it a name, a personality, you would call it Leonard Bernstein. The Harvard piano prodigy, when you were still starting out at Juilliard. Comparisons were made. You both played piano, both wanted to conduct. And Bernstein worked hard to play the Street Kid Made Good. Never mind that everyone knew the truth: His father was a businessman who bought his son his own radio show (a *radio show*!) when he was still in his teens. Went to the same Boston school as half the founding fathers. Got himself a classical education. Was studying at fucking *Harvard*.

Bernstein is the other motorist you look at, sideways, from

the driver's seat of your own career; always watchful of how fast he's going, how nimbly he manoeuvres from lane to lane. Same age as you – several months younger, in fact – but with two symphonies, a handful of ballets and a Broadway show under his belt; not to mention the concerts he's conducted in New York, Boston, Cincinnati and London… London!

You haven't spoken to your parents in years, but it's a good thing they never knew much about music. Imagine the comparisons they would make.

"That Bernstein boy was on the radio again. They say a second symphony he's written."

But if Bernstein (and Copland, and Stravinsky) were working either in or with Hollywood it was possible to come here and retain some integrity. And okay, in doing so you might have to make sacrifices, play by their rules, but if you do that, the world is yours. At least, that's how it was sold to you. But you've been here over a year, and have nothing to show for it except an empty house.

What will it take to make this work?

Chapter 15:
LENINGRAD, JULY 1938

The afternoon is sultry, the tram's windows ochre with the summer dust. Beneath an angry sky, Leningrad waits for purifying thunderstorms and cleansing rain. Sergey steps off near the Alexander Garden and walks the rest of his journey to the building where Vikor Remizov lives. He's waiting for Sergey by the elevator.

"So good to see you, comrade. This way."

He shows Sergey to his apartment, a few rooms facing out over a busy junction. It's smaller than his last place, which was cavernous, almost extravagant. The Union Secretary has lived here since his divorce, the causes of which remain mysterious. Sergey knows only that Anya Remizova was allowed to remain, while Viktor Remizov moved here.

Remizov was, at one time, a composer. Studied piano and composition with Yavorsky. He wrote a few chamber pieces that still get played from time to time, but by thirty he'd already begun manoeuvring his way through the union, his career gathering momentum each time a senior name was scratched off an office door.

He's forty-two now, though if he didn't already know this Sergey might struggle to pinpoint his age. Bald, what's left of his hair dyed the colour of Indian ink. Paunchy, but with a certain imposing heft, like a retired boxer.

"Would you care for a drink?" Remizov asks. "It's such a

hot day. Iced tea, perhaps?"

"No. Thank you."

He wants this over as quickly as possible.

"Are you sure?" says Remizov. "A glass of water?"

Sergey's mouth is suddenly very dry.

"Water will be fine."

Remizov brings him a glass of water, and together they sit near an open window. Sergey hears children playing in the street below.

"So you changed your mind," Remizov says.

Sergey nods without meeting his gaze.

"Splendid. I thought you might. Oh, Sergey Andreievich, you look ashamed. Please, don't. There's nothing to be ashamed of. People spend so much time and effort pretending this isn't how the world works. It's absurd."

Sergey says nothing.

"Come," says Remizov. "Follow me."

Another gulp of water and he follows Secretary Remizov to his bedroom. Remizov begins unbuttoning his shirt, all the time holding Sergey with his glare. He's enjoying this. Of course he's enjoying it. And not just the thrill of what might happen next, but Sergey's submission. His look says, "I broke you, eventually." Yet beyond that, something else. A note of shame; both aroused and repulsed by his own desire.

"You should undress," Remizov says with an anxious gulp.

Sergey begins unbuttoning his own shirt. Remizov is already naked and sprawling across the bed.

"Sit next to me," he says. "Please."

Sergey looks down at this pale and paunchy man, spread clumsily on silk sheets, working away at a stubby erection with one hand and stroking his own flabby chest with the other. He looks like a pig's carcass hanging in a butcher's shop. Does Remizov want to be fucked by him, or to fuck him? None of this was discussed. He imagines kissing him; Remizov's lips like raw liver. He's wearing some sort of perfume. It's impossible. Sergey feels sick.

"I'm sorry," he says. "I can't."

Remizov stops what he's doing and sits upright.

"What do you mean?"

"I can't go through with this."

"Go through with what? We're talking about a fuck, not a bank robbery."

"I'm sorry."

Remizov swings his legs off the bed and sits, hunched over, his sagging chest resting on his paunch, his paunch resting on his thighs, like a comic allegory of dejection.

"Why?"

Sergey looks away.

"Tell me, Sergey. Why? You've had everyone else. Tatiana and fucking Vasily and who knows how many others? Why not me?"

Sergey slips back into his shirt, the traces of sweat now cold against his skin, and he leaves the bedroom before he's finished buttoning it. Remizov follows, plucking a silk dressing gown from a hook on the door.

"Have you forgotten what we agreed?"

"Of course not."

Sergey fumbles with the door handle, opens the door and walks out of the apartment. The elevator is only a short distance away, but it takes an age to arrive. Remizov goes no further than the open door, watching Sergey with an expression that curdles from one of acute sadness to one of loathing. There may be no coming back from this. He remembers what they agreed. This was the condition, and he's broken it. It's over.

The chime of the elevator. The doors open. Sergey steps in. The doors close and the elevator goes down.

Chapter 16:
LOS ANGELES, NOVEMBER 1950

Midnight. San Bernardino. A motel room shaped like a wigwam. An hour's drive from the city, but by no means beyond it. In recent years, Los Angeles has begun spilling out through every valley and canyon like floodwater. It took an hour to drive here, but at no point did it feel as if you'd left LA.

You picked this place because Angie saw it in a magazine and thought it would be funny. Why either of you thought "funny" was appropriate for your wedding night remains unclear. Perhaps "funny" would defuse the tension of what was guaranteed to be an unusual day.

Tonight will be the first you've spent together. Perhaps there's something romantic in waiting, unlike so many couples these days. Perhaps these traditions are there for a reason, and not just because some rabbi or priest says it's the correct way of doing things.

The ceremony took place at City Hall in the presence of two witnesses; a college friend of Angie's who moved out here a few months ago, and Howard Greenbaum, a colleague at Capitol. Angie's folks live in Chicago, yours in New York, and neither pair are inclined to travel. She wrote to her parents telling them all about you. You told her you'd written to yours, but you hadn't.

You check into the motel as Mr and Mrs Conrad. The man

on reception takes one look – you in a grey suit, white shirt, yellow tie; Angie in a pale blue suit and pillbox hat – and says, "Newlyweds?"

"Yes," you tell him, proudly. "Yes we are."

"Well, sir, I'm afraid all of our wigwams are the same. We don't have a honeymoon suite, as such. But I can offer you a complimentary bottle of champagne."

Except for its sloping walls, the room looks nothing like a wigwam from the inside. You were expecting something made of canvas, but the walls are painted plaster on cement.

It's getting dark. You close the curtains, cutting off the view of Foothill Boulevard, and for a moment you and Angie look at one another from either side of the bed, as if considering a complicated chess move. The bottle of Paul Masson bobs unopened in the ice bucket. Angie unbuttons her jacket, draping it across the chair beside the dressing table, and begins unbuttoning her blouse in an almost business-like manner. You take off your shoes and unbutton your shirt, and watch her in the mirror as she removes her blouse. You're drawn to her breasts, so much fuller than you'd imagined; broad and heavy-looking. You take off your pants and shorts and slide into the bed before she has a chance to see you naked.

It isn't Angie who turns you on so much as the idea that what you're doing, or what you're about to do, goes against every desire you've ever had. Something about this feels forbidden, though it's the very opposite of that.

Unclothed, Angie stands before the bed, the light from the bedside lamp catching the side of her body and her breasts in golden waves and crescents. She touches herself with her fingers, looking down at you with a hesitant desire; confidence and caution mixed in equal parts. She gets into the bed and her touch makes you shudder with pleasure and shame. When you kiss, her mouth feels small.

Chapter 17:
MANHATTAN, OCTOBER 2001

Washington Square Park. New York's centre of gravity, the place where it was pinned to the map. The city might have other landmarks, recognised around the world, but to Natalie this was where New York was most unapologetically itself. Or, at least, it had been.

It had none of its usual spark that night; none of the buskers and students, dealers and tramps, chess hustlers, bag ladies, pigeon-covered hobos. Before September, Washington Square was like a nightly carnival, but now everything about the place felt wrong. The music people were playing, either on instruments or old portable stereos, was sombre, downbeat. If she'd heard *Everybody Hurts* once she'd heard it a thousand times. People were still lighting candles and wearing peace sign t-shirts as if it might make a difference somewhere in the world. In the distance, there was a gap in the skyline that made her stomach lurch each time she saw it; the empty chair at a dining table following a death.

Where could they possibly go from here? What next step would make sense of it, or draw a line beneath it? It often seemed they would have to live through all this – the sombre songs and candlelit vigils, the shrill news bulletins and war rhetoric and flags, *so* many flags – forever.

She and Pavel crossed the park to the Library, a walk she could take without thinking, her feet leading the way unconciously. If they hadn't, she may have had to fight the urge to turn back. She knew the library, but each step forward was a step into the unknown.

For three years she had visited this place almost daily, a sanctuary from her neighbours in halls or the turbulence of other people. It was how she'd met Tyler. Bringing books back, checking them out. He was one of the few faces she saw each day, one of the few people with whom she had any sort of interaction. He asked her out for coffee, then a movie. She said yes both times. They dated.

But what if Tyler wasn't there that evening? What if he was no longer at the library, or even in New York? She'd heard of college friends and acquaintances leaving the city in recent weeks, going back to their home towns or away to wherever seemed safe.

She and Pavel passed through the revolving doors. There were three people on the information desk and one of them was Tyler. Natalie breathed out. He was still here, and he hadn't changed a bit. Same mop of wavy brown hair. Same glasses. He was wearing a stripy sweater that looked three sizes too big, just as he always had. He saw Natalie and did as much of a double take as anyone does in real life.

"Natalie?"

He looked at Pavel, realised they were together, and his smile faded a little.

"Hey, listen," he said. "You know, I was meaning to call you or email. Just to make sure you were okay. But I didn't know if you had the same number and I only had your old NYU email and –"

"It's fine," said Natalie. "I was the same. Didn't know who to call, who to check up on. But you're okay."

"I'm okay."

"I'm glad."

"Me too. It's great to see you."

A pause. His smile seemed almost to erase the last three years completely. She could imagine she was back at NYU, carrying more books than she could manage, hoping she didn't have any outstanding fines, knowing he'd cancel them if she did.

"So," he said, arms spread in an exaggerated greeting. "What brings you to the Bobst?"

"We need a favour."

Tyler lowered his arms and grimaced.

"What kind?"

"We need a book. Maybe two. Or three."

Tyler's voice dropped to a whisper and he leaned forward. "Wait. You graduated *when*? Like, almost three years ago?"

"Two and a half, actually."

"Even so. You know the rules. Students and faculty only, unless you have an appointment. You guys should probably, you know, go through one of your old professors... get a permit..."

"We don't have time. And it won't take us very long. We'll be in and out before you know it. And I promise I'll bring them back."

"No," said Tyler. "No way. Look, I know you *were* a student here, but I can't make exceptions. I mean, do you even know what would happen to me if they found out I'd let a… you know… *civilian* take books?"

This was a stupid idea. Their time together hadn't ended with the neatest of breaks. She simply let him go; rarely ever calling, taking time when replying to calls and emails. In the end, he had to ask her if it was over, and she told him it was. And now she wanted a favour?

"Please?" Natalie said. "I'll bring them back Monday. I promise."

Tyler sighed, leaning back with his hands clasped behind his head.

"Okay," he said. "But if you're not out of here in an hour, I'll come looking for you. And two books, max. Okay?"

"Okay. And thank you."

There was something comforting about being here again. The Bobst Library belonged to a time when things were simpler, calmer. No-one ever demanded anything of her in this library. The world would leave her alone while she was here. Now that anxiety was everyone's default setting and nobody stopped asking how she was, what she was doing, what she was thinking, there was a reassurance in finding the library exactly how she'd left it.

The floor they visited was empty but for a young woman in a woollen beret, a book of Respighi scores cradled in one arm. Only a few years younger than Natalie, but she had that lightness, that untroubled air that only undergraduates ever seem to have.

"That guy," said Pavel. "Downstairs. He is a friend of yours?"

"We dated," she explained. "This was years ago."

"He likes you still," said Pavel. It wasn't a question.

"No," said Natalie. "He doesn't. I mean, we haven't seen one another in a while, and no. It was a long, long time ago."

Pavel grinned. "He does. He likes you very much." He leaned in close to her, and whispered, "I think he was jealous." The words brushed featherlike against her neck.

Though smaller than its counterpart at Columbia, the music section was vast. So many lives stored there, so much more tangible than a mausoleum. The known facts, the photographs, the first-hand accounts. Yet still, frustratingly incomplete. Every biography is missing something; the gaps left behind by secrets and lies.

The book on Bernard, the one she'd searched for fruitlessly in Sol's library, was sandwiched between a book about Irving Berlin and three separate biographies of Leonard Bernstein. She took it from the shelf and skipped whole chapters about Bernard's childhood, his teenage years, his time in Paris after the War, meeting Duchamp, Picasso and Gertrude Stein, his marriage to the heiress, Margaret Vandemeer. She was looking for 1938. Bernard was thirty-seven years old and already a success. His *Mill Neck Concerto* had premiered the previous year, and he'd begun work on his opera *Jason and Medea.*

"Here," she said, holding the book open for Pavel to see. He leaned in close, his shoulder touching hers.

"You read it," he said. "I would read too slowly."

She dragged her finger across the page: "In March and April of 1938 Bernard was one of a number of American artists and intellectuals who visited the Soviet Union at the invitation of Stalin's State Committee of the Arts, and as an assignment for *Modern Music* magazine."

She waited for him to grin, or laugh, or even cheer, his voice echoing across this almost deserted section of the library. He did neither of those things. If anything, it seemed as if he might cry.

"This is it," he said. "This is the proof."

"It proves nothing except a connection," said Natalie. "Bernard was in the Soviet Union in April 1938. That doesn't mean he was at the Kirov. And besides, what are we saying? That he came back, hummed the melody to his student? That just doesn't make sense."

"Then we need to know more about this," said Pavel, prodding the page. "This trip. Bernard. We need to know where he went and what he did."

She skipped to the notes. The main reference for that chapter was a book about the relationship between the Soviets and their supporters in the West. They took the biography of Bernard and ran across the library, only slowing when one of the guards told them to.

It took a while, but presently they found the book in question and searched its index for *Bernard, Ronald*. And there he was. Multiple mentions in more than one chapter. A picture of him in its glossy middle pages, with the caption:

"April 1938. A party at Leningrad's Hotel Astoria, following a performance at the Kirov Theatre (now the Mariinsky). Clockwise, from top row: Doris Fanshawe, Charles Fanshawe, Ronald Bernard,

Lawrence J. Black, unknown, Langdon Brunel, unknown, Dorothy Markham, Penelope Markham-Riley, William F. Kaufman, Viktor Remizov."

She pointed to the back row. "That's Bernard."

Pavel gasped and placed his hand over hers, moving it across the page until she was pointing to one of the two unknown figures.

"That's my grandfather."

"Well, now, look. It says here 'unknown', so…"

"You don't think I recognise him?"

"It isn't that. I just don't know what he looked like."

"You think I'm lying?"

She looked again at the photograph. Standing beside Langdon Brunel was a young man, smartly dressed but his tie askew and his face a blur. At the precise moment when the picture was taken, he'd turned his head to look at something or someone to his right. He was the second unknown.

"Okay," she said. "Listen. We'll take these books, and tomorrow we'll start making calls, yes? I've a friend who teaches at Columbia. This is her area. If I show her this I'm sure she'll be able to find out if it was taken the night they performed your grandfather's ballet."

Her words were tripping out of her. She hardly knew what she was saying. She was talking about her friend Carol and making plans as if she intended to see them through, as if she intended to help Pavel until the very end. Perhaps she did.

"But I *know* this was his ballet," said Pavel. "Look. April 1938. There's Bernard, there is Sergey. This is the proof."

"I believe you."

She said those words unconsciously, but they changed the air between them. Pavel leaned towards her and kissed her on the mouth. She put her arms around him, the books falling to the ground, and they stumbled back into the bookshelves. When they parted again they looked at one another as if seeing each other for the first time.

Down on the ground floor, Tyler scanned the books out on his own card, telling them they had until Monday, and no later, to return them. Natalie promised she would do just that and Tyler made a face, goofy and tender: *You'd better.*

It was dusk, the day receding in a blaze of pink over one corner of Washington Square. As they passed beneath the memorial arch Pavel took her hand in his, and they stayed that way, holding hands, all the way to her apartment.

Chapter 18:
LOS ANGELES, FEBRUARY 1951

The day Ron finished the *Inferno* oratorio, he said nothing, not immediately. He nudged the score across the desk and smiled at you. Even then, just sight-reading it, you heard his music as clearly as if it were being performed right there in the room, and you knew this was the piece for which he'd be remembered. The scale and ambition of it were like nothing he'd attempted before, as if he'd thrown away all uncertainty and put every last thing he had into a single work. But that joy was tempered, as you read its last movement, by knowing he'd left, encoded within it, a message. Something personal. Something cruel.

As such, *Giudecca* is an impossible piece, something you can hardly listen to, let alone contemplate conducting with a full orchestra and choir. You tried persuading Margaret Bernard to choose another piece, perhaps an earlier movement, but she was adamant. The oratorio is Ron's greatest work, and *Giudecca* its highlight. To not include it in the concert would be a travesty.

And now it consumes every evening, every weekend, not to mention those working days when no-one at Capitol pays much attention to what you're doing. The movement's transitions are like algebra or molecular physics; they may as well be written in hieroglyphs. For all the hours you spend staring at the score, it eludes you.

Ron was a man of contradictions, in his life and in his work. The scion of an old Cornell Republican family; his father a classicist, his grandfather a professor of philosophy. His shift towards radicalism came from nowhere. Even when he'd pinned his colours to that mast, his subject matter remained arcane. Euripides and Dante. In conducting any piece of his, let alone *Giudecca,* you'll have to meet those contradictions, and navigate your way through them.

A vacation could be the answer. A few days out of town, away from the city's distractions. Henderson needs no persuading; he'll relish a break from you. Angie is a little more hesitant, but after some deliberation she tells you that she understands.

"You do whatever it is you have to."

She might miss you while you're away, but the New York concert represents so many things for her, not least of all her husband conducting at Carnegie Hall and a trip to the East Coast. Late one night, in the moments before you both fall asleep, she tells you she'll feel more at home in New York than she ever has in LA, she's sure of it. Now, whenever you're studying the score at home she beams at you with pride, in a way she never did in Room 01B. Like Margaret Bernard and her Uptown set, Angie believes this is what you were meant to do, and as the days and weeks go by you come to believe it yourself.

Studying the oratorio does, at least, allow you to spend time with Ron. The days and weeks before you got married meant removing every trace of him from the house. The pictures, those that looked like photographs of two friends, were taken from their frames and placed in albums. Any in which a deeper intimacy was hinted at were burned, along with his letters, and after burning them you wept for hours.

It wasn't the first time you'd burned letters.

This is a clean start. This is your life now. You are a husband. You hadn't even thought of Nick in months, or if you had it was in passing, wondering if he might still be in Los Angeles, if his acting career ever took off. You dread the unexpected knock at the door. Nick asking to stay. Angie's questions. *How do you know this young man?* But those moments pass quickly enough. It's only as preparations for the concert grind to a halt and work at Capitol slows to a trickle and you and Angie settle into married life that you begin thinking of him again.

When Angie is out, running an errand or visiting a friend, you rush to the bathroom and masturbate, thinking only of Nick. With your eyes closed you go through every moment you spent together, embellishing those few encounters with added details, extra scenes. You can't stop thinking about him. You need time away. The solution was staring at you the whole time.

You have no destination in mind until you come across the black and white image of a mushroom cloud. You're getting your shoes shined outside Bullock's, flipping through *Life* magazine, and there it is. A story about the atomic tests in Nevada, accompanied by that photograph, spread across two pages. You've seen such images before. You read John Hersey's account of Hiroshima in *The New Yorker*. There's something strangely beautiful about them, columns of smoke towering impossibly above the landscape, pushing apart all other clouds and cresting at the edge of heaven.

The following night you tell Angie you're heading down into Beverly Hills to visit Herb Borowitz, a veteran conductor and a passing acquaintance of Ron's. She believes you, because she has no reason not to.

You drive, instead, to Pershing Square. Nick is there. Leaner than you remember him; not quite gaunt, but sallow, hungry. A kind of seedy, strung out look. He sees you but doesn't react. Instead he carries on talking to a group of men, laughing at their jokes, only acknowledging you when it might become embarrassing or dangerous not to.

"What the hell are you doing here?" he says.

"I wanted to speak with you."

"We got nothing to talk about. You made that clear last time."

You ask if he'd like to get a soda or a milkshake. You'd have suggested a beer, but that seems like the last thing he needs. You're sorry. You can explain everything. He hesitates, looking across the square to his friends. He says yes, perhaps to avoid a scene as much as anything, and you walk over to a diner at the corner of Hill Street and 6th.

There, you tell him about the night you wouldn't answer the door, and the days and weeks preceding it. You tell him about Mary, and the Buick, and the men in the snap-brim hats.

"You thought I was mixed up in all that?"

"Yes."

For a moment he says nothing. He looks out through the window, diagonally across the square towards the lights of the Biltmore. He taps his fingers restlessly against the table. You tell him you're leaving town for a few days, a road trip to Nevada, and ask him if he'd like to join you.

"Will there be a pool?"

"I don't think so."

"Casino?"

"Unlikely."

"But it'll just be the two of us?"

"Just the two of us."

"Then okay," he says. "I'm in."

Chapter 19: LENINGRAD, JUNE 1938

It's late, the union offices otherwise deserted for the weekend. Its stairwells and corridors are silent and dark. Remizov's office is the very model of austerity. On the walls, the obligatory portraits of Lenin, Stalin and Kirov. Doesn't have a telephone. Nothing on his desk except a lamp, a notepad and pen, a box of cigarettes and the message Sergey received almost an hour ago.

Герой тура отменен.

Hero tour cancelled.

Even before Sergey speaks, Remizov's expression is one of weary impatience, as though they've been having this discussion for hours on end, as if he anticipates everything Sergey is about to say and hasn't the time for it.

"Why is it cancelled?"

"Does it really need spelling out to you?" says Remizov. "The subject matter was deemed inappropriate."

"What do you mean, 'inappropriate'?"

"The subject matter. The *tone*. You took a single chapter from a pre-revolutionary work about the bourgeoisie. What were you thinking?"

"It wasn't inappropriate when I first proposed it. It wasn't inappropriate when we performed at the *Kirov*. Why is it suddenly inappropriate?"

Remizov sighs. "People can get awfully excited about a new work. But when that excitement dies down, well... sometimes we're forced to see the work for what it is. Now, there isn't much we can say or do to Comrade Lermontov about the vulgarity of his novel. But this ballet, on the other hand…"

"Vulgarity? How is it vulgar?"

"How is it not, Sergey Andreievich? Look at it from our point of view. Pechorin is a nobleman, an individualist, who gallivants around behaving as he wishes. What sort of a hero is that?"

"The title is ironic."

"And that's another problem. Irony. You see, irony plays well among the intelligentsia in, say, Paris or Vienna, but if we're creating music for the proletariat, that sort of thing can be mistaken for sincerity, can it not?"

"If you say so."

"You know I'm right."

Sergey braces himself with both hands against the back of a chair. He can't bring himself to sit. The room is smaller than when he entered it. Remizov opens the wooden cigarette box and takes one. He turns the box toward Sergey.

"No, thank you."

"Please. It'll calm your nerves."

"I'm not nervous."

"You should be."

Hesitantly, Sergey takes a cigarette, and Remizov lights it for him.

"So. Is that it? Is my career over?"

"Stalled, perhaps," says Remizov. "But not beyond redemption."

"Then what should I do?"

"Well, first you must renounce the thing itself."

"Renounce my work?"

"Of course. It has left rather a sour taste on the Soviet palate, which you must cleanse; first by renouncing your more recent work, then by eclipsing all memory of it with something more appropriate. There may be an interregnum, of course, but I'm sure you'll find work. A few months writing film music, for instance. Lenfilm are *always* looking for composers, and they're really not that fussy about former indiscretions."

"I can't."

"It's really not so different to writing for ballet, or –"

"I mean I can't renounce my work."

Remizov leans back and laughs, the cigarette bouncing in the corner of his mouth, raining grey ash down his shirtfront.

"You're being ridiculous," he says, brushing the ash away with his knuckles. "You make it sound as if renouncing your work is a physical impossibility, when all you have to do is say the words. 'I renounce my work wholeheartedly. I am ashamed of what I've done, and I promise never to do it again.' That's all. What's so difficult about that?"

"It's my *work*," says Sergey. "And I'm proud of it. Really, I am."

"Well, I wouldn't go bragging about *that*. Listen. Frankly, Seryozha, I don't care what you think or how you feel about your work. It really doesn't matter to me. What matters is that publicly you are ashamed, and that you demonstrate your shame. That's all."

"I can't do it."

"You can. You've done it before."

Sergey draws the chair away from Remizov's desk, and slumps into it before he can fall.

"I saw your file," says Remizov. "From when you were at the academy. I read the notes about your visit from the GUGB, or the OGPU, or..." He waives his hand dismissively. "... Whatever they were calling themselves back then."

Something catches in Sergey's throat, as if he's choking on a peach stone. With little effort, he can smell the bleached grey linoleum of the academy's corridors and see the winter light creeping in through its high windows. The long walk from his classroom to the principal's office. The agents waiting for him. The paperwork, the denunciation, on the desk, waiting for his signature. He was fifteen years old. They told him to sit. The principal got up and placed his hand briefly, sympathetically on Sergey's shoulder before leaving the room.

"Unfortunate business, all that," says Remizov. "What is it they say? You can choose your friends, but not your family?"

"That was ten years ago."

"Your point being? The files still exist. And they're worryingly prescient, given the nature of your work. I wouldn't want people to link the two unnecessarily. You know what I mean. 'Oh, his family were *kulaks*, therefore he was bound to produce a work like this sooner or later.' That sort of thing."

"You think they would say that?"

"Of course. You know how people are. They'd forget how you washed your hands of them. Or they'd say you were simply saving your own skin. What was your brother's name? Mikhail, wasn't it?"

"Misha."

"Not very old, if I remember rightly. But then, that was the difference between you. He stayed with your father, carried on being influenced by him, you came to the city. Don't get me wrong, the zealousness of those officials was regrettable. I mean, your brother was practically a child..."

"He was a child."

"But a child raised as a *kulak*. A very unfortunate business, all round. You must feel very lucky to have come to the academy, to have missed out on all that."

Sergey says nothing. His hands are shaking and he hides them beneath the desk. He wants to hurt Remizov, to get up and hit him from his chair, and when he's on the floor and curled up in a ball, to start kicking him until he hears the sound of breaking bones. Instead, Sergey takes a deep breath and holds it till it feels as if it's boiling in his lungs.

"Still," says Remizov. "It was a wise move, distancing yourself. To have done otherwise would have ruined your life, not to mention your career. Instant dismissal from the academy. Exiled to somewhere up north, or out in the east. You'd have been lucky to get a job teaching piano to schoolchildren after that. But now look at you. The world, Seryozha, is yours. If you want it. This whole business with the Lermontov ballet, it could be a minor setback if you do things properly."

Sergey stubs out his cigarette when he's smoked only half of it, and brings his hands together, cracking the knuckles.

"I won't renounce it," he says. "I don't care what you say, what anyone says. I won't renounce it. Not that. It's the best work I've done."

Remizov laughs. "You say this as if you're the elder statesman of Soviet music. How old are you? Twenty-four?"

"Twenty-five."

"Good grief, we really did spoil you, didn't we? Putting your first ballet on at the Kirov. Trust me. Everyone thinks they're a genius at twenty-five, but very few are. Forget about Lermontov and Pechorin and Princess fucking Mary, and all that nonsense. Write something else. Something better."

"Very well," says Sergey. "I'll write something else. But I will not renounce *A Hero of Our Time*. I can't."

Remizov sighs, flinging up his hands in showy despair. "What am I to do with you?" he says. "There is a tried, tested and time-honoured route to rehabilitation in this country, and I've spelled it out to you quite clearly. That said, if you're *adamant*..."

"I am."

"Well, if you're *adamant,* there is one alternative."

"Which is?"

"I can have a word with the union. My star is in the ascendency there, I feel. I can speak to them, perhaps persuade them that while *A Hero of Our Time* isn't in line with current tastes, it may one day become so. When the work of the revolution is complete and we can better appreciate its irony. That sort of thing. And perhaps, with that in mind, it shouldn't be denounced altogether. How does that sound?"

Sergey nods. "That's better."

"Better?" says Remizov. "I'd say that's an excellent offer. Should they agree to it, of course. However, I will need some guarantee that I can trust you to work in a more suitable vein from now on."

"You have my word."

"That isn't good enough, I'm afraid. I'm not calling you a *liar.* Far from it. But you are an *artist*, and artists are fickle, unpredictable. I want some means by which I can know that we are bonded in our discretion."

"What do you mean?"

"Oh, come now."

Remizov smiles, and draws another cigarette from the open box. He holds it to his lips, and pauses before lighting it, never once breaking eye contact. That single look, dark and mocking, is all the explanation he has to give.

Sergey leaves Remizov's office without giving him an answer, telling him instead that he would like to sleep on it. If the arrival of the note sobered him up, his walk back to his rooms tips him back into a heavy, sluggish stupor. This is bad. No mistaking it. He'd thought he was immune, invincible, and that the worst days were behind them. The revolution's work was complete, they said. But now it seems the revolution will never be over, and that no-one, least of all Sergey, will ever be safe again.

Chapter 20:
INDIAN SPRINGS, FEBRUARY 1951

Angie watches you pack. A big, proud smile for her husband the conductor. The man about to be the toast of New York City. The guilt coils in your stomach like a viper. Another secret, another thing to be hidden.

You collect Nick from a rundown-looking bungalow in Edendale. As he leaves the house he yells angrily at someone inside. He gets into the car with dark shadows beneath his eyes and a few days' worth of stubble, and though it's early in the day he smells strongly of marijuana, sweat and booze.

Driving through the morning and early afternoon, you stop for lunch on the outskirts of Barstow before heading out across the desert. In the diner you ask Nick about the argument he was having when you picked him up.

"Aw, it ain't nothing," he says. "Just some people can be assholes, is all."

You agree and don't ask any more questions. When you leave the diner Nick climbs onto the back seat of the car and falls asleep. It takes three hours to reach Indian Springs. The sky is vast and many stretches of the Death Valley road seem endless, tapering off towards the distant hills. You could do with someone to talk to, to keep you focused and alert, but Nick just snores away on the back seat, and doesn't wake up again until you pull up outside the Cheyenne Motel.

"Where are we?"

"We're there."

You check in as Sam and Bob Maitland – names taken from two brothers who lived in the apartment above yours on Clinton Street. The most goyish, straight-laced, white bread names you could think of.

"Room 37," the manager says. "It's away from the road, so it's nice and quiet. You here for the bomb?"

Nick is about to ask what he's talking about when you interject.

"Yes, we're here for the bomb."

"Should be a humdinger. Last one lit up the sky like the Fourth of July, and they reckon this one'll be even bigger."

He hands you the keys and you and Nick walk across the parking lot to your room. Nick says nothing until you're through the door.

"What's he talking about? Which atom bomb?"

"They're testing a bomb, fifty miles north of here, tomorrow night."

"Then why the hell did we come here?"

"I thought it would make a nice surprise."

"Surprise? It's a bomb."

"It'll be something to see, won't it?"

"It's a fucking bomb."

"It's not like they're bombing the motel."

"How far away are they testing it?"

"Fifty miles, like I said."

"You have any idea how powerful those things are?"

"It's a safe distance. You think they'd let that guy carry on running a motel if they thought it was gonna get blown up?"

"I think accidents happen is what I think."

"Come here."

"What?"

"I said come here."

You put your arms around him and tell him everything will be okay, and that he can trust you.

"Cross my heart and hope to die."

"That is a bad choice of words."

You kiss, and something lifts; a weight, or a darkness. Just lifts away and floods everything with light. The way he turns you on is more than just a physical response. You've missed him terribly. You stagger across the room and fall onto one of the two beds. With his body still reeking of a late and sleepless night he pins you down, his strong hands clutching your wrists. He takes off your clothes and turns you over and then he fucks you. The curtains are open, and you can see out across the parking lot to the manager's office. The thought that he may step out into the sunshine and see what's happening in Room 37 of his motel only turns you on even more.

★★

"So what is that?"

You look up from the score, whatever it was you were thinking, whatever idea you had, lost in an instant. Nick sprawls naked, arms crossed behind his head. Fixed to the wall above him, the sun-bleached skull of a deer; like something from an O'Keeffe desert painting.

"It's for a concert in New York," you tell him. "I have to conduct this, and it's a difficult piece."

"Did you write it?"

"No. A friend did."

"Why can't he do it?"

"He passed away."

"I'm sorry."

This was a terrible idea. How can you even begin to concentrate with him lying there? Even when you're not looking at him, he's all you can see, each time you close your eyes, even when you blink. You ask him to get a soda from the vending machine outside the manager's office. Just a minute's peace might be enough.

"I'm butt naked," he says.

"Then put some pants on."

"Why did you bring me here?"

You put the pencil down and shift around in your chair.

"What do you mean?"

"You bring me all the way out here, and now it's like I'm in the way."

"I told you I had work to do. I told you that."

"You *did*?"

"You know I did."

"I don't recall."

"What's the matter with you?"

"The look you just gave me. Like you didn't care if I was here or not."

"Listen. Of course I want you here. I asked you to come, didn't I? I just have to do this. Only a few more hours. Then I promise, I'm all yours."

Nick rises from the bed. He crosses the room and puts his arms around you.

"*All* mine?"

"*All* yours."

"Why, Mr Conrad," he says. "You oughtn't go saying such things to a man. Makes it hard for him to control himself." He leans across and kisses you on the mouth. "I'll go get your soda."

He walks back to the bed, slips into his jeans, and leaves the room shirtless and barefooted.

★★

Walking away from the motel and the road feels like walking backwards in time, away from civilisation. The sand beneath your feet is the same sand that has been here for a million years. The telegraph wires and electricity pylons and the lights of the motel are far behind you now. You and Nick hold hands. A light breeze whispers through the scrub. The clarity of the stars and constellations turns the sky into a bottomless ocean of light, and gazing up at it inspires a thrilling dizziness, like vertigo. You close your eyes, and with Nick's hand still in yours, you hear the opening of *Giudecca.*

"Vexilla regis prodeunt inferni..."

The banners of Hell's monarch come forth toward us...

Beneath it, something else, a drone, like something coming up through the arid soil. When Ron pushed the score towards you his expression was not only one of pride – of *course* he was proud – but of cruelty. He knew you'd understand the significance of *Giudecca,* the realm named after Judas, reserved for those who betray their benefactors. *Giudecca*, like the old Jewish ghetto of Venice. Layer upon layer of meaning, and he wanted you to understand each one. *Giudecca* for Judas. *Giudecca* for those who betray their benefactors. *Giudecca* for the Jews. This was his dedication to you, to what you'd done. "It didn't happen," he'd told you. "It's gone." But he lied. It was forgiven, perhaps, but not forgotten, and Ron's unwillingness to forget was now galvanised in his greatest work.

You could never have written a piece as complex as this, so how can his widow – or anyone else – expect you to conduct it? When you sight-read it in his study you were awed, dumbstruck simply by being in the same room as him while he wrote its final bars. It's still too much for you.

Back in the motel room you and Nick make love again, and he lets you fuck him for the first time. He gasps as you enter him and you ask if he wants you to stop, but he shakes his head and says, "No… harder" He needs this, and it's as if something has changed or been reversed between you. Your bodies move in time with the perfection of clockworks. You want to come at the same time as him and you do, and when it's done you fall back onto a bed now damp with sweat, and he lights you both a cigarette. On the radio, Sinatra is singing *If I Had You*; always your favourite song of his. It breaks your heart.

Perhaps you shouldn't tell him. Just leave it, and tomorrow or the day after drive back into Los Angeles. You don't have to see him all the time. Just occasionally. Whenever you need him, whenever that need is impossible to ignore. He's a kid. He'll have others, just like you. There always have been. He doesn't need commitment, or some parody of marriage. There could be some arrangement. Maybe in time he would understand.

"I have something to tell you," you say, hoping it won't sound too loaded, too melodramatic. Nick sits, resting on one elbow. He smiles hesitantly. You breathe in. "I got married."

He laughs – you're teasing him – but when you don't laugh back his smile vanishes. He pulls himself further up the bed and folds his arms across his knees.

"When?"

"December."

"Then what the hell are we doing here?"

"I had to see you."

"You made it sound like you missed me. Like you wanted to be with me."

"And I did."

"For how long?"

"Look, I'm sorry…"

"Does she know you're queer?"

"No."

"Well, ain't that typical? Do you love her?"

There are no words.

"You can't even answer that," he says.

In a way he's right. You want to tell him that you love her, but in ways that are different to whatever exists between the two of you; that people are capable of many different kinds of love, but that we confuse them. You want to tell him that in those moments when you and Angie are intimate, when you're inside her, in those seconds before climax you are always, without exception, thinking of him.

It would be easier if he was angry, really angry with you. Started shouting, started hitting you. Instead, he falls silent, and you feel the plans you made, the futures you imagined, falling away beneath you. And, of course, there's nowhere either of you can go, nothing outside this room but dust in all directions. Even Indian Springs, the nearest town, must be fifteen, twenty miles away.

The bomb is scheduled for the early hours, and with nothing else to do, the two of you dress and leave your room as planned, but this time you're not alone. There are other guests staying at the Cheyenne Motel, and together you form a strange procession marching out across the dunes. The others, perhaps twenty in all, talk excitedly among themselves, but you and Nick say nothing to one another, speaking only when spoken to.

"Say, where you boys from?"

"Los Angeles."

"Hear that, kids? These fellas came from Los *An*geles. We drove down from Park City. You know Utah at all?"

"I don't. Sorry."

"Took us… say, Alice, how long would you say it took us to drive here?"

"Seven hours?"

"Seven hours. Maybe more. And let me tell you, it is one heck of a lot colder in Park City. Oh, boy. The winters there. We've still got snow on the ground that'll come up to your knees. This is like summer to us. Ain't that right, Alice?"

"That's right."

"But we just had to see this. I mean, it is a miracle of technology. And Alice and I, well, we've spoken about it, and we've both said – haven't we? – we sleep easier in our beds knowing we have the bomb and the other fellas don't. Either of you fellas see any action?"

You both shake your heads. Nick was too young, of course. And you… you're sick and tired of saying '4F' so you'll just leave the man from Utah to draw his own conclusions.

"Well, I was on Guadalcanal," he says, "and I do not want my boys to experience anything like that; no, sir. I just do not understand why we haven't deployed it in Korea. How many thousand dead? Those lives could have been saved if we'd dropped just one of these here bombs on those Communists."

"George…"

"Alice. We've spoken about this."

Presently, the crowd stops on a ridge two hundred yards from the motel, facing west. Some brought foldaway chairs and cushions. Some of the men have bottles of beer. Tired children yawn and rub their eyes. No-one quite knows what they're about to witness.

The time given for the test was approximate, and so you wait, staring into the silent black, hardly daring to blink in case you miss something, as if it could all be over in a split second. A nearby family brought a picnic hamper, and the mother begins laying out plates and Tupperware boxes on a tartan blanket. The initial excitement dies down and a kind of ambient, pervasive tedium sets in. Men check their wristwatches, women keep tired children entertained. Then, carried on the breeze, a distant siren, like a baying animal. Not one siren, but several, or perhaps its echo, overlapping. A pack of these immense, unknowable creatures, howling in the desert.

Nick looks at you, his eyes glistening, and with an expression somewhere between hatred and undiminished love he whispers, "You know, you really broke my heart."

His timing is almost Biblical; the light from the west so sudden, so brilliant it turns everything into a blank page. You screw your eyes shut and put your arm across your face but you can still see it, that light; an orange glow that permeates every skin cell, every blood cell, even your bones. When you open your eyes again a globe of fire is forming over the horizon, turning the night sky a deep and bloody shade of red. It swells and churns, flaring yellow and white in its core, gorging itself on light.

Nick can't take his eyes off it, and you watch a single tear escape and trickle down his cheek.

"It's beautiful," he says.

You look again as a cloud shaped like an oak tree rises and blooms over the desert and the craggy hills. The crowd around you *oohs* and *aahs* as if they were watching fireworks. One of the younger children, a little girl, begins to cry.

You know exactly how she feels.

The glow fades and is followed by a deep rumble, like thunder, which builds to a cacophonous boom, the air around you stirring with dust and sand in the passing shockwave.

"Can you imagine," Nick says, his voice low and trembling. "Can you imagine what would have happened, if it fell on us?"

You tell him you'd rather not.

"There'd be nothing left," he says, regardless. "Nothing but ashes. Not even ashes. Who comes up with a thing like that?"

He looks at you again, his expression empty.

"Why would you want me to see a thing like that?"

Your hands and forearms are covered in a brownish dirt, and when Nick wipes his hand across his forehead it comes away even dirtier.

"I'm gonna take a bath," he says, and he starts walking back toward the motel.

At first you don't dare follow him. There's nothing more you can say after this, nothing that can be said after what you just witnessed. Is that why you brought him here? Because watching the materials of the universe ripped apart renders everything else absurd?

Back in the motel room the bathroom door is shut. A tap is running. It's either very late or very early, that point when night seesaws into day, but you sit near the window and read the score of *Giudecca's* opening bars and you hear the choir sing:

"Vexilla regis prodeunt inferni…"

You close your eyes and the night sky bursts with light, as if somebody had punched a hole right through it, and you hear that drone coming up from beneath you and rising in pitch, shifting like an ocean of sound.

Coney Island. You and your brother, Zack, racing down Stillwell Avenue ahead of your mother; lips and fingertips sticky with the mustard from a shared Nathan's hotdog. Down onto the beach. Soft sand. The noise of the city drowned out by waves. The waves get louder, and you're on another beach. Patchogue. Blankets and windbreakers. Cocktail shakers of martini brought down from the beach house. Someone – who was it? – grappling with a box Brownie. "Fellas. Say cheese." And you both smile, and Ron's smile was always easier, more sincere than your own. Another beach, but in winter. East Hamptons. The trees leafless and brown and snow all the way down to the sand's edge. The car parked a short distance away. You couldn't face driving all the way back to the city, not right away, and so you came here, to this beach, still wearing your black suit and your black tie, the order of service folded and tucked into the breast pocket, and you looked out at the sea.

You open your eyes again and hear the pattering of water. A dark puddle has spread out from beneath the bathroom door and into the bedroom. You leave the desk, cross the room and knock at the door. You tell Nick to open up, but there's no answer. Your knuckles are tender – you hit the door much harder than intended – and so you kick at it, but still no reply. The water spreads even further into the room, making islands of your feet. You hit the door again.

"Nick, please."

Asleep. He fell asleep. Too tired to notice what was happening, he's in there now, asleep, the water spilling out from his bath and onto the floor. Or else he's doing this to make a point. Trashing the place, knowing you'll have to pick up the tab.

The first charge achieves nothing except a throbbing shoulder that you know will bruise badly. Second attempt and something splinters, but the door remains firmly in place. Third time around the door bursts open and you stumble into the bathroom, slipping and falling on the wet tiles and almost cracking your head against the toilet bowl.

The bath is overflowing with pinkish water. Nick's face is white and his pale eyes stare unblinkingly at a fluorescent strip on the far wall. You run, or rather crawl to him and try lifting him out of the water. The pocket knife he used, the kind most boy scouts carry, lies open on the tiled floor beside the bath. There is a pool of blood around the knife and a large crescent of blood dripping down the bathroom wall. The wound in Nick's wrist is so deep you can't bear to look at it for more than a second, let alone feel for a pulse.

Back in the bedroom you pack away your notepad and pencil and the score and you change into clothes that aren't wet with bathwater or stained with blood. You leave Nick's belongings exactly as he left them, and go to the car without locking the room or turning out the lights. All this happens in minutes, and as you drive away from the Cheyenne Motel you pray the manager didn't make a note of your registration plate.

A few miles before Pahrump you pull in and walk out across the scrub carrying a bundle of wet and bloodstained clothes. You place them on the ground, douse them in gasoline and set fire to them. You walk back to the car and brace your hands against the fender and you scream until it feels as if the veins in your throat might rupture. You get behind the wheel and begin driving again. You can still see the column of black smoke when you're ten minutes further down the road.

Chapter 21:
MANHATTAN, OCTOBER 2001

She woke with a start, her sense of relief unsteady. The dream had ended with an approaching cloud of smoke and debris, rolling towards her like a sandstorm crossing a desert. She was safe, but only a second ago the threat was real. Her body was slicked with sweat, the bedclothes clinging to her skin. She shivered and moved around until she felt dry again.

The nightmares had been persistent these last few weeks. She often forgot them as she woke. If her pillowcase was damp, she might have been sobbing in her sleep. The dreams she remembered were never subtle. Fires, clouds of smoke, great edifices collapsing. Confinement. Darkness.

Her memory of that day felt every bit as dreamlike. A power outage before her train could pull out of Union Square. Complete black for a moment before the emergency lights came on. They called everyone off the train and told them to exit the station. She heard someone complain about the MTA, how they kept raising the price of their tickets but couldn't "run things for shit". Another person was talking about a fire at the World Trade Center. In Union Square she saw people crowded around the window of a TV store, but couldn't see any of the TVs. She walked along Fifth Avenue to Washington Square. As the towers came into view she saw the smoke. She stayed there until the smoke was all that remained.

There were phone calls. She called the house on East 73rd Street and told Rosa what had happened. Rosa told her not to make the trip across town. "It's too dangerous." Then her mother called her. "Oh, thank goodness." Said with disappointing understatement. Most of those watching from the square had company. People were hugging, crying on one another's shoulders. Natalie watched it alone. A part of her wanted to go up to the nearest stranger and ask them if this was really happening, but she felt as if she was gate-crashing a funeral. She went back to her apartment around midday and flicked through channel after channel showing the same images, over and over. The second plane, slicing into metal and glass like a knife. The North Tower opening up like a terrible grey lily as it collapsed. A man or a woman – she couldn't tell which – tumbling forever. She turned off her TV and hadn't turned it on again since.

Pavel's body was warm next to hers, and she curled in close to him. The morning light made a sand dune of his shoulder; his shallow breathing the sound of waves. Through the window she watched steam rise up through the building's airshaft. From neighbouring apartments came the muffled sound of TVs and radios.

What happened the night before felt as unreal as her dream, and almost as unsettling. How long was it since she had taken someone home with her? That in itself made the night unusual, a change from her routine. But more than this, there was something familiar about the way he touched her and the way he responded to her touch. It felt as if they had known one another for months, years, the intimacy between them was wordless, instant.

She left Pavel sleeping and went to the kitchen. The books they'd borrowed were there, on the rickety chrome dining table with its matching rickety chairs. She drank orange juice and flipped through one of the books, pausing on the picture taken at the Kirov. Ronald Bernard and the man Pavel said was his grandfather. There was a likeness; no denying that.

Pavel appeared in the doorway a little after eight. He saw that she was looking at the picture and sat next to her, his chair wobbling on its uneven legs.

"It *is* him, you know," he said, tapping the page.

They kissed. If he didn't go immediately she would never want him to leave, and so she told him she had things to do. Not entirely untrue. She had to call her friend, the one who would help them. What else? Other stuff. Better to avoid too much detail, in case she forgot any of it. He left the apartment, pausing on the stairs to wave goodbye. She stepped out into the hall to see him just a fraction of a second longer.

★★

She and Carol Sorenson had met during Natalie's final semester at NYU. There was a recital at the Lincoln Center and then a party. They had a mutual friend in one of the violinists. Natalie wasn't sure how or why they'd gelled. Shared tastes, perhaps. Or maybe it was Carol's tendency to monologue. She could talk for hours, and Natalie was happy to listen, to take it all in.

Carol was one of the Effortlessly Smart. One of those people who never seem to have taken a wrong turn or made the wrong decision. She had everything – tenure, her next publishing deal – mapped out before her. The apartment where she lived with Louise was in one of the more recently gentrified stretches of Harlem and took up a whole floor of their building. It even had a small, unkempt garden out the back. Louise played viola in a successful string quartet. Whenever Natalie and Carol met, Carol had invariably been somewhere or done something exciting, while – work aside – Natalie had barely left the East Village.

It was unusual to see Carol twice in the same week, but these last few weeks had been anything but usual. Each Monday since September had been loaded with meaning. Remembering the banality of September 10th, going to bed clueless of what the next day would bring. Even that get-together, only a few days ago, seemed more purposeful than just a dinner party.

Natalie had prepared for it by stopping at a bar on 110th Street. It was just about the only way she could face walking into a room full of people, all desperately pretending they were happy. Just happy. No reason. And all that conversation. Even before September Natalie had always struggled to make small talk. She was happier as a wallflower. But September changed all that. Being a wallflower was no longer an option. Everyone wanted to speak to you, ask how you were. Everyone had an opinion and wanted to know yours. She told herself she would only have one drink, but one drink turned into four. She was drunk by the time she got there. No wonder she'd made such a bloody fool of herself.

She contemplated beginning her phone call with an extensive apology, trying to find the right words while she listened to the dial tone. Carol answered.

"Bonjour?"

"It's me. Natalie."

"Ah, Natalie. *Notre bon vivant!*"

Natalie winced. Carol sounded cheerful rather than angry. Any apology might only make things worse.

"I was hoping you might be able to help me with something."

"Anything, Natalie. Anything."

"I'm looking into something for a friend."

"Anyone I know?"

"He's from Russia. His grandfather was a composer, and he wants information on a ballet that was performed at the Kirov."

"What was his grandfather's name?"

"Sergey Grekov."

"Hmm."

If she'd known right away who Grekov was, Carol would have said something, perhaps named a work of his.

"And this ballet?"

"Based on *A Hero of Our Time.* The novel by –"

"Lermontov, yes."

A pause. From the other end of the line, the sound of Carol tapping at her teeth with a pen.

"We should meet," she said. "Brunch?"

"Great. Where?"

"You know Amy Ruth's, on 116th?"

It would take two hours, give or take, for her to walk from East Village to Harlem. No cab, no bus, no subway. Definitely no subway. Not that she'd tell Carol any of this. No-one knew that she was walking everywhere. She didn't want anyone to think she was weird.

"Could we maybe meet somewhere closer to the Park?"

"How about Tavern on the Green? I've not been there in a while."

"Perfect."

She called Pavel and told him how she and her friend were meeting the next day. She still hadn't mentioned Carol's name.

"It looks promising," she said.

She could hear him smiling. He suggested they meet up, get some food, a few drinks. If she saw him again, she would want to see him another time, and another. A familiar force, like gravity, pulling her away from herself. From everything.

Chapter 22:
NEW YORK, APRIL 1951

Your mother wore a fox fur stole that night, and an embroidered black cloche. It made her look old fashioned, though you'd never say so. She was wearing her very best while you wore the suit bought recently for your bar mitzvah. It was your first time at Carnegie Hall. You rode the subway. The train was crowded, standing room only, the two of you pressed in among Wall Street men heading to Uptown and gasworks crews and secretaries going home to Queens. Why couldn't you get a cab? Wouldn't that have been a more dignified way to arrive, right outside the concert hall? Not jostling your way up out of the 57th Street subway.

You didn't know it, but there was no way your mother could have afforded a cab that night. She and your father spent every penny buying those two tickets, and they were far from the best seats in the house. You were up in the nosebleeds and had to climb a hundred steps just to get there.

Down on the conductor's platform, Toscanini; a tiny black speck with an even tinier shock of grey hair. You'd learned about the speed of sound and wondered how many fractions of a second it would take for the music to travel from the orchestra all the way up to the top tier.

Tonight you'll stand in the same place Toscanini stood eighteen years ago, but there'll be no subway ride. Your hotel is only a few blocks from Carnegie Hall, a distance you'd have walked easily as a kid, but a car – rather than a cab – will pick you up and take you from one door to the next.

It's still two hours till the concert begins, but you pace the room restlessly. For half an hour or more you fiddle with your bowtie, and you're still not wearing any pants.

"It's straight," says Angie, attaching the second of her pearl earrings at the dressing table.

"No. It's off. See?"

Her reflected eyes meet yours. "It's going to be fine," she says. "Trust me."

"You're sure of that?"

"I was at the rehearsal, remember? It sounded *great*."

You adjust your tie again, if anything only making it worse. Angie stands behind you, resting her chin on your shoulder. She squints at the tie for a moment and then, reaching around with both hands, fixes it in an instant.

"There," she says. "Done. Now don't touch it."

She's been in New York a week; you've been here almost a month. An unpaid sabbatical from Capitol. She brought with her a sense of order and calm, not to mention company. Before she got here you spent a few evenings at the Village Vanguard, had several dinners with Margaret Bernard and her friends and some of the orchestra stalwarts, but you've led an otherwise monastic life, divided between this hotel and the rehearsal rooms.

Not long after your arrival you took a 6 Train to the Upper East Side, and walked around its streets, looking for the home of Dr Lowe, but it was no use. You'd forgotten the house number, and the markers you might have used to find it have all since gone. There's something about that part of town that makes your heart ache, more so than anywhere on the Lower East Side. You thought you would be living in a place like that by now, before you ever dreamt of going to the Coast. Fame and fortune were just around the corner. They are always just around the corner.

So what is tonight, if not a symbol of fame and fortune? The concert was mentioned in the *New Yorker* and *Musical America*. You've had letters wishing you good luck from those who knew Ron personally and those who admired him. You even got a brief note *("Best wishes for Carnegie Hall")* from Leonard Bernstein. Isn't that fame? And Ron's estate and the New York Philharmonic helped keep the wolf from the door while you've been away from Capitol. Not a fortune, but you're hardly the starving artist in his garret. Why should some house you can't find on a street you've half-forgotten even matter to you?

You're trying to distract yourself. That's all this is. When the concert is finished you'll be travelling not to LA, at least not immediately, but to Washington DC. There'll be no chauffeur-driven car, and the hotel room is one you'll pay for yourself.

The pink slip arrived two months ago. A subpoena to appear before the House Un-American Activities Committee, either in Los Angeles or DC. The dates were so close to the concert, you decided DC would be more convenient. And maybe there was a safety in keeping it all at arm's length, in some city which means nothing to you.

You could ask why you were selected to appear. You have no affiliations. You've never been a member of any society or club. Politics is a game for those who have everything or those who have nothing, and you were dealt a half-decent hand. The problem is, you're caught in a crossfire of associations; with Ron, with Mary. And there's one more thing they might have on you, if they were thorough.

If you were a card-carrying Red you might ask what power they have over a man's thoughts, because that's what this amounts to. By deciding that one kind of thought – not action, but *thought* – is dangerous, toxic, harmful, are they saying such thoughts can be removed by the weight of the law? A thought isn't tactile, something physical. A thought hangs in the silence between moments. A thought can be anything, about anything. Trying to stamp it out, to punish it, is about as futile as waging a war against memories and dreams.

Angie tells you it's just a hearing, you're not on trial, but that's what everyone's wife or husband says. You stopped seeing the Buick and the men in the snap-brim hats as soon as you received that slip.

Chapter 23:
LENINGRAD, APRIL 1938

The Princess swoons into Pechorin's arms, her death accompanied by a sustained A from the strings, a vertiginous glissando from the horns and a final, thunderous roll of timpani. The lights become a cold and deathly shade of blue shifting to a bloody red, and the stage falls into darkness.

From the wings, in what little light is left, Sergey sees the conductor, Feldt, lowering his baton. In the absence of the orchestra's roar and the glare of the spotlights the world becomes dark. Only when the lights come back, the dancers standing side by side, arms linked, ready to take their first bow, does he hear the applause.

The Kirov audience is on its feet and cheering, but he's drawn to the box on the first level. There they sit; the "old men" (none of them any older than fifty) of the Union of Soviet Composers. Standing and clapping; not with too much enthusiasm, but Remizov looks pleased. Next to him: Klepov. Stony faced as ever. Rarely smiles, rarely frowns. Next to him, Ilyin, Kozlov, Yenin and Khromov. All clapping. Ilyin and Kozlov exchange words. Ilyin nods, then Kozlov. Still clapping. Yenin says something to Khromov, and Khromov laughs, but it's a warm kind of laughter, nothing callous.

Everything is good.

Sergey turns now to the front row of the first tier. The guests from America and England. They look funny to him;

different, somehow. The way they dress, perhaps. Trying to look austere, less colourful than they might back in New York or London, but still like peacocks; so colourful, so bright. All of them beaming down at him and clapping.

Feldt is away from the podium and at Sergey's side, and he hooks arms with him.

"Come on," he says. "They're clapping for you, you know."

They step out into the spotlights and someone in the stalls cries "Bravo! Bravo!", and the rest of the audience follows his lead.

"Bravo!"

"Bravo!"

"Bravo!"

Chapter 24:
NEW YORK, APRIL 1951

This is it. Hallowed ground. You wish you could remember just how many names you've seen standing where you are right now. Men who occupied the same space. Breathed the same air. The auditorium at Carnegie Hall is the closest thing to a grand synagogue, temple, or cathedral that you'll ever know.

She joins you on the stage, announced by her footsteps on the wooden boards.

"Mrs Bernard."

"Mr Conrad."

"Nervous?"

"A little."

"You shouldn't be. Tonight will be marvellous. I'm certain of it. Will your family be in the audience?"

"My family?"

"You're a New Yorker. I assumed you would have family here."

An invitation was sent to Mr and Mrs Yitzhak Cohen of 26 Clinton Street, but they never replied. You imagine they'll spend the night in their apartment listening to your father's old radio, and not NBC (who are broadcasting the concert live), but one of the Yiddish stations based over in Brooklyn and Queens.

Angie suggested you visit them – she still has an eye on

moving here one day – but you made excuses, as if Manhattan was simply too vast and your schedule too busy, and she seemed to understand the finality of your answer.

In much the same tone, you tell Margaret you won't have any family in the audience, other than your wife.

"Ah, yes. Another composer, I'm told."

"That's right."

"From Los Angeles?"

"Illinois, originally, but we met on the Coast."

"And is she aware of your… I hesitate to call it a 'lifestyle'…"

"She is not."

"Good. Knowing one's husband is so inclined can be a burden."

"You could have divorced him."

They are words you've wanted to say for many years, but Margaret simply laughs.

"Good lord, no. I wouldn't have dreamt of it. Oh, if he'd run off with some pretty young slip of a girl, then yes. I'd have divorced him, and I'd have had the sympathy of every woman and most of the men in Manhattan. But our situation was very different. Were it known that our marriage had been… let's say *'compromised'*… by a *boy*… Well. How would that have reflected on me?"

"I don't follow."

"Vulgar as it may seem, Mr Conrad, when a woman's husband leaves her for another man people assume the source of his corruption is the marital bed. Leave a man unsatisfied *there* and there's no telling what he'll get up to. Do you follow?

No. I wouldn't have pressed for divorce on *those* grounds."

She pauses, once again peering out across the dim red gloom of the stalls, her hand held to her brow like a visor.

"Are you happy now, with *Giudecca*?" she asks.

Typical of her to ask this twenty minutes before the house opens, as if she had to plant a seed of doubt. You tell her you're very happy, and that you're glad she talked you into including it.

For the first time since joining you on the stage, Margaret faces you, and the two of you exchange a smile that's neither warm nor hostile, but something mysteriously in between.

★★

The auditorium falls silent. Someone, perhaps a hundred feet above and behind you, clears his throat. One of the cellists shifts in his seat and the stage beneath him creaks. You breathe in deeply, close your eyes. And you begin.

This isn't, of course, the first time you've heard it; it's not even the first time you've heard it today. Even so, the sound of the choir causes you to lose focus, if only for a second, and the flesh along your arms and shoulders becomes taut with gooseflesh.

You can feel the paper of that first draft score as you turned its pages. You can see Ron's expression, looking at you from across the desk, waiting for your verdict and your understanding.

"It's incredible," you said. "Simply incredible."

The first performance in Boston. Outside the concert hall, the rain fell in silver pinstripes and the puddles were inches deep. By the time you took to your seat in the front row you were drenched. Margaret Bernard was there – this was long before the separation – placed as far from you as possible. She didn't notice those moments when her husband, sitting beside her, glanced across at you and smiled.

The choir sings Dante's words and the orchestra plays Ron's music. This is what the absence of genius feels like, and how it will always feel. Ron was the one who could write music fit for Dante. For you, such confidence was impossible, until you saw the sky burst into flames above the scrublands of southern Nevada.

Ron's music, written after the obliteration of cities and the liberation of the death camps, was never concerned solely with a medieval Hell. It was as much about the Hell we make for ourselves and others here on Earth; the Hell of wars and massacres, the Hell of jealousies and betrayals.

The choir sings *"Io non mori' e non rimasi vivo"* – I did not die and I was not alive. You're holding Nick, trying and failing to lift him out of the water; his skin cold and soft and horribly like butchered meat. That is what death feels like. Soft, but cold. No life, no tension behind it. The flesh giving way, giving up, submitting to whatever comes next.

You're wrapping a veal cutlet behind the counter of your father's shop. A Western Union van pulls up outside. Your father stares at the van but says nothing. Your mother steps out from the storeroom and makes a sound in the back of her throat, neither a cry nor a gasp. The bell above the door jangles and the Western Union man enters and asks for Yitzhak Cohen. He hands your father the telegram and apologises as if it could possibly be his fault. He leaves the store with the expression of a man not yet numbed by being the bearer of bad news. Your mother begins to cry. Doesn't even have to read the telegram. You take it from your father's shaking hands and read it, picking out only your brother's name and those words that burst from the page before coalescing into a single, inescapable fact.

This music was always there, beneath each moment, long before Ron wrote it. The choir's voices fill the auditorium, transforming it into a space without gravity, and you are watching an event that occurs almost a mile above the desert, a single atom shattering, triggering a series of events that fills the night with fire. This isn't a moment of destruction, but rather an act of terrifying creation; another sun being born and living only a fraction of a second before consuming itself into nothing but dust. If you took the sound of that moment and drew it out over minutes, rather than millionths of a second, what you would hear is the *Inferno* oratorio, sung by a one hundred-strong choir.

★★

You last saw Doris and Charles at Ron's birthday party, back in '47. The Fanshawes. Connecticut and affluent, but involved in good causes and activism, much like Ron. They were in

Paris when he died, and so couldn't attend the funeral.

"We were devastated, of course," says Doris.

By Ron's death or the awkwardness of their absence?

They're a dapper enough pair. You'd mistake neither for members of the proletariat. Charles teaches architecture at Yale while Doris collects art and recently had one of her "people" pick up a Jackson Pollock at auction.

"Can't *stand* the stuff, myself. So self-indulgent. But it's all the rage. And that sort of thing can only ever increase in value."

After an aside about Pollock's work – "Like something the cat hacked up" – Margaret steers the conversation onto the subject of tonight's concert.

"Well, I thought it was top drawer," says Charles. "Wasn't it darling? What do you think?"

"Sublime," says Doris.

"Of course," says Charles, "the only shame is that Ronald wasn't there to hear it for himself."

"Well, yes," Margaret says curtly. "But it *was* a memorial concert. His being around to hear it would have defeated the purpose of it somewhat."

You feel yourself blushing. Angie suppresses a laugh by turning it into a demure cough. Doris and Charles don't react at all.

"So," says Charles. "What next for our young maestro?"

You ask what he means.

"You're based in Los Angeles, yes?"

He pronounces 'Angeles' with the same hard "g" as Margaret. You tell him that's correct.

"Yes," says Margaret. "Mr Conrad composes music for the motion pictures."

"For *movies*?" says Doris. "You mean musicals?"

You tell her it's mostly westerns and crime movies, actually; an exaggeration after months of being blackballed at Capitol. Even then Doris looks startled, as if you'd told her you write jingles for soap commercials.

"Well, now," says Charles. "I don't suppose you'll be writing that sort of thing for much longer."

"Meaning...?"

It comes out a little aggressively, but Charles takes it in his stride, laughing through his nose and taking another sip of his Old Fashioned.

Doris answers for him. "What my husband means is that now you've made your New York debut there's no need for you to waste your talents on something as disposable as the cinema."

"Disposable?"

"Why, yes. What was it you said? Westerns? Cops and robbers?"

"Among other things."

"Well, there you have it. The movies are all well and good, but there isn't a single film starring Humphrey Bogart or John Wayne or, what's the other fella called? Cary Grant. There isn't a single film starring any of those characters that'll last as long as the *Eroica*. Even when a composer such as Copland works in Hollywood, he produces only minor, forgettable works. Can you imagine going to a concert to hear the music from

Fort Apache?"

"I rather enjoyed *Fort Apache*," says Charles.

"You *enjoyed* it," says Doris. "That's not the same as considering it beneficial to the common man. You *enjoy* a hotdog whenever Harold – that's my brother – whenever Harold insists on taking you to the Yankee Stadium. That doesn't mean we should start handing out free hot dogs on every street corner."

"Man cannot live by hotdog alone," Charles smirks. He looks at you for a moment, narrowing his eyes. "Say. I just thought. Weren't you the young man who joined us on that trip with poor old Larry Black and Dotty Markham and her sister and… who else? When was that, Doris? Thirty-six?"

"Thirty-seven."

"As late as that? You're probably right. Spring, if I recall. Was that you?"

You shake your head, offer an apologetic shrug.

"Oh well," says Charles. "Must have been another of Ron's young men."

Doris shoots her husband a caustic sideways glance and Charles sips his cocktail without as much as a blink. Margaret Bernard remains stoic.

You make your apologies, avoiding Angie's gaze, and walk away without a destination in mind. Your bowtie is too tight and your feet feel very suddenly compressed by your dress shoes. At Capitol, this concert was both a tacit confession and a potential embarrassment. In Manhattan, the movies make you a vulgarian. Hollywood judges you because you're queer and because Ron was a Red. New York judges you because you're a cog in capitalism's grotesque machinery. Perhaps Doris and Charles would approve if you were writing music for films about factory workers and collective farms.

Wasn't changing your name enough for them? Abandoning Cohen for something more goyish? Ron's suggestion. "Look at Copland, look at Gershwin." Though, to your mind, Gershwin still sounds pretty Jewish. You looked around Ron's apartment for inspiration and saw the spine of a book, *Under Western Eyes*, by Joseph Conrad. Later still you learned the author was born Józef Korzeniowski, which had a certain irony. Your father's expression, when you told him what you'd done, was enough to break your heart, but you wouldn't relent. Your name was now Sol Conrad. And things were never the same after that.

Was all this not enough for the Uptown set, for Ron's friends at the Century Club, for the WASP sponsors and donors and patrons of the arts who make up maybe eighty percent of those milling around the bar here at the Waldorf?

In the restroom you take a piss you don't really need, glad simply to be away from those people. A Negro attendant hands you a towel and some soap, and as you wash and dry your hands you're joined at the washbasin by a guy you first noticed in the bar. Not part of your group. He was sitting at the bar, looking over at you, and your eyes locked just once. You didn't dare look again, in case Angie noticed, but now he's staring at you in the mirror.

He's dressed smartly enough. Pinstripe tailored suit, good

shoes. His grooming is old-fashioned for his age; you'd guess he's about forty. Handsome. A businessman, most likely, from out of town. Chicago or Detroit. In New York for one night only. Probably has a room here, and as you walk back to the bar he'll ask if you'd like to join him upstairs for a drink. Forward, and confident, because he can afford to be.

He'll invite you to his room and you'll go there, and the whole thing will be over too quickly because however drunk you might be you'll still remember that Angie is waiting for you downstairs, talking to – or being talked at by – Margaret and her friends.

The guy – you've decided his name is something butch like 'Bob' or 'Frank' – smiles at you and you look away. You felt something you don't want to feel. It's always in the eyes. Across a room, across a bar, across some shady path. You're thinking of another night, a long time ago. Hours you will never forget. Walking along the frozen river as the sun began to rise. Or Pershing Square, a group of men standing around the statue of Beethoven, and one of them looking over. That first lecture at Juilliard. A famous tutor with a name you'd heard on the radio, looking around the class, familiarising himself with his students, his eyes resting on you a beat longer than anyone else. You once lived for those moments, but things are different now.

You clutch another paper towel and dry your hands a little quicker, still staring into the basin. Your hands aren't properly dry, but you throw a dime into the attendant's tip tray, and leave the restroom as if fleeing the scene of a crime.

Chapter 25: MANHATTAN, OCTOBER 2001

They began at a ramen bar in East Village, the staff barking at them in Japanese as they entered. The waitresses looked like something from Anime; bobbed pink hair and bright plastic accessories.

Pavel asked her how she came to New York, what kind of work she'd done before becoming Sol's assistant. She went through her CV. Much of it felt like several lifetimes ago. Waiting tables part-time in a self-styled bistro in Chipping Campden. Had he heard of the Cotswolds? (He hadn't.) In New York she worked weekends in a shop that sold "ethnic stuff" and incense sticks. Then, after graduating, she applied for the job as Sol's PA. It had little to do with her degree in musicology, but she didn't want to teach. Working for Sol seemed a happy compromise.

Pavel asked how much she earned and Natalie coughed and laughed and told him he was being forward.

"What does this mean – 'forward'?"

"Rude."

"Why is it rude?"

"It's… we don't… that isn't something people talk about."

"Why not?"

"Because… it isn't. It makes people uncomfortable. Especially the English. It's like this unwritten rule we have."

"But not for Russians."

"I'm not Russian."

"But I am. So how much does he pay you?"

She told him how much and Pavel almost choked on a steamed dumpling, his coughing fit brought to an end only when he spat it out and took a swig of water.

"What's so funny?"

"He is a wealthy man. He should be paying you more."

"I get by."

Pavel nodded. He wouldn't press it any further. He ate another dumpling and smiled at her with his mouth full. Beneath the table, their knees touched. Natalie couldn't remember the last time she had talked this much about herself. Ordinarily, it was the sort of thing she would shrink from, changing the subject as quickly as she could, letting others do all the talking, but with Pavel it felt different. She didn't mind.

A moment's silence was broken when the bell above the door jangled, more customers entered, and the women with the bobbed pink hair yelled, *"Irasshaimase!"* Natalie and Pavel nearly jumped out of their seats. They looked at one another and laughed.

After another moment's quiet, Pavel said, "Why is he alone?"

"Who?"

"Mr Conrad."

"I don't know. How does anyone end up alone? He was married once. But they divorced. He doesn't have any family. There was some rift between him and his parents."

"That is sad," Pavel said. "A man his age, having nobody."

"That's not true," said Natalie. "He has me."

Pavel nodded slowly. He was staring into some far corner of the restaurant, lost in a thought. Now was the time.

"What is it you want out of all this?" she asked.

"What do you mean?"

"I mean *this*. Your grandfather's music. Proving the connection with Mr Conrad. What is it you actually want?"

She'd allowed a trace of anger into her voice. She wasn't angry with Pavel, as such, but if she was going to carry on helping him, she needed to know.

"Lots of things, I guess," Pavel said. "Money, obviously. If there is money that should be ours, my family's, we should have it. Is that wrong? We were never rich. My grandfather, my father, my mother's family, always poor. But it's not just that."

"Then what is it?"

"I feel like people should know who he was. Sergey. Because everyone forgot. Almost like he'd died. Like they'd killed him with all the others. But they didn't. He lived. And he married. And he had children. And his children had children. And nobody knows."

Why couldn't he have left it at "money"?

"Do you remember him?" Natalie asked.

Pavel nodded. "He was a quiet man. I think he was a good man. Not always. He told my father that before they sent him away he was *mudak*. An asshole. But that's not how I remember him."

He reached across the table and held onto her hands,

squeezing them gently. His hands were warmer than her own. She didn't want him to let go.

"Thank you," he said. "For helping me."

There was nothing she could say. She smiled. If this carried on she would cry. She gestured to one of the women with pink hair and mimed signing a cheque, even though she would pay their bill with a card.

From the ramen bar, they zigged and zagged their way across the Village to Pier 45. She half-expected the place to be deserted, fenced off with a sign that said, *"Merriment cancelled until further notice";* the city draped in widow's weeds.

Instead, in the greenish light beneath its pavilion, they found people slow dancing to a Sinatra song. Young couples and old couples, straight couples and gay couples. The kind of scene New York does so well. Across the dark river, the lights of Jersey shimmered against the water. To the south, at the far end of Manhattan, there was a sad, black nothingness of sky between the towers.

She invited Pavel to dance. They'd had a few beers at the ramen bar and she was already feeling a little drunk.

"I do not dance. I would be like a dancing bear."

"Come on," she said, grabbing him by the hands, dragging him towards the music. He didn't put up too much of a struggle. They slow danced and they kissed and Natalie closed her eyes and listened to Sinatra and the sound of water lapping and gurgling against the pier.

The moment soared with happiness, a breathless joy that washed over her, surrounded her. It wasn't that her time in

New York had been unhappy, but rather that she had been resistant to happiness. Yet out there on the pier she was overwhelmed by a sensation of living in the present, her future as black, as unknowable, as the night sky or the water below.

She insisted they walk to his hotel, telling him it was too lovely an evening for the subway. Winter would kick in soon enough, and then it would be too cold to walk anywhere. "Let's enjoy this while it lasts," she said, and so they walked.

Natalie still hadn't told him Carol's name. How would this play out? Carol seeing the score and confirming everything. The story going public. A whirlwind of academic interest, maybe even a few column inches in the *New York Times*. Then plans to perform Sergey Grekov's ballet, either in St Petersburg or here in New York. Or St Petersburg *and* New York. A joint production between the Mariinsky and the New York City Ballet. And of course, the authorities would have to let Pavel stay on in the States, so that together he and Natalie could tell his grandfather's story. And Sol wasn't getting any younger. By the time the truth – whatever the truth might be – came out, he'd be way past understanding. His most famous work plagiarism? The network would pick up the bill, pay any royalties, settle everything out of court. What difference would it make?

There was never even a moment's hesitation before she got into the elevator that night. They began kissing and undressing as it went up to his floor, and they ran the short distance from the elevator to his room.

The physical act itself was something wordless, instinctive. Not sex, not love, not even fucking, but something closer to a dance, and it terrified her. It terrified her with its perfection, with its rightness. It terrified her with its promise of a beginning.

Chapter 26:
WASHINGTON D.C., APRIL 1951

A wet spring day in Washington; the trees coming into leaf and its streets slicked with rain. The city is coldly unfamiliar to you, its marble facades grey beneath a clouded sky. You were here once, in the early '40s, but came late in the afternoon, travelled straight to the concert hall, and went back to New York the same night.

The twelve hours before the hearing are spent in your hotel room, leaving it only for a joyless supper in the hotel's restaurant. There is little conversation between the two of you. If your marriage is built on anything, it's an ability to talk to one another for hours on end, but you have nothing to say. The noise of tomorrow drowns out everything.

In your room she tries to instigate sex, kissing you on the mouth and placing her hand on your crotch, but you tell her you're too tired. She accepts the apology and falls asleep in minutes, but you're incapable of sleep. How much longer can things go on with you turning her away like this? Tonight there's an excuse, but on other nights, after all this is over, what then?

You can't tell her the truth; that each moment of intimacy takes you back to that night in the Nevada desert, that thoughts of sex, of fucking, of making love are now entangled, inextricably, with the memory of Nick's cold flesh. In quieter moments, when alone, you wonder how long it was before they found him. You picture the stillness of the bathwater; how it must have settled and become glass within minutes. The awful emptiness of that room in the hours that followed.

You spent those first few weeks scouring newspapers for reports of a body found in a southern Nevada motel. The dead man's identity a mystery or – if Nick had any ID – his reasons for being there under a false name unknown.

"Said they came to see the bomb," the motel manager would tell authorities. "Said they were brothers, but now I ain't so sure."

"They seemed friendly enough," the husband and father from Utah might say. "Real strange turnout of events."

But how could anyone connect you with Nick? His friends don't know you and your friends don't know him. That is the nature of this life; the threads that bind people together simply aren't there. Death made him an island. And if the men in the Buick were watching the whole time, they simply didn't care.

In the morning you drink coffee and put on the same suit you wore to Ron's funeral, but accompanied by a blue silk tie. You take a cab from Kalorama Heights to Independence Avenue, Angie sitting next to you, but when you ask if she'll be there in the caucus room she shakes her head.

"Why not?"

"Because if they say anything to you, anything hurtful, I swear to God…"

She looks away, dabbing at her eyes with a handkerchief, and you tell her everything will be fine. This isn't Soviet Russia. This isn't Nazi Germany. They can't make you disappear, and it's not like you sold atomic secrets. What's the worst they can do?

But there's plenty they could do, and both you and Angie know it.

At Cannon House the corridors smell of wood polish and cigar smoke. You use the men's room several times before the hearing, the last time staring down as nothing comes out. You're standing there with your nervous, shrivelled dick in your hand when a familiar voice says, "I'm surprised you got anything left in there. What is this? Comfort Break Number Five, or Six?"

Roy Carmichael, Capitol's Head of Security. His back against the wall, his arms folded across his chest. What the hell is he doing here; and not just this restroom but D.C.? You don't even need to ask him; it's as if he can hear your thoughts.

"Didn't anyone tell you?" he says. "It's Capitol day in Washington. I think they're going studio by studio, so Capitol sent me here."

"But why?"

"To talk to those artists who are appearing before the House Un-American Activities Committee. Such as your good self."

"I still don't get it."

"Mr Conrad. Your presence here, appearing before the men of the committee, may be an inconvenience to you, but it's a cause of embarrassment for the studio. There are many at Capitol who would rather you were cast out into the wilderness. There are others who believe the current climate is unnecessary and bad for business."

"Which are you?"

"I care only about protecting the property, personnel and reputation of the studio. While you are contracted to the music department at Capitol you are my business, but your continuing employment depends upon one thing."

"Which is?"

He adopts a stentorian boom, his voice echoing off the tiled walls:

"Are you now or have you ever been a member of the Communist Party?"

"No."

"See, that *sounds* convincing, but you and I both know that men of your, uh, *persuasion* are born liars. Comes with the territory. So I'll ask again. Are you now or have you ever been a member of the Communist Party?"

"No."

"And that's the answer you'll give out there?"

"It is."

"And there is nothing, and I mean *nothing* they could have dug up that'll contradict that?"

"No."

"Good. That's good. Well, while we're here, and we have the privacy of this delightful men's room – and I mean that, by the way… I mean, jeez… if this is what my tax dollars pay for… But while we're here, I should tell you that if, for whatever reason, you come out of that room stained with even the slightest hint of red, you might as well stay here on the East Coast, because you will never work in Hollywood again."

He turns toward the door, pauses.

"One last thing," he says, gesturing to your crotch. "Don't forget to do up your fly."

Chapter 27:
MANHATTAN, OCTOBER 2001

It was a Sunday, and the park was full of families. Typical for a weekend, but this was something else. There were so many of them, and it just kept getting busier. Children in cycling helmets riding stabilised bikes, people pushing prams. Old couples holding hands and struggling to keep up with their grandchildren. An almost forced normality. Everyone making that extra bit of effort to get things back to how they were.

She reached the restaurant before Carol and took a seat near the window, looking out across the road to the far meadow. A little boy in an orange GAP hoodie was trying to get a kite in the air, but to no avail. After a while, Natalie found herself willing the bloody thing to take flight.

Carol arrived, and after their greetings and double kisses they spent a moment scanning their menus. Natalie waited for Carol to suggest the drinks and Carol ordered them a pot of tea to share.

"So," Carol said, eventually. "I have been very busy with this assignment."

Carol's accent was three parts French to one part Norwegian. She wore a uniform of black t-shirt and black jeans, and today she had on a black leather jacket. She'd always reminded Natalie of the heroine from a foreign detective novel, and today more than ever.

Carol pursed her lips and breathed heavily through her

nose. Without taking her eyes off the menu she continued:

"The name. Sergey Grekov. It was familiar. I've seen him mentioned here and there. In some places, a violinist. In others, a composer. Perhaps one of the 'disappeared'. I don't know. But then, we are talking about the Soviet Union in the late 1930s..."

"Pavel said his grandfather was sent away, to a prison camp."

"And the connection is Bernard?"

"We think Ronald Bernard may have attended a performance of his grandfather's ballet."

"Ah, yes yes yes!" said Carol, slamming down her menu. "April 1938."

"That's right."

"The Kirov staged a ballet, based on Lermontov's *Un héros de notre temps,* ah... *A Hero of Our Time.* Very unusual for the Kirov to stage a debut composer. This suggests perhaps the ballet was considered a prestige work, the sort of thing they staged for visiting dignitaries. And we know that Bernard was in Russia at this time. But typically, *Modern Music* has no online archive."

The tea arrived, and Carol poured them each a cup, very aware that she was keeping Natalie in suspense. Only when she had finished did she go on.

"Fortunately, Columbia has the microfiche of the entire back catalogue."

Natalie breathed out.

"So I looked up the fall issue of 1938. And yes – Ronald Bernard writes about new Soviet music. And he mentions a... wait, I have written it down..."

Carol lifted her handbag onto the table and began rooting around in its contents. The chaos of that bag and the personal organiser she kept – its elastic band straining against notes and receipts – was surely a part of the act; the illusion of disorder, when Carol was anything but disorganised. She flicked through her notebook, found the page she was looking for, and read aloud:

"'Though their Union of Composers frowns upon atonality, there is a great deal of invention to be found in Russian music, and from the next generation of Soviet composers. In Leningrad, formerly St Petersburg, this reviewer saw an excellent new ballet based on a chapter from Lermontov's novel *A Hero of Our Time*.'"

"That's it. That's his grandfather's ballet."

"Well, you see, that's the interesting part. I searched everywhere, and do you think I could find any mention of the composer? No, I could not. There are mentions of the ballet, but no mention of who wrote it. You'd almost think Bernard liked the ballet but not the composer."

"But you're saying it *was* the ballet that Bernard saw at the Kirov?"

"Certainly. *Geroy nashego vremeni*. A few people have wondered who the composer was over the years, so we're not the first. Some thought it was adapted from music for a play by Meyerhold, before he was…" Carol drew her finger across her throat and pulled a face. "Impossible to say, of course, without there being a score. Talking of which…"

Natalie nodded and reached into her handbag. As she placed

the score on the table she heard Carol draw breath.

"May I…?"

Natalie pushed the manuscript towards her, as if passing an enveloped bribe. Carol opened it and began leafing through the pages. Her breath trembled and her eyes glistened.

"It's genuine, yes? Not some… some *hoax*?"

"I think it's real."

"This could be very important. You do realise that?"

Natalie nodded.

"A composer hardly anyone has heard of. A piece of music very few people will have heard. Remarkable."

Natalie's pulse quickened. With each page, Carol drew closer to the *Pechorin March*. If she saw it, she would recognise it and she would know. No alternative then but to announce this to the world. Journalists would begin scratching away at the story. Sol might not be a household name, but he had one claim to posterity and it was right there, on the page.

But how? Natalie thought she had it. She had spent much of her walk from Midtown to the park going over everything she knew, until it came together, each piece slotting neatly with the last.

"And the man who wrote this. You say his grandson is here, in New York?"

"That's right."

"Why did he come to *you*?"

Natalie thought she detected a note of envy.

"Mr Conrad," she replied.

"It's very sweet, you still calling him that."

"It would feel strange calling him anything else."

"But still, it is sweet. So… Sol Conrad. Ronald Bernard. I see."

"Pavel thought perhaps Bernard may have mentioned the ballet while they were together."

"Of course. But Mr Conrad remembers nothing?"

"Unfortunately."

"This is tragic."

"It is."

"I wonder," said Carol. "What is left when the memory goes? Not a person, surely."

"Oh, he's in there. It's still him."

They ate their food and settled the bill. Outside the Tavern on the Green they hugged. Carol was effervescent.

"This is so exciting," she said. "Please. Let me know what happens, and if you need any more help… oh! This is wonderful. *Formidable! Incroyable! Joyeux!"*

They embraced once more and headed off in their separate directions; Carol going to the nearest subway and Natalie to the nearest bar. Her cell phone showed three missed calls from Pavel. He'd left a voicemail asking where she'd taken his grandfather's score. She thumbed a short reply, telling him that she and her friend were spending the rest of the day at Columbia; that she would take good care of the manuscript and return it to him the following day. As soon as the message was sent she turned off her phone and left it at the bottom of her handbag.

The bar was an "Irish Pub". Neon shamrock in the window. Bare brick walls, wooden floors. The music just a little too loud for anyone to hold a conversation. The clientele consisted largely of tourists with Bloomingdales bags, ordering platters of overpriced, under-fleshed Buffalo wings. The jukebox was playing a strange medley of Lynyrd Skynyrd, Britney Spears and Chuck Berry.

Natalie drank a beer and chased it down with vodka. The song on the jukebox came to an end and she heard familiar strings. It was the same Sinatra song they'd danced to on the pier.

She wasn't superstitious. It couldn't mean anything. Just coincidence. She turned to face an emptier part of the bar, away from the tourists and the bartenders, her jaw trembling and her eyes beginning to burn. Why couldn't Pavel have told her he was in it for the money and nothing else? It would have been easier then.

When her tears had dried, Natalie turned back to her drink. She was nearing the bottom of the glass. The temptation was to order another, to keep drinking until she no longer knew where she was. That desire to numb herself was getting worse, and it wasn't just sadness she wished to numb, but every last troubling emotion.

Chapter 28:
LENINGRAD, APRIL 1938

One glass of champagne, and he's intoxicated. The ballroom's chandeliers spin like fireworks. The string quartet plays the *Gopak* with such gusto it's as if the whole room is dancing around him. Strangers shake his hand, kiss his cheeks, tell him his ballet is a triumph, simply a *triumph*, but their compliments feel distant, as if they should be offering them to someone else.

Remizov takes his arm and walks him around the room. Here are men from Moscow, "important men", who toast his good health and tell him they expect great things in the future. Here is the committee he was telling him about. Here are the people from *Ogoniok*.

Remizov smells strongly of French cologne. Whenever they stop to talk to someone new he places his hand in the small of Sergey's back. Sergey shifts awkwardly and Remizov's hand falls away. They move on, from a party man and his wife, and Remizov murmurs, "I'm sorry."

"What for?"

"You know what. You must know. I find you very attractive."

He's a comical figure when he's like this. Desperate for affection. He could have his pick of the boys in the reserve troupe. None of them would dare turn down a union secretary. When did this infatuation begin? Sergey laughs.

"Is that so?" he says. "I never would have guessed."

"I do," says Remizov. "And I suppose it's too much to hope you feel the same way about me."

He avoids giving an answer.

"Where are these Americans you keep telling me about?" he asks.

Remizov takes a moment to collect himself. His rigid smile returns, his chest and shoulders expand, and he takes Sergey on another breathless sweep of the room.

Exhausting. The day began early, and he spent last night staring at the shadows on his bedroom ceiling. He should have gone to the brothel on Kazanskaya Street. They know him there, and the girls are cleaner than some other places. A quick fuck and he might have slept – it usually does the trick – but instead he lay there and imagined, over and over, everything that could possibly go wrong. An audience of bored faces. The orchestra playing out of time or out of tune. The dancers lumbering around the stage like graceless apes.

None of that matters now that he's the toast of the Kirov. No! *Leningrad*. There will be a review in tomorrow's *Pravda*, of course; written by Remizov, or another of the Old Men of the Union, declaring *A Hero of Our Time* a triumph and its composer the heir to Mussorgsky. He will win prizes and become the youngest person accepted into the union's inner circle. From there, it's merely a case of biding his time. People like Remizov are politicians first, artists not even second or third, and politicians come and go. But a composer could climb the ranks quickly and stay there, if he knows how to play his hand. And Sergey has always known how to play his hand.

"This way," says Remizov, squeezing Sergey's arm. "This way!"

Another group. The peacocks from the Kirov.

"Here," Remizov says, and then, in English, his voice raised: "Let me introduce our young maestro. Sergey Andreievich Grekov."

The guests put down their drinks and applaud him again, and Sergey bows. It's the sort of gesture that would be frowned upon elsewhere; too old fashioned, too much like the old way of doing things. But here it's accepted, even encouraged. This whole evening is a performance; not just what happened on stage and in the orchestra pit, but here in the ballroom of the Hotel Astoria. This is a pageant of Old Russian hospitality, culture and charm, preserved for the sake of outside eyes.

"And these people," says Remizov, switching back to Russian, but giving each person their title in English. *"Meester Charles Fanshawe* and *Meeses Doris Fanshawe. Meester Lawrence Black. Meester Langdon Brunel. Meeses Penelope Markham-Riley. Meese Dorothy Markham. Meester William Kaufman. Meester Ronald Bernard.* And *Meester…"*

His mouth falls open. The last person he introduced, Ronald Bernard, smiles. Sergey has heard of him. An American composer. Not as old as he'd imagined, perhaps late thirties, but serious, professorial. Beside him, a young man with dark brown hair that falls across his eyes in a long fringe.

"I am very sorry," says Remizov, in English. "Your name?"

"Solomon," the young man replies, a little sourly. He glances at Bernard with a flicker of resentment. "Solomon Cohen."

Remizov beams. *"Meester Solomon Cohen."*

The young man and Sergey exchange a smile. The visitors take it in turns to approach Sergey and tell him how much they enjoyed his ballet. All in English, of course, until he comes to Bernard, who speaks in near-flawless Russian.

"A great work," says the American. "I mean it. If this ballet is anything to go by, you are destined for great things."

Great things. A world tour. Lauded in the cities of America and Europe. The deck of a steamship, sailing into the harbour of New York City. An aeroplane, taking off from Shosseinaya airfield and touching down at Le Bourget. Crowds gathering to greet him.

"We must have a photograph!" bellows Remizov, again in English. "Photograph! We must have a photograph!"

The photographer scurries over, attaching the flash to his camera. He jerks his head this way and that, sizing up the group.

"Yes, yes," he says, and then, in Russian, "Closer together. Everybody closer."

Remizov translates, orchestrating the group into two rows, with Sergey at the back, situated between the Americans.

"Please, everybody, look straight at me," says the photographer, again in Russian, though the guests appear to understand. Almost everyone faces forward, frozen in the moment of performing for the camera. The flash explodes, flooding their eyes with light, and the photographer moves on to another corner of the room.

"Splendid!" says Remizov. "Splendid!"

Sergey rubs his eyes to wipe away the flashing blotches of purple and green. The guests begin talking among themselves. The young American is talking with Bernard. They seem familiar. Not just familiar. Bernard places a hand on Solomon's shoulder and leaves it there. He whispers something in his ear. There has been an argument.

Two American women are speaking to him, and Sergey pretends to listen, but his eyes remain fixed on the boy. They exchange another glance, both now pretending to listen to someone else. Will these two women ever stop talking? Solomon looks over again and rolls his eyes. Something catches Sergey's breath. Finally, they approach one another and meet in the centre of the room.

"Solomon, yes?"

"Sol."

"I am Sergey."

"I thought your ballet was wonderful," Sol says, his eyes bright and glistening in the soft light of the ballroom. "How do you say 'wonderful' in Russian?"

"*Chudesniy,*" says Sergey.

The lad repeats it back to him.

"Perfect!"

"And the theatre," says Sol. "It's splendid I mean it's just so beautiful we don't really have anything like that in New York I mean there's Carnegie Hall I guess and there's Radio City Music Hall and the Metropolitan Opera House and I guess the Met is kinda similar but they're really nothing compared to that place…"

"Slow down," Sergey laughs. "My English. Is not so good. You say something about Carnegie Hall?"

"Yes," says Sol, and then, more slowly, "Your theatre, the Kirov, is very beautiful. What's 'beautiful' in Russian?"

"*Krasiviy*," says Sergey. "*Ochyen krasiviy.*"

"*Ochyen krasiviy.*"

"That's it! Now you are Russian!"

There's something tangible in the air, the space between them charged, like the moments before a storm.

"How are you here?" he asks. "You know these people?"

Sergey gestures to the other Americans.

"Mr Bernard is my tutor at Juilliard."

"I have heard of Juilliard," says Sergey. "And he brought you to Russia, your teacher?"

Sol nods: Yes.

"He is communist?"

"I… well… I don't… I mean, that is to say, I think he has opinions, but…"

"It's alright. It is not test. You don't have to say anything."

"That's okay. I guess what I mean is that Mr Bernard, Ronald, he has opinions, but coming here, it was more about the music. He wanted to hear the music you make in Russia. We don't always hear a great deal of it in America."

"It is same here. We do not hear much American music. I hear of Mr Bernard, but I do not think I know his music. And you? You are composer?"

"I don't know whether I'd call myself *that*," Sol says, his cheeks flushing with colour. "I've written a couple of pieces. Nothing good."

"That will come," says Sergey. "Everything I write before now is… what is word? *Dyermo*, we say in Russian. Not good."

Sol laughs, his cheeks and throat turning pink. He sweeps his fringe nervously to one side. Again, their eyes meet, and they become two magnets, trembling in the seconds before they spin together and lock.

"You are enjoying this party?" Sergey asks.

Sol nods without conviction.

"Very much so," he says.

"You are a bad liar," says Sergey. "It is boring party, I think. No?"

"I'm having a splendid time."

"But you are young, and everyone here is old."

"You're not."

"No," says Sergey. "This is true. What are young men like us doing here?"

Sol laughs. "I don't know."

They leave the ballroom and step out onto a narrow terrace overlooking Vorovsky Square. The night air is cold, and the younger man shudders, patting his arms to keep warm. Sergey takes off his jacket and hands it to him. It's several sizes too big. They talk about music, their favourite composers, their favourite symphonies. Sergey asks Sol when he first heard an orchestra.

"Carnegie Hall," Sol replies. "Toscanini was conducting. They played the overture from Dvořák's *Othello*. It was incredible."

Sergey smiles. "My first time?" he says. "Otmichi People's Orchestra. In an old village church. *Nutcracker.* It was terrible."

Remembering the orchestra makes him laugh. In a flash, he sees the expression on his father's face; a sort of pained grimace each time the celesta player hit the wrong note, or the pizzicato fell out of time. Even though Sol can't possibly picture the scene, Sergey's laughter is infectious, and soon the pair of them are laughing at the thought of it, their laughter carrying across the square.

What brought Sol here? Who is he? Sergey doesn't recall seeing him at the Kirov. And now he seems like something impossible, miraculous. More than that, he's untainted; by the Kirov, by Leningrad, by Remizov. Entirely pristine. Someone they can't touch.

They go back inside. At the far end of the ballroom Tatiana and Vasily are conspiring like naughty schoolgirls, glancing occasionally at Sergey and Sol. At the other end of the room, Remizov has his ear cocked towards Ronald Bernard, but his eyes are on them. Tatiana and Vasily and Remizov aren't the only ones watching them.

Enough. This is no longer his night. It never was. Everything has been in the service of the union and the republic. His work is done. He whispers in Sol's ear:

"I'm leaving."

"But it's early."

"You could come with me."

Sol looks across to Bernard and Remizov. Sergey is still

leaning in close and when he breathes he feels his breath rebound off the boy's skin. The urge to kiss his throat is overwhelming.

"Okay, let's go," Sol says. "But he can't see me leave."

★★

The night is cold, and Sergey immediately sets about lighting a fire and two paraffin lamps. When he's done he and Sol stand either side of the room, as if neither of them dares to move. Always the chance, in a moment like this, that he might have misread things. Make the first move, and he might be snubbed, pushed away. But surely not this time.

Sol makes a face – *What now?* – and Sergey crosses the room and kisses him on the mouth. He pauses, waiting for rejection, and Sol cups Sergey's face in his hands and returns the kiss with greater force, the kind of kiss given after years of absence.

They don't make it as far as the bedroom. Their clothes fall in unkempt piles and they make love on the hard floor next to the fire. Sol's skin is soft, but beneath it is a wiry strength, his body tensing in moments of pleasure. They become an island in the middle of this darkened room. Everything else goes away. This is the first and last night they will ever spend together, and they make love knowing this, unable to forget.

Chapter 29:
MANHATTAN, OCTOBER 2001

Natalie could hear Rosa and Jamilah laughing as she entered the house, but as she walked into the kitchen the laughter stopped. Rosa smiled at her. Jamilah held up that morning's edition of the *Wall Street Journal.* Natalie had enough time to catch the word KABUL before the paper was slapped back down against the table.

"Can you be*lieve* this bullshit?"

Natalie nodded and shrugged at the same time.

"How many people from Afghanistan were flying those planes? Zero. Not one of them. And now we're invading Afghanistan and raining bombs on them and what good'll it do?"

"I don't know," said Natalie.

Rosa clutched a blue dish towel against her chest like a rosary. "It's terrible," she said. "Just terrible. But these people. These Taliban. They harbour terrorists. This is why. This is why."

"That's if you believe Bush's bullshit," said Jamilah.

Rosa winced.

When they'd left, Natalie made Sol a cup of tea and joined him in the study, taking the books she had borrowed from the library.

"How you feeling today?"

"Oh, yes, you know," he said. "Funny thing this morning.

A Cape May warbler, right outside my window."

It was a good day. Not just a good day, but one of the better ones. She asked him what a Cape May warbler was.

"A bird. What else would it be?"

"What kind?"

"Bright yellow. Yellow and brown. You don't see many of them in the city."

He drifted for a moment, gazing at an upper corner of the study as though the bird itself was perched there.

"You wanted to ask me something. What is it?"

She sat close by and opened one of the books in her lap, showing him the photograph taken at the Kirov.

"That's you, isn't it?" she said, pointing to the blurred figure, the second "Unknown", standing beside Langdon Brunel.

He moved slightly. Rested again. What was going on in there? No trace of anything in his eyes. No sadness, no joy, no familiarity. How was he meant to recognise a blurred face?

"It is you, isn't it?" she asked again. "You remember this, don't you? You went there with Ronald Bernard. You lied about it later, but you went to Russia, and you heard that music..."

"The march," said Sol.

Natalie drew breath. She hadn't mentioned anything about the *Pechorin March*. Not now, while they were looking at that photograph.

"Sergey," Sol said.

"You remember."

He moved again and began shaking his head.

"Why are you looking at me that way?"

It was the most she would get from him. She had been lucky to get this much. Besides, it took little effort for her to imagine how it would have happened. A morning in the summer of 1978. Sol sitting at his desk to begin work on this new project. They wanted something epic. They wanted something almost exactly like *Star Wars.* He had nothing. He listened to Holst, to Stravinsky, Strauss. Nothing. In interviews, he would talk about inspiration, how the word means to literally inhale an idea, breathing in whatever the muse has to offer. But there was no inspiration that day. He could go for a walk, listen to music. Most likely, he cracked open a bottle of Johnnie Walker. He was still a heavy drinker in those days. A functioning alcoholic by some accounts. He would have lost a day, and then another day, and then another.

Deadline looming. Still no theme. And what was this show, anyway? A pilot, the script cranked out to cash-in on the latest big movie, till the kids stopped caring about spaceships and robots and the next big thing came along. Probably wouldn't even go to a full series.

What did a theme for something like that even matter? And who would be watching it? Kids too engrossed in rock music or disco music or whatever they listened to these days to care. How many of them had known the *Lone Ranger* theme was by Rossini? And that's when it came to him. A piece he'd carried around for years. A fanfare and a march; a little bombastic, perhaps, but underscored with melancholy.

It was perfect.

Did he hesitate before beginning? Did he worry that someone, *anyone* might know? How could they? The months and years had passed without word from Sergey Grekov. His name and music simply vanished. And even if he was still alive, they'd never see this show… what was it called again? *Battle Station Alpha*? They'd never see it in Russia, anyway, so…

He wrote quickly and without compunction, and by the time he'd finished, adding his own little touches here and there, perhaps he convinced himself it was entirely his own work.

Natalie took the book away and left it face down on the kitchen counter. She made coffee and went up to the roof terrace. Still that murky haze to the south, but a clear sky, two white jet trails forming a cross.

This could all be done in minutes. Call Pavel. Tell him what she knew, or what she thought she knew. Call Carol. Call the *Times* or the *Journal* or CNN. But all those questions. All those conversations she would have to have and explanations she'd have to give on Sol's behalf. And for what? However good Grekov's ballet might be, no-one had chosen to remember it but his son and grandson. Sol's music was loved by millions.

This wasn't just about a piece of music. She realised that now. It was about a decision; one choice representing familiarity, routine, the other offering change, but a change she couldn't control.

And so much had already changed. She kept hearing people say it. Everything changed in September. September changed everything. Change was the altered skyline and the yellowish pall hanging over the city. Change was the sense that nothing could ever go back to how it was.

She took Sol to a deli a few blocks away, where he ate his favourite lunch – pastrami on rye with mustard and gherkins – served with black coffee and followed by a slice of key lime pie. The waitress knew him by name.

"Haven't seen you in a while, Sol," she said. "How you doing?"

Sol frowned at her and looked out through the window.

He wouldn't know. If she made it public, he wouldn't know. It wouldn't make any difference to him.

Natalie picked at her own lunch, taking only a few bites from her sandwich. Sol finished every last crumb. The key lime pie revived him. Maybe it was the sugar. He still didn't remember the waitress's name, but he recognised her and gave her a kiss on the cheek as they left.

"A penny for them?" Sol asked, as they were walking back to East 73rd Street. It wasn't often he asked her anything like that. She wasn't even sure he wanted or expected an answer.

"Oh, nothing," Natalie replied. "Nothing at all."

She took him the long way home, walking along Fifth Avenue by the park. Orange and yellow leaves gathered at the sidewalk's inner edge. The wind ruffling through the trees sounded like the pages of a manuscript falling to the ground.

"I love the changing colours," said Sol. "The seasons are what I always miss in LA."

"Miss", not "missed". He was there, but only just. At the corner of Fifth Avenue and East 74rd Street they came upon a payphone, and Natalie stopped to use it.

Chapter 30: WASHINGTON D.C., APRIL 1951

There's a heat given off by this concentration of people gathered in a single room. If this is what it's like in April, imagine how it'll be if the hearings run on through July. Ron once told you that Washington D.C. is a southern swamp pretending to be an East Coast city, and you can believe it. The room simmers. So many spectators and press.

You're not the big draw here today – there's a well-known character actor from New York scheduled to appear this afternoon – but the press learned early on that even some nobody can dish the dirt on a major star. No-one wants to miss out on that moment. Anyone can become famous in this room.

"Order! Order!"

John Wood. Grey-black hair slicked across in a side-parting; mouth like a sea bass. He slams his gavel three times and the chatter fades to silence, or the closest thing to silence a room of five hundred people can muster.

"Order!" he says again, and then, turning to the man seated to his left: "Mr Tavenner?"

Frank Tavenner – jowly and jug-eared with the shoulders of a movie mobster – leans into his microphone.

"Could you please state your name?"

"Yes, sir. Solomon Conrad."

"And was that the name you were born with, Mr Conrad?"

"No, sir."

"In that case, could you also state the name with which you were born?"

"Cohen. Solomon Cohen."

"Cohen?"

Jews, queers and unionists…

"Yes, sir."

To Wood's right, Francis Walter. White-haired, weak-chinned and wearing heavy, black-rimmed glasses. He leans towards the microphone.

"And why did you change your name?" he asks.

You tell him you were encouraged to.

"By whom?"

"A teacher, sir. At Juilliard."

"Gentlemen," says Wood. "I believe we're getting ahead of ourselves. Mr Tavenner?"

"Of course," says Tavenner. "Mr Conrad. What is your present occupation?"

"I'm a composer."

"A film composer, is that correct?"

"Yes, sir."

"And how long have you been a composer of film music?"

"Almost two years."

"And is that also how long you've lived in Los Angeles, Mr Conrad?"

"It is."

"And before then you lived in New York City?"

"Yes, sir."

Tavenner pauses to remove his glasses. You know the next

question before he asks it.

"And are you now or have you ever been a member of the Communist Party?"

You tell him, "I am not."

"Not now, but have you ever been?"

"No, sir. Never."

You feel like a child.

"And do you presently know the names of any writers, actors, fellow composers… do you know the names of *any*one working within the motion picture or entertainment industries who is, or has been, a member of any branch of the Communist Party?"

It has come to this. You haven't rehearsed anything, not even in private. You didn't come here with answers, only with a fork in the road, the possibility of two paths.

"I would kindly ask that you be more specific, sir," you reply.

"Very well," says Tavenner. "Did you know a woman by the name of Mary Lafitte?"

"I did."

"And could you explain, for the benefit of the committee, the nature of your relationship with Miss Lafitte."

"She was my neighbour."

"And Miss Lafitte passed away in January of this year, yes?"

"That's right."

"While she was a patient at…" He consults his notes. "The Camarillo State Mental Hospital."

"Yes, sir."

"Would you say that you and Miss Lafitte were close?"

"Close?"

"Were you on friendly terms?"

You think about the phone call from a hospital administrator, telling you that Mary had died, and that they were burying her on the hospital grounds. There was something unspeakably sad about her being buried in the grounds of a hospital, but you apologised in advance for your absence.

"I suppose so," you reply.

"And before her admittance to the Camarillo State Hospital you spoke with her often?"

"Fairly often, yes."

"And did she ever mention her involvement with an organisation called Bundles for Britain?"

"She did."

"Mr Conrad, were you aware that Bundles for Britain was a front for the Communist Party?"

"No, sir."

"Were you aware that Miss Lafitte was a member of any communist organisation?"

A deep breath. This is the beginning of a descent.

"I had my suspicions."

"Suspicions?"

"From certain things Mary said. I thought she may, at some point, have been involved in communist activity. But I never knew for certain. She didn't say as much to me."

"And did she ever name any friends or acquaintances of hers who were Communists?"

"No, sir."

A chorus of whispers passes over the room. You're pretty sure 'audience' isn't the proper word, 'spectators' or 'observers' being preferred, but it's difficult not to see or think of them as an audience, or this hearing as theatre.

"And when was the last time you saw Miss Lafitte?"

"November of last year."

"And that was at the Camarillo State Hospital?"

"Yes, sir."

An afternoon visit. The hospital's white stucco walls reminded you of the Alamo. Mary was catatonic, saliva dribbling from the corner of her mouth, staring out through the barred windows as if she was the witness to something terrible.

Tavenner puts his glasses back on, adjusts them. Makes a face as he reads his notes again. "I'd like to turn now to your time in New York, Mr Conrad, when you were a student at Juilliard. While in New York did you know a person by the name of Ronald Bernard?"

You spit out your reply: "You know I did."

"Mr Conrad, I am asking not for my benefit but the committee's. Would you like me to ask the question again?"

"I knew Ronald Bernard."

"And what was your relationship with him?"

"He was my teacher and my friend."

"And is it correct that you lived with Mr Bernard?"

This is it. He's about to ask how many bedrooms there were, how often the bedding was changed in each room. How big were the beds? How often was Mrs Bernard present? What kind of books did Mr Bernard read? What kind of artworks did he have on the walls?

You reply: "That is correct."

"And how long did you live with him?"

"Six years. Until his death."

"Six years. Isn't that somewhat unusual? For a teacher and pupil, I mean."

"By then I'd graduated from Juilliard."

"I see. And as well as being his pupil and his friend, you were professionally close, yes?"

"Meaning?"

"Mr Conrad. Only last week you conducted a concert of Mr Bernard's work at Carnegie Hall, yes?"

A collective chuckle passes across the room.

"Yes, I did."

"And were you aware, while Mr Bernard was still with us, that he had visited the Soviet Union?"

"Yes. I was aware of that."

Tavenner studies his notes again.

"April of 1938," he says. "He visited both Leningrad and Moscow."

"If you say so."

That was unwise. Tavenner eyeballs you over the frames of his glasses. Another cursory glance at his notes.

"And did Mr Bernard ever discuss the trip with you, at all?"

"He mentioned it."

"And what did he say? Was he *approving* of what he saw in the Soviet Union?"

"I don't recall. It was my understanding he went over there to review ballet. I don't remember him talking about anything else."

Walter's turn to lean forward again. He scratches at the top of his head, straightening out a few errant strands of hair, and he speaks into the microphone.

"Now, you say he went there to review Russian ballet. Would you consider Mr Bernard's own music to be in any way influenced by Soviet composers?"

"I'd say he was influenced by Russian composers."

"The difference being…?"

You resist the urge to sigh.

"He liked Mussorgsky and Stravinsky. Both Russian, but I'd call neither of them Soviet."

"But Ronald Bernard visited the country in 1938, did he not? The music he listened to during his visit would have been Soviet, yes?"

"I guess so."

"You guess so. And Mr Bernard was still your tutor at that time?"

"He was."

"Would you say your own work is influenced by his?"

"I suppose it must be."

"Mr Conrad. Is it possible that some of Mr Bernard's Soviet influences could have found their way into your music?"

"Soviet influences?"

"Themes. A certain *style* the Soviet composer has."

"Mr Walter. I am a film composer. I write music for Westerns. Can you imagine what the producers would say if I wrote music for a John Wayne flick that sounded like a Cossack dance?"

Another ripple of laughter from the spectators and the press, but not the committee.

"Order," says Wood, gavel at the ready. "Mr Conrad. This is not an audition for *The Ed Wynn Show*. Just answer the question."

"No," you say. "I don't believe any Soviet influences have crept into my own work."

Tavenner sticks his thumb down into his collar, as if letting out steam. He smiles at Wood and Walter before asking his next question.

"And have you, yourself, ever visited the Soviet Union?"

A fork in the road, like something from a cartoon. A gnarled old wooden signpost with arrows pointing off in each direction. You feel as if you've been standing here forever.

★★

It was a good half hour before Ron spoke.

When the broadcast was over – a performance of Shostakovich's *Leningrad* symphony – he simply crossed the room, turned off the radio, and sat back down in perfect silence. You knew then not to speak to him, that you should allow him some time to gather his thoughts, for remembered passages of it to settle like autumn leaves. Ron wasn't given to first impressions or gut reactions. No good, he maintained, could come from a world in which people are no longer allowed the time to *think*.

The story behind the symphony was remarkable in itself. Composed in a warzone, a city under siege, smuggled out on microfilm. That night was the first time it had been performed outside Russia.

Only when Ron had poured you both a drink and you were seated on his couch did you pluck up the nerve to ask what he thought of it.

"It's excellent," he said. "So much dignity. I'm sure people will say it's trite, that it's propaganda and so on, but can you imagine writing a piece like that in those conditions?"

You told him you couldn't.

"Such a tragedy," said Ron. "Such a beautiful city. And those poor people."

He lit a cigarette, the smoke drifting in a bluish-grey ribbon before settling, blanket-like, in the middle of the room. Earlier that day, you'd visited the Metropolitan Museum of Art to look at illustrations from the *Inferno* by Blake and Dore, and later you took lunch at the Tavern on the Green. You and Ron spoke of many things, about the sketches, the food you ate, how oppressive New York summers can be, but you discussed nothing of importance. Now that you were both thinking of serious things, Ron took the opportunity to ask about another.

"How is everything at home?"

"I can't stay there," you said. "You don't know what it's like.

My Dad... He can barely bring himself to speak to me. And Mom just cries all the time."

It was a betrayal, telling him this, as if you'd invited him into the apartment to snoop on them.

"But your family," said Ron. "They need you now, yes?"

What family? Thinking of what your brother left behind as a family was like describing a half-demolished house as a home.

"Need me?" you said. "They hardly know I'm there. My Dad just sees me as another pair of hands in the store, and my Mom, well... She's half-crazy with it."

"They lost their son."

"You say that as if I didn't know. As if they don't remind me of it every goddamn day. And now I've got my Mom telling me to run away some place, so I won't get called up. I said to her, I said, 'Mom. Where the hell am I gonna go?'"

"She's frightened. And can you blame her?"

"Of course not. I'm frightened too. I keep having these dreams..."

"You were restless again last night."

"I know. I lay awake at night, scared that when I fall asleep I'll have the same dream. I keep having the same dream."

You wanted to tell him about it. The metal room tipped on its side, seawater gushing in around the edges of its only door. The stench of smoke and engine oil. The groan of metal being bent out of shape and the sound, from other decks, of men screaming.

"It's just a dream," Ron said.

"It's more than that," you tell him. "And Zack's out there now, somewhere, at the bottom of the sea. And if I'm not dreaming about that, I'm thinking about it, wondering how many miles down he is, how dark and cold it must be. And I keep imagining myself down there with him in the dark. What happens if I get drafted?"

"It won't come to that."

"You can't know that for certain."

Ron took a final draw on his cigarette and stubbed it out. He paused, gazing at his shoes, lost in a thought. In moments like this he could seem so academic, so detached. It would always be a source of tension between you. Ron was born at just the right time; too young to get drafted in the last war, too old to get drafted in this one. Wealthy, and with the kind of old money that wasn't tied up in anything risky. The Great Depression had meant little more than one less member of staff.

Men like him were on a conveyor belt of good fortune. You had friends like him at Juilliard. Kids who found it *fascinating* that your father was a butcher on the Lower East Side, that you still lived with your parents, that you could, if necessary, walk home after a day in school. You doubted any of them were worried about the draft, and they certainly weren't wrapping veal cutlets and chicken livers to earn their allowance.

"There is one way you could avoid the draft," said Ron.

Here it was. He was going to say exactly what your mother had been saying for weeks. Run away to some place in Latin

America, somewhere the war will never touch, and stay there till it's over. He'd probably have some friend, some Argentinian or Brazilian academic, who could find you a job, help set you up.

You asked him what he meant.

"If you were medically unfit," he said. "They couldn't draft you then."

You laughed. "Medically unfit? Ron, there's nothing wrong with me."

"But if there was paperwork. A doctor's report."

"Doctor Lowe's known me since the day I was born. And he may be a friend of the family and all, but there's no way he'd sign something saying I was unfit for duty. He just wouldn't."

"I'm not talking about him. I have a friend, in Florida. He runs a hospital for those suffering from tuberculosis. He and I go back many years. He would do this for me, I know he would."

"But, Ron. This is serious. I mean..."

"Please, Sol. Think of your parents. Think of me. Some of us are old enough to remember the last war and everything it left behind. I couldn't bear it if that were to happen to you."

"We're talking about draft evasion. You know what the penalty is for that? And if they found out it was your idea..."

"They would send me to prison. But what's prison? How could prison be any worse than the alternative, for either of us? I've thought about this, Sol. I've been thinking about it for some time. We tell them you had TB back in '38 and spent three or four months in hospital. You were out of New York for some of that time, so it's perfect."

You started to speak, but he cut you off.

"The way things are going, a trip like that, going to Russia, could ruin your career before it's even started. It may still ruin mine. But if we tell them you were in Florida, no-one will ever know and you'll escape the draft. It's perfect."

"But there'll be paperwork, documents..."

"We can make them disappear. There are favours I can call in. That's one of the few benefits of this lifestyle."

"And he'd do all this, your friend?"

"In a heartbeat."

Another secret, another lie. Was this all life ever amounted to? A steady accumulation of untruths, the sculpting of separate lives, public and private? Nobody would ever truly know who you were. Even Ron, sitting there and looking at you with such affection, didn't know everything. And from now on there'd be a noble, perfectly reasonable explanation as to why, unlike your brother, you didn't become another name etched into marble.

"If we do this," Ron said, "Leningrad didn't happen. Do you understand?"

There was now something different in his expression; something harder, almost cruel.

"It didn't happen," he said. "None of it. It's all gone."

You knew exactly what he meant.

★★

Tavenner, his thumb still jammed under his collar, asks, "And have you ever visited the Soviet Union yourself, Mr Conrad?"

And you reply, "No. I have not."

"I would remind you that you are under oath." Tavenner glances briefly at Wood with the suggestion of a smile.

You tell him you are very aware of that.

"You see, while we were compiling information for this hearing, one of our investigators spoke with a Mrs Edna Stowe. Do you know Mrs Stowe?"

"I do."

"And could you explain, again for the benefit of the committee, who she is?"

"She was Ronald Bernard's secretary at Juilliard."

"Now," says Tavenner. "Our investigators spoke to Mrs Stowe and she recalled that when Mr Bernard travelled to the Soviet Union he took one of his students along with him."

"Really?"

"Sadly, the passenger records for the flight were unavailable and Mrs Stowe is getting on in years. She could not remember the student's name. Were you that student, Mr Conrad?"

"No I was not."

"Do you know the name of the student Mr Bernard took with him?"

"No."

"In that case, are you able to confirm your whereabouts in the April of 1938?"

"Yes, sir."

"You must have a very good memory. Where were you at that time?"

"I was in hospital. Fort Lauderdale. I'd contracted TB... uh... that is to say tuberculosis in the February, and I was sent away to convalesce."

"I see. And where was this exactly?"

"Sunny Glade Tuberculosis Hospital. Umm, that's Oakland Park Boulevard, sir."

"And who was your physician, while you were staying at this hospital?"

"Dr Clarence Buckley."

"And if we were to contact Dr Buckley he would vouch for your being at the Sunny Glade Hospital in the April of 1938."

"He would, sir."

Tavenner chews on a thought as bitter as sherbet lemons, and Walter takes the lead.

"Going back to Ronald Bernard," he says. "Was Mr Bernard ever a member of the Communist Party, or any affiliated organisation?"

And you reply: "Yes, sir."

"And can you name any friends or colleagues of Mr Bernard's who were also communists."

"Yes, sir."

The audience breathes in as one, loud enough for it to echo. Ronald Bernard might not have been a Hollywood star, but his name is famous enough for this to matter. You imagine – you hope – that somewhere in the Hamptons or on the Upper

West Side, Margaret and her friends, the Dorises and Charlises of this world, are listening to it on the radio.

Fuck them. All of them. The past is the past and the dead are dead and this is your life, so fuck every last one of them. If this is what it takes, burn every last fucking bridge.

Chapter 31:
MANHATTAN, OCTOBER 2001

She was on hold for what felt like an age. Sol was waiting outside the phone booth, gazing up to where the sunlight and shadows met on an apartment block. A troupe of Hare Krishnas in saffron gowns went by on Fifth Avenue, singing and dancing and hitting tambourines. Sol saw them and laughed, and he waved at Natalie to get her attention. Natalie nodded and smiled. *Yes. I see them too.*

Thirty seconds of Mozart's Flute Concerto on a loop, crackly and punctuated with thanks for her patience. As if they wanted people to hate this music. Just background noise. Something to fill the silence.

Finally, someone answered. She paused a moment before speaking. She could just hang up. Hang up and walk away. What difference would it make?

Outside the phone booth, Sol was getting restless. The Hare Krishnas had gone, but he could still hear them, and he was beginning to wander off towards Fifth Avenue. He looked lost, helpless. Natalie hit her hand against the glass until she had his attention and she waved, signalling that she would only be a moment. She couldn't tell if he understood.

"Hello...?"

"Yes, I..."

Sol began wandering off again, and Natalie beat the glass until he stopped. She mouthed the words: *One minute. I'll be with you in a minute.*

"Hello, ma'am?"

Deep breath. She began.

★★

They were in the study; Sol listening to Schubert, Natalie going through old letters, shredding anything they didn't need to keep. It was a day much like any other. And there was something immensely satisfying about watching those old bills and circulars sliding into the shredder, the crackle of the paper passing through its metal teeth. What if you put everything into one of these? Birth certificate, driver's licence, social security, everything. Every photograph, certificate and diploma. Just fed it into the shredder and watched it turn into confetti. Would you become someone new, or would everything remain the same?

The music came to an end. Natalie left the shredder chewing up another circular from Juilliard and went over to Sol's record player.

"More Schubert?" she said.

Sol made a face. "That was Schubert?"

"That was Schubert."

"Not Schubert, then," he said. "Mozart. One of the piano sonatas."

"Which one?"

"Eleven."

"Which recording?"

"Anything but Glenn fucking Gould. Life's too short."

Natalie laughed. He was having a good day. She put Schubert back on the shelf and looked for the Murray Perahia recording of K.331. She held it up.

"Yes, yes, good, yes," said Sol.

Natalie placed the record on the turntable and lowered the stylus. The music began and she closed her eyes and listened to it for a while. She felt an almost unfamiliar sense of calm, the world settling all around her with the grace and elegance of the leaves on Fifth Avenue. When she opened her eyes again, Sol was tracing invisible curlicues in time with the music. Life's too short, he'd said. She wondered how much time he had left. No-one could say. There wasn't a timer, counting down. There was just this. The two of them alone together, listening to music. She was happy with that.

Pavel would be on the plane by now, or at least she hoped he would. How long did that whole process take? Before September they might have dragged their heels, passed him around from pillar to post, but now? Now she imagined it would be quick. INS vehicles and police cars outside the hotel within minutes of her call. Officers rushing into the building with their badges ready, beating on Pavel's door and, if he answered, cuffing him immediately. They'd gather his things while he sat there, handcuffed, on the bed. He wouldn't understand. Why had they come for him now? Who sent them?

Maybe he told them what had happened. There was always that chance. It wouldn't be grounds for them to let him stay, but it might be enough to prompt a visit from the police. They would ask if she had the manuscript.

"Some ballet score, or something?"

And if they didn't come asking for it, Carol might. She wouldn't let this go so easily. Natalie would have to lie, but it wouldn't be a first.

"He went home," she'd tell her. "He wasn't interested in publicity. He took the score with him before I had a chance to get it scanned."

It was sitting there, on Sol's desk. Purple card and yellow paper. It must have been a beautiful object when it was new, when Sergey Grekov made his first mark.

So many things had already been lost, destroyed. What difference would another make?

Chapter 32:
LENINGRAD, APRIL 1938

Thin traces of the dawn, splayed across the ceiling like fingers of light. Outside, an early morning tram jangling its way along Volodarsky Prospect. Sol stirs, mumbles something and draws Sergey's arm around him, and they lie like this a moment before Sergey gets out of bed.

Neither of them says much as they get dressed. He senses Sol's guilt, or his shame. Will there be a scene when he gets back to the hotel in last night's clothes? Does he regret what happened here?

Sergey regrets nothing. If he feels anything at all, it's a sense of injustice; that the world could be shaped in such a way to force them apart, that these moments together will be their last. How many minutes do they have? How many seconds?

When they're dressed and ready, Sergey walks Sol back to his hotel, and they stroll along the Palace Embankment, side by side, without touching. It is a sunny morning, and a light mist clings to the Neva. Along the river wall fishermen are angling for *koryushka* or whatever else can be caught this early in the year. Broken ice sheets drift downstream, clunking into one another as they move. The sun is low in the sky, and Sol and Sergey's shadows are drawn long and indistinct before them as they walk.

Outside the hotel Sol asks, "How do you say 'goodbye' in Russian?"

"*Mi ne umeyem proshatsya.*"

"All *that* means goodbye?"

"No," Sergey laughs. "It is from a poem. It means, 'We do not know how to say goodbye'."

Nothing more can happen. They shake hands, like two travellers who exchanged small talk while waiting for separate trains. Sol enters the hotel alone, pausing briefly to look back through its revolving door as it turns. Out in the cold street Sergey watches Sol's face flicker with his own reflection, one face replacing the other, over and over, until he's gone.

THE END

Acknowledgements

An earlier version of the second chapter of *A Simple Scale* originally appeared in a short story collection, *Speak My Language*, edited by Torsten Højer (Robinson, 2015). An abridged version of chapter 21 appeared on the Wales Arts Review website.

About the Author

David Llewellyn is the author of three novels published by Seren: *Eleven, Everything is Sinister* and *Ibrahim and Reenie*. He has also written short stories, scripts for the BBC and novelisations of the Torchwood and Dr Who tv series. He was born in Pontypridd and is a graduate of Dartington College of Arts. A freelance writer, he lives in Cardiff.